D0284724

DARK
RIVERS
TO CROSS

DARK RIVERS TO CROSS

A NOVEL

LYNNE REEVES

CROOKED
LANE

NEW YORK

Copyright © 2022 by Lynne Reeves

Published in the United States by Crooked Lane Books, an imprint of The Quick Brown Fox & Company LLC.

Crooked Lane Books and its logo are trademarks of The Quick Brown Fox & Company LLC.

Library of Congress Catalog-in-Publication data available upon request.

ISBN (hardcover): 978-1-63910-121-4
ISBN (ebook): 978-1-63910-122-1

Cover design by Meghan Deist

Printed in the United States.

www.crookedlanebooks.com

Crooked Lane Books
34 West 27th St., 10th Floor
New York, NY 10001

First Edition: November 2022

10 9 8 7 6 5 4 3 2 1

For women torn between
impossible choices

Content Warning

This story sensitively explores issues of family violence and inherited trauma.

All those years
listening to those
who had
nothing to say.

All those years
forgetting how everything
has its own voice
to make itself heard.

—David Whyte, *The Winter of Listening*

CHAPTER

1

Boston—1993

*I*T HAPPENS IN *November. You are walking down Beacon
Street when you feel a chill settle deep within you. It's the
kind of feeling you know won't let go till the warmest spring
day arrives with plans to linger. Or perhaps you are being
followed. You tell yourself, "No, don't be paranoid." Still you
look left, then right, scanning streets and scrutinizing intersec-
tions. Tentatively you relax, because sidewalks are dotted with
the usual Brahmins and their designer dogs and BU students
taking the shortcut to the Charles River Esplanade. All harmless, these people. You recognize the look on the faces of women
just like you, eager to head home and fill a wineglass to the
brim, the night's companion.*

*Despite your uneasiness, you tell yourself he is not lurking
behind a column, a lamppost, an elegant tree. He is not inside
a neighbor's vestibule or hiding on the far side of that unfamiliar van with no identifying logo. You haven't seen him in
one hundred and eighty-two days. Let go. Move on.*

*You open and close the door to the brownstone. Quickly.
When all three locks are firmly set in place, you lean against*

dark oak, taking in the rambling place left over from your marriage. It always felt too big for two, and now, six months into living alone, its echoes and shadows make being there harder than you thought it would be. It should be a relief, shouldn't it? This place planted in the Back Bay nearly two hundred years ago, with its Italian influence, should suit you. It is stable, solid; it has stood the test of time. Unlike anything else you have known.

With your husband gone, you should finally be able to draw a deep breath. Yet your lungs won't fill, and you wonder if perhaps your body senses traces of him clinging to the drapes, worked into the fabric of the sofa. His scent still hangs on the air. Sometimes, like now, you think you can smell him as if he were standing right there.

Flick, walk, flick, walk. You turn on lights as you go room to room; your high heels sound out a path to the only other entrance. The back door is locked. Double-bolted. See? Nothing but fatigue playing tricks with your mind. It's the cold gothic spaces that have you down, that's all. Or something to do with changing seasons. Oriel windows that like to hug the outside, beckoning in Boston's humidity during summer, and today, as the leaves finish their fall, allowing winter wind to take its place right on schedule.

Within seconds of turning up the heat, the pipes whine and moan, as if they're annoyed to be roused from their slumber. You can almost hear your lover, Nic, whisper softly, "Relax, *cara mia*—a hot bath is all you need. Everything is fine."

Moving on to someone new was never what you had in mind. It isn't your style to rebound. You wanted your marriage to work, to be wonderful like that of your dearest friend, who is married to your husband's brother. Was it so foolish to expect that things would turn out the same for you? No one can say you didn't try to make it work. When it didn't, you swore off men—all of them suspect to you after Davis. None to be trusted. Until you met Niccolò Conti.

With the faucet all the way up, you watch the steam climb its way out of the clawfoot tub. As much as you care for Nic— and you truly do—sometimes you wish you could vanish as easily as the vapor does. It is all too complicated, your story, your life. As you trade your sweater dress for a plush robe, you think, Yes, the wine will help. *It often does. Why not light the sweet honeysuckle candle? Erase the smell memory of one man while luxuriating in the recollections of being with another. Make the best of this night to yourself, for as hard as it is to be here, it is increasingly difficult to stay at Nic's. As much as you take pleasure in his touch, he longs for things you are not yet able to give. May never again be able to give.*

Hurry to pour the wine. Check the tub. With the glass down on the vanity, beside the candle casting a delicate glow on the noble floor and ceramic tile, you drop your robe and ease your weary body into the bath; your arms and legs create known rivers as you sink into calm.

You should not have closed your eyes.

You should have come home earlier, later, not at all. If only you had invited Marli to dinner, he would not be slam-ming your head against the porcelain tub. Promising to hurt you like you have hurt him. Why didn't you stop at the Lenox for a drink? Go shopping for things you do not need. You could've stayed at Nic's, and accepted his generous offer to move in. But you—you weren't ready. You were trying to make things work on your own.

You think you will fight. Claw, bite, scratch, beat your way out of the inevitable. But he has always been strong in body. And the mere presence of you has been known to push him over the edge. He is frightening enough on the brink, the permanent place where he lives now. It doesn't help to remem-ber he wasn't always this way.

You think you will feel something. Fury. Hatred. Fear. At the very least, the pain of it, your body splitting in two from the force of him. Instead, you watch a lonely maple leaf attach itself to the transom. At first it grips the glass, trying to hold on against nature. And then the wind and rain come. The sky is shedding tears for you. Still you feel absolutely nothing. The leaf lets go; it slides down the glass, urging you to do the same. Surrender, it says as it falls. You think, Yes, letting go is an option, a good idea. It's the right thing to do. *You slip under the water, slowly, an inch at a time. Staying quiet so he won't notice what you are plotting. You needn't worry. He has become preoccupied, intimate with his own cruelty.*

You think you will struggle. That the lack of air is as much your enemy as he is. But you don't need to breathe. Even that is unimportant now.

The last thing you remember before losing consciousness is being thankful you never had children with him.

crosscurrent—*noun*. A stretch of turbulent water in a river or the sea caused by one current flowing into or across another current; see *riptide*.

Millinocket, Maine—2012

LUKE

"NOT EVERY PERSON who's adopted wants to know where he came from," Luke said, turning his back on his brother. Bending down, he took hold of the gunwale of an Old Town canoe, pulled it from the river's edge, and in one swift motion hoisted it onto his thighs and up over his head.

"Listen, you don't have to look for your birth parents if you don't want to," Jonah said. With a lit cigarette dangling from his lips, he heaved another canoe from the water, then followed Luke up the incline toward the rows of bunk storage racks they kept wedged into the pine grove.

When the last of the boats were pulled from the river and stowed, Jonah squeezed Luke's shoulder and pointed to his hangout, telling him to take a seat, like he had countless times before. The salt-and-pepper rock he called "*the office*" jutted over their corner of the Penobscot. It was the place Jonah dragged his brother whenever he needed to tell him something out of their mother's earshot. His brother's next move was predictable. He reached behind the weathered stone, his hand disappearing into an underwater net he'd jerry-rigged to the rock three years ago when Luke was still in high school and Jonah was about to leave for college. From his secret cooler, he pulled a beer. He held the dripping can out to Luke and with his eyes asked if he wanted to join him for a cold one.

Luke shook his head. "We came from the same foster home. If you learn stuff, I'll have to know it too. And what about Mom? Do you even care how she'll feel when she finds out you're doing this?"

Luke knew she'd be hurt Jonah wanted to find his first mother. For years, she'd been evasive about the details of his adoption, every time he asked.

Behind them came the delicate *snap snap* of twigs, then silence. Like a reflex, Luke turned to be sure it wasn't their mother checking up on them. It would be like her to catch them in the act of doing nothing. When she didn't materialize, Luke tried to guess which little creature would emerge skirting the mudflats—short-tailed weasel or fisher cat? He waited. Nothing there.

The leftover light on the late August horizon, a mix of blue-gray and orange bands, told him it was after seven. In less than an hour, shadows would come from a half moon surrounded by bullets of stars. Nights like this Luke couldn't understand why Jonah wasn't happy living and working at their family inn. If only he could see Church's Overlook—and all there was to lose—through his eyes, he'd be content. He'd know, no questions asked, that they belonged right there, sheltered by acres of pine forest that stretched along their waterfront. There was nowhere else Luke cared to be.

"Why can't you make your documentary for school about something else? Like the history of Katahdin," Luke said.

What he really wanted to know was why Jonah couldn't leave this alone. It wasn't fair for him to do this, to risk hurting their mother. And he had no right to push Luke into thinking about the past if he didn't want to.

"There's plenty to know about the mountain, its Indigenous people, and legends," Luke said. "And you wouldn't be causing anybody any pain in the process."

"This isn't about my senior project, and I'm not doing this to hurt Mom," Jonah said. "I'm not really doing this to find them. I'm doing it to find *me*." He held a fist to his mouth, but Luke heard him loud and clear. "In filmmaking, you have to care about your subject," he said.

Jonah's head snapped to the left at the same time Luke's did, both of them sensing the danger before actually seeing it. A peregrine swooped out of a cluster of red spruce, down toward a loon riding the current, a chick on her back. As quickly as the falcon took the nose-dive toward its prey, mother and baby vanished under the surface. Forty-seven seconds went by—the hunting thwarted and the bird long gone—and fifty feet from where the pair went under, two heads popped up.

"How can you not think things like that are amazing?" Luke asked.

"She protected her kid—so what? That's what she's supposed to do. That's what our real parents should've done."

"Maybe they did."

"How can you stand living with the idea that you have a family out there someplace?" Jonah asked. "You may not need to know, but I do. That'll be enough for me."

Squatting down, Luke cut the smooth glass surface with his hand, obliterating their reflections, the reminder that he and Jonah were brothers of circumstance, not blood.

Inside and out, they were nothing alike. At six one, Jonah had three inches and thirty pounds on him. By the time Luke got to high school, he knew size-wise he'd never catch up. So he decided at least he could be the stronger of the Blackwell boys. Luke volunteered to take tourists on nature hikes over rocky footpaths, adding in hilly terrain that would strengthen his legs and reward guests of the inn with picturesque views from the mountain in his backyard. Without being asked by their mother or their groundskeeper Coop, Luke spent Saturday mornings loading bulging suitcases into mini-vans and SUVs, hitching kayaks, bikes, and fishing gear to roof racks and truck beds.

Then Jonah took the whitewater job. In a matter of weeks, guiding rafts through Rip Gorge, down the Exterminator and Staircase rapids, he was bragging to his friends, showing off how easily he could throw Luke over one shoulder.

What bothered Luke more than them laughing at his expense was that Jonah didn't have to know much about the river to lead people down it. True, Luke envied his way of tapping into people's adventurous spirits, putting them at ease in the water—and he did have a solid record of keeping everyone in the raft, which had to come from some natural instinct. But for as many times as his brother had traveled the West Branch, no matter how often he'd rested in an eddy or paddled flatwater, Jonah couldn't name a single plant or bird.

Streaky blond hair and light eyes, Jonah was the fair-haired one, but only in the looks department. Even he'd have said he was the black sheep. At two years older than Luke, and a senior in college, Jonah had worried their mother in every way a kid can, and still he griped that Luke was her favorite. To him, their mother was like the hiker who chooses the easiest trail around a hill; the lion's share of her affection naturally made its way toward Luke because he was her path of least resistance.

Or maybe because Jonah barely made an effort to stay out of trouble's way, Luke worked extra hard to please her.

"Christ, how long are you gonna think about it?" Jonah leaned over to nudge Luke's arm. "I'm not asking you to kill someone. I just need you to get some information out of her for me. If I ask, she'll know I'm up to something. She'll never suspect you."

Jonah took another swig of his beer. Even above the water slapping stone, Luke could hear the liquid travel down his throat in a series of anxious gulps. The wind picked up, rustling the brush behind him, and the loss of light was changing the temperature of the air.

So Jonah planned to do this without telling her? And Luke was just supposed to agree to help him? The idea of coaxing details out of their mother about the time before they came to Church's Overlook didn't sit right with him. Until his brother told him he was going to search for his birth parents, Luke had always liked the idea that Jonah's adoption was tangled up in his. They called the story "The Adventures of the Blackwell Boys." It all started with Lena Blackwell—a woman with no living family, no brothers or sisters, her parents and grandparents long passed—going to a foster home to meet the two-year-old child she'd chosen from a series of photographs offered to her in advance by the state of Maine, and there Jonah was, holding tight to Luke's little baby hand. Two boys, not related yet inseparable.

Luke owed Jonah. If it weren't for him all those years ago, insisting in his little kid way that they were a package deal, he might never have come to be part of this river in Maine.

"You gonna help me or not?" Jonah asked.

"Depends on what I'm supposed to do."

"Find a way to get her out of the inn tomorrow so I can look for my adoption papers, health records, things like that. Most of the guests will be out on hikes. I'll have plenty of time to scope out the office. Once I know what I've got, I'll let you know what questions to ask her over dinner."

"I hate when you do this. You had all summer to get what you needed. Why are you roping me into this right before you leave for school?"

"I tried. It's like she has some kind of radar rigged to the office. Every time I try to get near it, she appears out of nowhere to ask me why I'm not doing some stupid chore. Look, I need you, Old Man Freshman," he said, throwing an arm around Luke's shoulders.

Jonah had been calling him *Old Man Freshman* since the day he'd first revisited the idea of applying to college. Three years after graduating high school, Luke was no more eager now than he'd been back then to trade in his naturalist routines for school ones. Lately, with Jonah about to graduate, he'd felt increasing pressure to get on with it. He applied to Bowdoin, never expecting to get in. With tuition for the first semester paid and housing chosen, everyone assumed Luke would follow Jonah there in two days. How could he tell everyone now that he wasn't ready to do it?

"Tomorrow night she'll be so bummed that you're about to leave home, even Lena Blackwell will be nostalgic. We'll pluck the heartstrings. I figure a couple glasses into the bottle of wine I've got chilling, she'll answer at least some of the questions I have about my adoption. Even if I do the asking. By dessert, I should have enough to get started."

"When was the last time you saw her have even one glass? Plus I don't know how much there is to celebrate." Luke muttered under his breath, "I've changed my mind. I'm not going."

Jonah slapped a palm to his forehead.

"I've thought it through. I'll have plenty of time to do what needs to be done around here if I get up extra early and take afternoon classes at U Maine."

"Are you kidding me? You would pass up a chance to go to one of the best schools in the country because of this place?" Jonah was on his feet now, beer in one hand, waving his cigarette in the direction of the main inn. Standing on the ledge, towering above Luke, he gestured wildly. "I don't get you. This is when I know we're not—"

Jonah didn't have to finish. Luke knew what he was about to say. But he was wrong. They *were* brothers.

"She made you feel guilty for leaving, didn't she?" he asked. "Coop's here to help her. You don't have to do this."

"Mom had nothing to do with it. It's what I want."

Shaking his head, Jonah was about to throw what was left of the cigarette in the river when he caught his brother's glare. Sighing, he dropped the butt into the beer can. It sizzled in backwash.

"Have you told her?" Jonah slid a fresh one from his pack of Kents and slipped it between his lips. The sharp angle of his jaw lit up on the second flick of his Bic.

Brittle branches snapped within a few feet from where they stood. This time there was no mistaking the sound for anything but a person. Their mother appeared from in between white pines, pulling her fleece jacket tight around her body.

*   *   *

LENA

She didn't ask her boys to elaborate on what they'd been talking about. Lena had heard enough. For over twenty years, she had cultivated this life to keep them safe. Now her boys were about to unwind it. Oscillating between being afraid and feeling betrayed, she did what she did best. She kept the focus on the inn.

"There's work to do. Scribner needs firewood. And there's a squirrel trapped in the living room at Thoreau. Put those away," she said, her eyes fixed on Jonah's beer and lit cigarette.

"Relax," Jonah said. "There aren't any guests left on the property. Coop must've told you. He ran everybody down to River Drivers for dinner."

When Jonah blew smoke in her direction, he was far enough away that it didn't come off as completely disrespectful. But his message to his mother was clear. *Don't tell me what to do.*

"I don't care," she said. "You know there's no drinking or smoking by staff on the grounds. Period. You two will have plenty of time together when you're at school."

"I'm not staff," Jonah said as he crushed the beer can with one hand.

Lena waited for him to add, *"I'm your kid,"* when what he wanted to say was, *I'm not your kid.* But he didn't make either declaration. He never did—at least not out loud to her.

"Come on. Let's do what Mom wants," Luke said. "I'll take Thoreau. Then I'll come help you finish stacking wood at Scribner."

Of course Luke would choose to deal with what was holed up in the cabin named for the area's famous visitor, to coax the wildlife back outside where it would be out of harm's way.

Moving away from Jonah, Luke looked overeager to climb the river bank to get back to work, and away from her. But the closer he got, the more he stared directly at her face, trying to gauge how much she had overheard.

Jonah came toward Lena too, adjusting his pace to keep up with his brother, their identical work boots alternating right, left, right. In the late afternoon light, all she could think about was that her lies were finally piling up in the present, setting the past to vibrate.

Lena fell in line with her boys, walking the forest floor among the ferns. Several yards from the main inn where divergent paths would lead Luke and Jonah to different cabins, different chores, Lena came to an abrupt standstill, using her hand on Luke's arm to stop him mid-stride on the trail.

"Jonah, go on ahead. I need to talk to your brother."

He sighed and took off toward Scribner.

Shielded by a giant maple, Luke didn't move. As Lena waited until Jonah went out of sight, she ran through her options.

If she encouraged Luke to stay at Church's Overlook, there'd be no telling what Jonah would do on his own back at college. If both boys went to Bowdoin as planned, she'd have more control over them, even from a distance. Except to get Luke to agree to thwart Jonah from unraveling their larger histories, she'd need to give him an inkling of the dangerousness of what his brother was about to do.

"I heard you two talking," she said finally. "You know it's a very bad idea."

"What?" Luke asked, playing dumb.

A quiet, skillful worrier, Lena knew how to bend words to conform to the shape of the trouble. To fit her concern to the moment, tapping into a person's anxieties or diffusing them, depending on her objective. For now she would let Luke think she hadn't heard that he wanted to abandon going to Bowdoin in favor of staying at Church's. She needed time to think.

"You can't let Jonah do it," she said. "The adoption is closed. Biological parents make that decision for complicated reasons. Trust me, what little I do know isn't good."

"You don't have to tell me my story," Luke said. "I don't need to know it. But give Jonah something. Anything, so he'll be satisfied."

For years Lena had represented to the world and her sons that her primary job was to do whatever it took to run a successful river lodge, when what she'd really been doing was keeping Luke and Jonah from the pain of their past lives. Her deception always backlit by love.

"I know it might not feel like it, but he isn't trying to upset you," Luke said.

"Whether he intends to or not, people are going to get hurt," she said. "I'm counting on you, Luke. We're a family. He trusts you, and I know you can keep him from doing this. It's reckless."

A few feet ahead of them on the trail, something disturbed the brush. Lena glimpsed the furry back of the dark presence, a shadow moving among other woodland shadows. Neither she nor her son reacted to it. Unlike Jonah, they were comfortable here. In this way they were alike; they were home.

CHAPTER

3

Millinocket, Maine—1999

LENA DIMMED THE light in the lobby of the main inn and took her position by a window, her body partially obscured by heavy drapes. Looking past the trees that stood like soldiers, she surveyed the grounds, accounting for guests, reconciling the number of cars. She verified each shadow, landing finally on Coop's cabin. From across the expansive property of Church's Overlook, she could see his outline inside. He flashed the sign.

Coop had finished rounds. Lena was safe, which meant so were her little boys. They had successfully completed this evening ritual for years now. Maybe it was time to let go of it.

Lena knew night well. Every sight and sound memorized. Every variance checked and rechecked. The groans and squeaks above her head coming from Luke's room were harmless. Her energetic sons were jumping on the bed.

Calibrating the sound of her steps, making certain they could hear her presence on the stairs, Lena had no desire to frighten the boys unnecessarily. There had been enough of that for a lifetime.

"We can't sleep," Jonah said, when he saw her hovering on the threshold. He kept right on jumping, his PJ bottoms getting lower with each bounce.

"Yeah, can't sleep." Luke kicked his legs out from under him, landing in a heap, the mattress cushioning his fall.

Before his bare feet could hit the plank floor, Lena looked away. To know about his foot was one thing; to see it, another altogether.

Jonah, the quicker and taller of the two boys, flew off the bed, reaching the shelf before his brother could pull their favorite book down: *The Legends and True Stories of Katahdin*.

"Read 'Lost on the Mountain,'" Jonah said.

"Not tonight" she said. "It gives Luke nightmares."

"How about 'The Storm Bird's Wrath'? Please, please, *please*."

Luke moved closer to Lena, elbow to elbow, as Jonah shouted out the terrifying titles. She sat down on the bed, accepting the book from him.

"It's 'Red Rose' or nothing," she said.

As the boys' mother opened to that page, to that legend, she could feel the tension flow from Luke's body. When one son became calm and the other settled, she pulled them close and began reading from the book.

Red Rose was a lonely girl who one day wandered into the woods a long way from home. She came to a place where Mount Katahdin was in view. As she looked at the mountain, she wished for a good man, someone to love her and be the father of her children. Very tired from the long journey, she fell asleep on a blanket of moss. In her dreams a native man appeared. He said, "I am the Spirit of Katahdin and you will have your wish."

Red Rose did indeed give birth to one boy and then, not much later, another. She lived in the lonely woods, as happy as she could be with her sons. Yet, as the years passed, Red Rose grew homesick. "I long to go back to my people," she said.

"You will have your wish," the Spirit of Katahdin said once again.

As a parting gift, he kissed the firstborn son, telling the boy that whenever he would pass a hand over his lips, he would speak the truth. Then he gave the second son the mark of the spirit, a sign meant to protect him from all danger found in the wilderness.

So Red Rose took the children to the banks of her Penobscot. When they reached her tribe, it was a time of famine. There was no game in the woods. No fish in the river. Everyone was distressed. Red Rose felt the desperation too, but then the firstborn son passed a hand over his lips and said, "There is game in the woods." At once the woods were full of game. Everyone was happy, and there was no more famine.

In time, Red Rose's tribe was attacked by other tribes from the east. In war, the second-born son shot arrows in every direction, trying to save his people, protecting the treasured land. And never once was the second son harmed.

Years passed and after Red Rose had gone beyond, and both of Katahdin's sons were very old, the first son spoke a truth. 'We will live forever,' he said. Then together, hands held, the brothers climbed the steep mountain to join the spirit who dwells beyond the stone doorway, and because of the second son's gift, never did they strain or stumble on the treacherous hike.

Now surrounded by his sons, Katahdin spends his days within and around the peak, for he is the spirit of the mountain.

Lena closed the book as quietly as she could. Jonah was asleep at the end of the bed. When that boy was awake, he ran at full tilt, but once his head hit the pillow, he was out like a light. She kissed him lightly on his cheek.

"How did I get this again?" Luke whispered, pointing to the scar that ran the length of his heel.

"You remember what I told you," she said. "It was an accident. It happened a long time before you came here with me."

Luke ran his finger up and down the fibrous cord. "I don't like it."

"If you want," Lena said, "we could imagine that, like the second son in the legend, you've been marked by the spirit. Which means you're safe now. This is your place, Luke. Your wilderness."

Her little boy smiled and nodded, and Lena pulled the covers down enough to slide Luke's legs under the sheets. She made a playful show of tucking him in tight.

"Tell me the 'doption story, again."

"*A*-doption," she said.

"Yeah, that one."

"I loved you from the moment I saw you. I knew you were meant to live with me. Just you and me and Jonah. One day, I brought you here, and the three of us took a walk together. It was sunny, and the reflection off the river was like something I had never seen. Little jewels, a watery treasure. You loved these woods the minute you heard the birdies sing. And that's when I decided this was our home. Now can you go to sleep?"

With her lips pressed against his silky hair, she felt him nod.

Off went the light, and with the book under her arm, she was about to pick Jonah up to carry him to his room, to tuck him into his bed, when she heard Luke whisper, "I like it when he stays."

She pulled the woolen blanket out from under Jonah and covered the boy.

Outside Luke's door, she leaned against the wall and opened the book. She ran her hand over the simple inscription: *To Lena. From Coop.*

Lena. The name wasn't that hard to get used to. Luke and Jonah called her Mom. Guests of Church's Overlook didn't call her anything, as if because she served them, she didn't deserve a name. Only Coop called her Lena, and even he didn't say it out loud very often. He was a gentle man. Kind enough not to remind her that's not exactly who she was.

entrapment—*noun*. Dangerous situation in which a part of a paddler's body is caught inside the hull while the paddler is attempting to leave the kayak or canoe; see *broadside*.

CHAPTER

4

Millinocket, Maine—2012

LUKE

LEAVE IT TO Jonah to think there was an easy way to get their mother out of Church's Overlook for a few hours.

Their place downwind from Baxter State Park in Millinocket was named for Frederic E. Church, a landscape painter from the famous Hudson River School. The decent-sized main inn was flanked by ten smaller, more rustic cabins and a groundskeeper's cottage. All of them built long after Mr. Church came to the Maine woods and stood on the shore of their Penobscot, aiming to capture Mount Katahdin in oil.

From what Luke had pieced together, around the time their mother adopted the boys, she bought the land, kept Coop on as her groundskeeper, and gave him the cottage in exchange for his service. Older than their mother by maybe ten years, Coop was native Penobscot and knew the area trail to tree. Together the two friends tore down most of the original logging camp and turned the new place into a stopover for nature seekers.

Luke understood why his mother kept busy, cooking her signature country breakfast day after day, taking reservations, supervising cabin turnover each Saturday between guests. Like the river, life at Church's Overlook had a rhythm of its own, a way of bending time. Routines were predictable, and their repetitiveness allowed the days to flow from one to the next without cluttering the mind with worry or stress.

Aside from Coop, his mother didn't have time to talk to people or tend to friends. She kept what some might call a low profile. The guests who came and went were good-enough company for her, and even with them she didn't mix much. She wasn't a shopping or primping kind of mom. The few pairs of jeans she owned and the collection of chambray shirts with the name of their inn embroidered above the pocket—shirts Jonah refused to wear—were all she needed.

Everything about Lena Blackwell was do-it-yourself. His mother's religion was her work. She didn't take time off.

So without having said he would help his brother—or his mother—but not having said he *wouldn't* help either one, Luke spent the night wide-eyed in his bed, staring at the little faces in the knotty pine ceiling.

He justified helping Jonah by telling himself a person had a right to know where he came from, even if Luke didn't want that for himself. He belonged here, content with the family he had.

Then there was his mother. It didn't take much to call up the way she'd looked on the trail. Every muscle of her face pinched tight, like she was afraid of something. Luke couldn't remember a time when he'd heard her voice so hesitant. He could almost still feel her grip on his arm. She had every right to feel hurt by Jonah wanting to know about the mother who had abandoned him, the one who'd chosen not to raise him. Still, what real harm would it do to let him look? And why explicitly ask Luke to stop him? It didn't seem fair.

He went back over his conversation with Jonah at the river's edge. If their mother had heard them talking about their adoption, then she knew about Bowdoin too. So why didn't she call him out?

Whether Luke decided to look the other way while Jonah searched, or he aided and abetted him, or actively thwarted him, he was already the definition of duplicitous. Accepting admission to Bowdoin, applying to U Maine, then pretending to different people that he'd picked classes at both places when he hadn't at either.

Luke wondered if there was a word for triple dealing, stacking one lie on top of another like a hiker's cairn. Even though it wouldn't solve his problem, he got out of bed to search out the word for lying exponentially.

He didn't need his brother or anyone else to tell him he didn't act like a typical twenty-one-year-old. His room provided the evidence.

Luke knew his way around a laptop and spent plenty of time online, but he preferred less connected ways of doing things. Like looking up words in a dictionary. His favorite was a tome of a thing, its cover with the look and feel of birch bark. It sat on an oak stand Coop helped him build when he was in fifth grade. That night, grappling with whether to help his mother or his brother, it was opened to the letter *P*—*privileged, probability, prodigal.*

In the beginning, the dictionary and its stand were all that filled the space in front of the bigger of his two windows, the one that faced east and looked down on the river. Now this corner of the room was overloaded with his collection of lost-and-found things.

The hand-drawn map of the northern-most stretch of the Appalachian Trail was so perfectly rendered, the rugged dips and climbs around lakes and ponds and streams so accurate, that if a guest hadn't left it behind in one of their cabins, and his mother hadn't seen him staring right at it, imagining himself hiking those places, it might well have been the first thing Luke stole.

It was a Saturday and he was ten, and they were cleaning the cabin named for Emerson. For a few seconds, holding that work of art, Luke forgot his mother was there. Then she tapped him on the shoulder and told him he could keep it if he got back to sweeping. "If she didn't take it with her," his mother said, "it couldn't have meant that much."

That map wasn't the only thing in Luke's collection of little abandonments that came to him honorably. The less-than-perfect wildflowers pressed between pieces of wax paper by the lonely girl who spent one week every summer with her grandparents had been left on the picnic table outside Roosevelt. The love letter Luke found bookmarking a page in one of the field guides to birds he'd borrowed from a shelf in the lobby of the main inn; its recipient must have had a fondness for the scarlet tanager.

And from the kitchen counter in Scribner, he'd snagged a random shopping list: *bread crumbs, ant cups, softer toilet paper.*

Cast off or left behind, Luke had become attached to these things, maybe to disprove the words his mother had affixed to them: *"Couldn't have meant that much."*

Then one day he stopped waiting for things to be discarded. Certain items he'd come across would insinuate themselves in his brain, nagging him, tempting him to take them. An August 1917 copy of *Field & Stream*, with two boys in a canoe on the cover, practically jumped out of the stack of vintage magazines a guest had spent the day collecting at a flea market in Brownville Junction and then left on the coffee table in Thoreau. The book of poems by William Carlos Williams, with notes in the margins— *imagism, idiom, double entendre*—words that begged to be looked up in his dictionary.

It's just a book. It's only a magazine, Luke reasoned. *I'll stop doing this the minute someone speaks up.* Should he get caught taking things that didn't belong to him, he'd feign ignorance. *Must've picked it up by mistake when I was tidying your cabin. Won't happen again.*

His wall of chosen things grew to mural proportions and became a kind of art exhibit, one he was more proud of than guilty over. He spent more time building it and admiring it than he did considering why taking these things preoccupied him. As far as Luke knew, nobody except Jonah ever said much about the items he'd adopted. Not even their mother, a woman who should know about such things.

A single knock on his wall disturbed the peace. Luke called it Jonah's chime; his brother's way of telling him to look at his texts.

What are you doing up?
Have you figured out how to get her out of here?
I'll need at least an hour in her office.

It bugged Luke that Jonah assumed he would help, and also that he was one room over and this was how they talked at night. But he texted back.

I never said I'd help you
Why can't you leave me out of it?

I'd do it for you, and you know it

I would never ask you to

Come on
Sweet talk her into going for a river run
She won't say no to you
She's not going to find out

Luke could've told him right then that she already knew what he was up to. Torn by this crisis of loyalty, he texted:

I'll think about it

By morning, Luke was off the hook. Jonah was in luck when their mother had to leave the inn to return a week's worth of fruit affected with fire blight. But then, during breakfast, the plan fell apart again when she put Jonah in charge of one last rafting trip before he had to head back to school.

Without a word to his mother or his brother, Jonah left the breakfast room to lead a half dozen guests outside, texting as he held open the door.

Luke looked at his phone, and sure enough there was a string of messages from him.

I need you in my corner
Would you do it for me?
You're good at poking around and lifting things

Luke took off out the front entrance. He began to stack the crates of apples—macs and goldens—along with some nectarines and pears into the back of his mother's truck. "I can bring this stuff back to Haverman's." Luke's offer was his last-ditch effort to get out of the bind.

"No, you stay here and man the reception desk," she said, pulling her keys from her pocket. "I've got errands to run on my way back. I'm making a special send-off dinner for you and Jonah."

She put her hand on his arm. Unlike the day before, her touch was light. "It means a lot to me that you see this thing with Jonah like I do," she said, smiling. "Trust me: Nothing good would come of it."

The lines of her face relaxed, and in that split second, she seemed happy. Tangible lightness was a rare and special thing coming from his mother. The hint of it sent him back into a spin over who to align himself with. After all, he'd never actually agreed to help Jonah get inside the office and snoop around.

"What exactly do you expect me to do?" Luke asked.

"Whatever it takes," she said. "Steer him toward another topic for his film project. Remind him biology doesn't matter. I'm your mother. I have always been your mother. I know you can sway him, Luke. There's no one he listens to more than you."

And that's where she left it. She was in her truck and down the drive before he had a chance to object.

It was Sunday and the guests who were early risers were up already, most of them out on the river with Jonah. The lazier ones wouldn't be milling around the lobby till lunchtime. His mother would be back by then.

Luke parked himself in the lobby behind Reception. Riffling the pages of the reservation book, he tried not to think about what might be waiting for him in the office.

With only one phone call, it took all of five minutes to reserve Roosevelt for the Winslows, who, in a last-minute booking, would check in on Saturday. The rest of the guests due to arrive next weekend had already been confirmed. There were no credit cards to run or brochures to address and stamp. The desk was neat and tidy. There was nothing to do.

Idle hands. And feet.

Luke backed out of the lobby, and before he'd thought it all the way through, he had entered the office he hoped would one day be his. Why not pretend to look, and then tell Jonah he didn't find anything?

With all his brother had left to do before leaving Millinocket—packing up his stuff and saying goodbye to his girlfriend—there wouldn't be time for him to prove Luke wrong. Without papers, he'd be forced to drop his plan to find his birth parents. He'd have to pick a more sensible topic for his documentary; their mother would be reassured.

If Luke came through for her, she would owe him. He could stay right here where he wanted to be.

The battered maple desk wasn't anything special, but it did a fine job of organizing her things. The top drawer held pens and pads and loose-leaf paper; nothing remarkable, nothing with names. Crowding the second drawer were bill folders filed alphabetically: cable, electric, health insurance, tax.

Luke had never had a reason to go through his mother's things before, and he felt a kind of relief to find it all so ordinary.

Until he decided to see what was left to pay off on the land and their inn.

People's United Bank with an address in Bangor headed the top right corner of the bill. Luke couldn't focus on the principle amount due because he was struck by the fact that his mother's name wasn't on it. Under the address on the "Please remit" line was their groundskeeper's name—Irving Orono Cooper.

Why was Coop the one holding the mortgage?

Outside, a deer moved past the window, momentarily changing the light in the office. Luke stuffed the pages into the folder and filed it back where it belonged. There had to be a simple explanation for why his mother's name wasn't on it. But then he checked the phone bill, the light bill, Jonah's truck payment, and his. Coop, Coop, Coop, and Coop.

He had the urge to text Jonah to tell him what he'd found, except Luke had no idea what any of it meant. Instead, he slipped out of her chair and, without engaging the noisy latch, closed the office door halfway and pulled the blinds. The bottom drawer had a trademark creak, so to avoid making it sing, Luke opened it slowly, taking his time to reveal the built-in safe where his mother kept cash and credit card receipts, and whatever else she might be hiding. He didn't have the combination but fiddled with it anyway, starting with random sequences, moving on to more complex combinations of birth dates and other favored numbers.

"Your mother know you're in here?" Coop's gravelly voice, as familiar as it was, caused Luke to slam his fingers in the drawer. With his stocky frame filling the doorway, Coop looked exactly like the same man Luke had seen every day of his life. Except now he wondered if he really knew him.

"I'm manning the desk," he said.

"I think she might have meant reception," Coop said. "Hard to man that from in here with the door part shut."

"I needed to—" Luke didn't bother to finish. More to the point, he couldn't think of what else to say. He walked out to the lobby, past Coop, trying not to make eye contact as he went.

*　*　*

LENA

Over the years, without meaning to, Lena had become as stony and aloof as the mountain landscape she hid inside. Living in a perpetual state of fear made it hard to be the person she was before she'd gotten to Maine— conversationally light and outwardly affectionate. So yesterday, when Luke had suggested that she give Jonah something to satisfy his curiosity, he'd broken through her toughness, and her next steps became clear.

Maybe Jonah had the urge to search for his birth parents because Lena hadn't done enough to show him she loved him. She needed to work harder to remind him this had always been and would forever be true.

Tonight Lena could stop Jonah's perilous pursuit by simply giving her son the kind of mother he'd been yearning for.

If simple evidence of honesty, generosity, and kindness would allow him to see she was more than bricks of strength, then she would paint a happy portrait at the family table. If Jonah wanted her undivided attention, then she'd close the inn to guests for dinner—something she had never done. If he needed to feel known, she would prepare his favorite meal. And if he craved an understanding of his past, she'd call up their best memories in good conversation over fine food.

Low clouds wrapped around her truck as she drove the south end of Ferguson's Lake and rolled into the driveway of Haverman's Farm. The steam fog that appeared this time of year when the air cooled before the river did couldn't rob the farm of its panoramic views.

Lena was still taking in the scene when Walt Haverman knocked on the passenger side window, motioning for her to meet him at the back of her truck.

Despite his bushy beard and bulging eyes, Walt had a kind face. "I feel terrible about your order," he said. "I got the blight isolated to a handful of trees in the north orchard. I didn't figure out that college boy had picked from that area till you called."

"No worries. I employ a couple of college kids myself," she said, her tone light. It was the best she could do to sound friendly.

"Yeah, except your boys are conscientious. This wouldn't have happened if you'd loaned me Luke or Jonah for the summer."

"Sorry—I needed them for my own peak season. I'll find out soon enough what busy looks like once they're off to school."

Side by side, Lena and Walt moved the rotten produce toward a dumpster around the back of the barn. Walt was strong, with thick legs and an even thicker middle, a shape that resulted as much from physical work as from too much beer. Lena matched him, crate for crate, because her power had been honed.

When the new crates of fruit were loaded in and tied down, Walt stepped back and folded his arms across his chest. "I'd like to make your second trip here in a week worth it to you. I've got some venison I'd be willing to part with, or maybe you want some of the trout I caught this morning. Take your pick."

Ordinarily, Lena would say, *"No thanks,"* but here was her chance to cater to each of her sons' preferences. "I was planning a special dinner for my boys—one eats red meat and one won't," she said.

"Well then, you'll have to take a little of each. I'll be right back."

While Lena waited for Walt, she toyed with the idea of leaving without taking his gifts. His attempt to be a good neighbor suddenly made her uncomfortable. She'd get around her dismissal of his kindness the next time she saw him by explaining she'd been called back to the inn suddenly. Something urgent having to do with a guest.

Before Lena could make her getaway, another truck pulled in next to hers. Sylvie Ellis. Jonah's girlfriend.

Lena liked Sylvie. Not only was she sweet and smart, but she was good at reining in her impulsive son. Or maybe

Jonah wanted to be better around Sylvie because he loved her.

"Hey, Ms. Blackwell. You get the bad fruit too?"

Sylvie wiped her palms on her jeans and then tugged at the hem of her shirt.

"I did," Lena said. "Just exchanged it for fresh."

"I only have one bag," she said pointing inside her truck. "I wasn't going to bring it back, but Mr. Haverman told my mom he'd rather be the one to throw it out. I guess blight can spread to all kinds of plants and trees if you're not careful."

Sylvie seemed relieved when Walt reappeared. Who could blame her? Lena wasn't the easiest person to make small talk with.

"This ought to make your boys plenty happy." Walt handed Lena a brown bag.

Sylvie leaned into her front seat to pull out the contaminated fruit.

"Let me get that, and then we'll go grab your replacement order," Walt said, motioning for Sylvie to follow him. "Enjoy your nice night, Lena. See you next week."

"Wait, Sylvie," Lena said. "Would you like to come for dinner? I've got plenty of food, thanks to Walt. It'll make Jonah's night to have you there."

"Well, I don't know about that." Sylvie crossed her arms.

"Please," Lena said. "I want to do this nice thing for him. And for you too. Plus, Luke will want to see you before he goes."

"I shouldn't," she said. "I have tons of packing to do."

"You still have to eat dinner, don't you? Please, I insist." Lena got into her truck so Sylvie couldn't keep pushing back. Before pulling out on to the rough road, she lowered her window. "Let's surprise him, okay? Come at seven."

broach—*verb*. When a canoe or kayak is pinned against an obstruction by the force of the wind, waves, current, or rocks; the prelude to a capsize.

5

Millinocket, Maine—2012

LUKE

I N ALL THE time he'd lived at Church's Overlook, Luke couldn't remember a single night when his mother had closed the main inn to guests so they could have dinner without being interrupted. They weren't the kind of family with much occasion to celebrate, and once his school news was out in the open, that would still hold true.

Even though he was the first one in the dining room, the smell of something sautéing in apples and onions, and the sound of someone working in the kitchen, told him he was on time. Luke stood in that familiar space, going over it. Whether or not his mother was guilting him into keeping tabs on Jonah, this was the night to come out with it. He wasn't going to Bowdoin. Alone there, he weighed the benefits of bringing it up before the main course, and he contemplated the upside of waiting till dessert.

Empty of people and with all but one table pushed back against the log wall, the room looked bigger than usual.

The remaining table, alive with candles, was parked in front of the window overlooking the river. The only thing partially obstructing the view was a potted mum sitting smack in the middle. Plates and napkins and glasses laid down for five confirmed that Coop would be there. Luke expected as much since he ate with them most nights, sitting at the head of the table opposite his mother. But who else had been invited?

"There he is," Jonah said, shaking his head, making a tsking sound through his teeth. He held the door open, and in walked Jonah's girlfriend and Luke's best friend since grade school.

"Look who I found, in the lobby." Jonah said. "People around here are good at keeping all kinds of secrets."

Sylvie elbowed Jonah in the ribs on her way through the door, and she gave him a look that meant his brother had already told her Luke wasn't going to school with him.

"Don't listen to him. Things'll turn out fine for you," Sylvie said, kissing him on the cheek.

Luke had known Sylvie since the first day of third grade, and she'd been a calming presence even then. Whenever he'd get nervous about a new school year or tough teachers, or he worried too much about an upcoming test, Sylvie would remind him that he worked himself up like this every fall for no reason. He always did fine. And there wasn't anything wrong with asking for help if he needed to.

When she'd told him, in the middle of their senior year of high school, that she'd been accepted to Boston University and would study to become a nurse, it made sense to Luke. One kind look from Sylvie, and your fears would up and disappear, your afflictions were healed.

"Where've you been, brother? I've been texting you." Jonah pushed a jumbo-size bottle of wine toward Luke with so much force he almost doubled over. "Say it's from you."

Their mother backed into the room by way of the swinging kitchen doors, carrying a basket of freshly baked rolls. "Wonderful—Sylvie's here." After handing the basket to Jonah, she wiped one hand on her apron, and with the wrist of the other, she brushed the hair out of her eyes. "Thank you, Luke," she said, accepting the wine. "How thoughtful."

It was strange to watch his mother care about the way her hair looked, acting like they did this every Sunday. Luke could've sworn he was seeing things when he noticed she'd dressed up for dinner.

"Thanks for inviting me, Ms. Blackwell." Sylvie's lips tightened, and she started fidgeting with her necklace.

"Of course. This will be nice." She turned to head back into the kitchen. "Give me a few more minutes to get everything ready. I'll be right out."

When she was gone, Jonah broke the silence. "Who took our mother and left us with *her*? Did either of you know she owned a dress?"

Jonah had a talent for saying what other people were thinking. Sylvie and Luke laughed and took seats next to each other, facing the river.

"I don't know whether to be glad she's in a good mood or offended," Jonah said. "It's like she's excited to get rid of me."

Next up, Coop came through those swinging doors. The man who'd taught them to haul canoes from the river, chop cords of wood, and pack a camper like a pro was the closest thing to a father they had. But Luke had never seen him—not once in his life—juggling a tray of noisy glasses and holding a bottle of wine by its neck.

"Hey, Sylvie, boys." Coop nearly lost two glasses on his way to the table. Jonah grabbed them in the nick of time and set them at his and Sylvie's places.

Coop's hands shook as he screwed the bottle opener into the cork. The twist and squeak sent a shiver down Luke's spine.

"When are you heading back to Boston?" Coop asked Sylvie, gesturing for Jonah to sit. "What year are you in again?"

"Saturday. I start classes the day after Labor Day. I'm a junior."

"Bet *you've* started packing your things. Maybe you can jump-start these two. Imagine leaving tomorrow, and not one damn thing's seen the inside of a box."

Jonah took a swig of his wine before he sat down across from Luke. He had *"I need a cigarette"* written across his forehead. Keeping his head down, Luke tried to avoid looking at Coop, but he didn't mean to stare at Sylvie's legs, and the creamy white gap of flesh between her jean skirt and leather riding boots. Then she went and made things worse for him. In an effort to reassure him, she took his hand under the table and squeezed it.

It wasn't right to like the feeling of her hand in his as much as he did.

Coop and his mother made three trips back and forth from the kitchen, setting down piping hot bowls of sweet potatoes and squash, platters of trout, and a Dutch oven filled with venison stew. Each time through, they refused offers of help. Theirs had always been an easy friendship. Neither one much of a talker, they seemed content with the sameness of their days. Or maybe they were mind readers.

In between disappearances, Jonah gave Luke directions:

"Get the name of the adoption agency.

"The foster home if you can.

"Even the hospital would be a start."

Luke didn't tell him there was no way he was going to steer the conversation in the direction he wanted. He had things of his own to say.

When their mother had taken her seat, Jonah went to pour her a glass of wine, but she put her hand over the rim before he could fill it.

"It's been a long time coming," she said, raising her empty glass. "To both of my boys at Bowdoin."

Jonah looked first at Coop, who had his glass held up in front of his face covering his expression. To Luke he mouthed the words, *You didn't tell her yet?*

No one said anything as they heaped their plates with food.

"Well, get ready for surprises all around," Jonah finally said.

"Don't," Sylvie said.

Jonah threw back the rest of his wine like he was drinking from a shot glass. "Luke, go ahead and tell them."

The way his mother pinned her stare on him confirmed what Luke already knew. She had heard what he'd told Jonah down at the water's edge. The look also warned him not to go through with it.

"Luke's traded Bowdoin for U Maine," Jonah said, sloshing more wine into his glass.

"That true, son?" Coop asked.

Luke could feel sweat sliding down the sides of his face as the attention shifted to him. Why was Coop acting surprised? If his mother already knew, wouldn't she have told him?

"Actually, no. That's not quite right," Luke said, pushing his plate toward the center of the table, bumping the mum and sending petals raining down on his food.

"I've decided not to go to college at all. I'm content to stay right here and work."

"You are going," his mother said. "It's been decided. I've already paid tuition for the first semester." Her voice carried the low notes she used when what he and Jonah wanted wasn't up for discussion.

"Most of it is refundable as long as classes haven't started yet." As soon as Sylvie's helpful commentary was out, she looked down at her plate and lifted a fork full of trout to her lips.

"For the last year you've been telling me I could change my mind anytime," Luke said. "So this has to be about what Jonah's planning to do."

His mother stared hard at him. "That's enough."

His brother pulled a cigarette from his pocket, ignoring the no-smoking-inside-the-inn rule. "Come on, you told her?"

As she so often did, his mother moved her attention right off Luke and onto Jonah.

"You haven't thought this through," she said. "Adoptions are closed for a reason."

"I'm not the first person to challenge that thinking. Plus, just because I learn the details doesn't mean I'm going to do anything with the information."

"Have you thought about me?" she asked, her voice cracking. "I raised you. I am your mother. Maybe I don't want you to do this."

"Look, I'm sorry this upsets you," Jonah said. "Contrary to popular opinion, that's not what's driving me."

"Then why would you set out to turn lives upside down? Yours. Mine. And whoever that other woman is, or was. If she was willing to face questions about her decision to do what she did, she would've left the adoption open. Clearly she didn't want that."

"Maybe back then she didn't. But she might not want to *be* found until she *is* found. Your family's gone, but at least you knew them. Good, bad, or otherwise, I have a right to know mine."

"You're being selfish," she said. "I'm asking you not to be."

"I'm an adult, and I want you to tell me what the foster care people told you. I want you to give me whatever records you have."

"There isn't anything I can say to you."

"Can't or won't?"

"I'm asking you again. Do not do this."

Jonah stubbed his cigarette out by impaling the flesh of his trout. He never broke eye contact with her.

Finally their mother looked away. She pressed her shoulders back, pushed her chair away from the table, and stood. In a gesture Luke had never once seen her execute, she smoothed out her dress and walked out of the dining room, not carrying a single plate or cup when she disappeared through those doors.

*   *   *

LENA

Pots and pans covered every burner of the stove, and the sink was piled high with dishes. Lena stood in the middle of the inn's kitchen, taking in countertops crowded with a cook's tools, and for the first time in a long time, she couldn't bring herself to clean up a mess. What was the point? All her hard work had been for nothing. Her special meal. Coop's behind-the-scenes efforts to get Luke into Bowdoin. Leave it to Jonah to jeopardize everything with his self-focused plan. She'd had such peace of mind knowing her boys would be together at college. Finally her responsible son keeping an eye on her rash one.

As much as Luke loved the Maine woods, she never thought in the end he'd choose Church's Overlook over being with his brother. She didn't expect Luke to disobey her either. Had he even tried to talk Jonah out of finding his birth parents?

Overwhelmed by the sweltering kitchen, she gave in to the urge to flee, exiting by way of Reception. Inside her room, with the door latched, she ran her sweaty palms down the length of her knit dress. No mirror required, she knew she looked foolish. Served her right, the way things were going. After all these years, Lena had dared to bring this remnant piece of clothing from her old life into her new one.

In a twist of fate—the story she'd concocted to keep the boys from learning about the horrible life she'd saved them from was the very one that had Jonah yearning to know the truth.

Lena fought to unzip the ridiculous dress. Pulling it from her body as though it were on fire, she dropkicked it to the back of her closet before reaching for a pair of well-worn jeans. A cotton jersey top was barely over her head when she heard a single rap on her door.

She opened the door to Coop on the threshold. Always patient, forever careful not to startle her, this was one of the many reasons Lena had let him into her life. And into her room.

Looking deep into his dark eyes, she could see he was worried for her.

"I'm okay," she said. "Sorry I made a scene. Think I can go back to the dining room and claim I just needed to change out of that dress?"

"Dinner's done. Sylvie and the boys are cleaning up. Grab a sweater and meet me down by the water."

That's what Lena and Coop did. When they needed to talk, they'd conference at the river's edge or hunker down in their office, away from the boys.

Lena slipped out the back entrance of the inn and made her way down a path that snaked the east side of the property. She didn't need moonlight or a flashlight to find the trail. It was as worked into her memory as the ground she walked on. Coop was already sitting on the bench he'd carved out of a fallen tree shortly after Lena and the boys had arrived at Church's Overlook years ago.

He had a tribal blanket over his lap, and when she sat down, he flourished it until it covered her too.

Coop's warmth was welcome; the sound of the river, a comfort.

"It'll be fine," he said, taking her hand.

"I thought after all this time I was free and clear. Neither of the boys has talked about the adoption in years."

"You still are in the clear. Even if he can't be talked out of it, Jonah will come to a dead end."

"How can you be sure? If there's a single thread to pull, that boy will yank it," Lena said.

"You've got nothing to worry about. Tracks have been covered. I've lived here a lot longer than you. Penobscots stick together."

At night all things were shades of black. When Lena turned to Coop, she realized then that the only time she ever really looked at him, he was a silhouette of shadows. During the day there simply wasn't time to focus on each other. Working with him to run the inn, one or the other of them was always off tending to the never-ending list of chores. And up until these last few years, she'd also been caring for the boys.

"I've never asked you why you helped me," she said.

Coop remained silent. Lena waited, unable to tell if he needed more time to form an answer or if he wasn't planning to offer one up.

Wood thrush called out their goodnights, and as the birds finished their duet, Coop leaned his head against hers. "You needed me. Out of the blue, I had a chance at a family. Every arrangement has its terms."

"What if Luke and Jonah find out what I did?"

Coop drew her closer to him under the native blanket. "Maybe you could tell them a few things."

"We've been over it. There's no way to explain what I stole them away from."

The Maine wind picked up, and from the south, there was a rumble of thunder.

"I'm getting that feeling again," she said. "Like I'm not safe here."

"I'll go back to making rounds at night. Flashing you the signal," Coop said.

It had been years since they'd adhered to that evening ritual; the habit they had practiced to teach Lena to know the night.

"You'll feel better if you do something too," he continued. "Maybe revisit the old cabin. You could stash food and store wood up there. I think you felt safe there right from the start."

Lena had no idea if Coop's suggestion was nearly robust enough for what she might be facing should her story unravel. Still, he was right about how she felt up river. It was something to do.

"You'll stock the place top to bottom and never need to shelter there. You know the boys," Coop said. "Luke will feel bad for you and talk Jonah out of dredging up the past. Even if he can't—Jonah will dig a little, hit an obstacle, and lose interest the way he's known to do. Next week his senior project will be about something else entirely."

Lena did know her boys, and sitting next to Coop, with his strong body firm against hers, she needed him to be right. Maybe the dinner hadn't been a total disaster. She'd made an effort to let Jonah know she cared. She'd objected strongly enough that he might have second thoughts and drop it. Jonah was more sensitive than he liked to let on.

Staring at the fluctuating surface of the water, across the dark river, Lena wanted to believe that the span of time between then and now had changed how afraid she needed to be.

She would create a safe house anyway.

6

Millinocket—2001

THE MINUTE HER little boys heard they might be able to pitch a tent alongside a stream in a forest of spruce and fir poised for glimpses of moose and deer, it was over. At first she'd wished Coop hadn't brought up his good-for-business idea right in front of Luke and Jonah over dinner. Yet reluctant as she was, Lena agreed to give the first Annual Hike and Camp for staff and guests of Church's Overlook a go.

It was the end of June, late into the evening, when she curled up on the couch in the lobby of the main inn to flip through some Baxter State Park guidebooks. It didn't feel like work. More like planning a vacation.

Lena couldn't let herself think about the last time she'd done that. Regrets were unkind visitors.

As much as she hated to admit it, she'd begun to look forward to taking the trip with Coop and the boys, including their guests of the inn. He always seemed to know what she needed to keep her spirits up. Life at Church's Overlook was crowded with routines and schedules, nothing unpredictable or spontaneous save for New England weather and cyclical bouts of loneliness.

Lena knew it would make Coop happy to form an official family with her and her sons, but that wasn't going to happen. Her heart had been hardened by romanticized love. Never again would she tether herself and the boys to anyone or anyplace. Lena needed to be free to run if that's what she decided to do. But that didn't mean they couldn't act like a family on occasion.

While only half of their ten cabins were rented this time of year, every last one of the scheduled guests was willing to join Lena, Coop, and the boys. Add in the naturalist guide they'd planned to secure, and that narrowed the list of campsites able to accommodate that many campers down to a handful.

For obvious reasons, Lena crossed her original cabin off the list of possibilities. It wasn't quite big enough to house their party, which was reason enough to exclude it, but in truth, since she'd moved into the main inn, Lena had no desire to go back to that part of the land.

Turning the pages of her guidebook, she noted that there'd be plenty of room at the Matagamon Lake site, except it could only be reached by truck and then water. Taking a few canoes out on the river at a time was one thing, but a traveling caravan that included novice paddlers and two young children seemed a little ambitious even for someone as capable as Coop. The boys were so over the moon about the trip, there was no telling if they'd have the wherewithal to listen to a single direction.

Since Lena had given the go-ahead on the campout, Luke had been preoccupied with writing out a list of things to bring. *What-her* for water. *Falashlite* for flashlight. Young as he was, she couldn't get over how he'd taken to sounding out things and scratching down letters on paper. Watching him, seeing his joy at discovering how to read and write all on his own, made her smile.

There was nothing funny about Jonah's preparation, which involved getting up in the middle of the night for a week straight, banging around the kitchen as he packed his backpack with snacks as if this were the morning they'd be leaving at dawn.

With days to go, Lena focused again on the guide-book, and right there on the opposite page, she found it. If Coop wanted remote, offering something other resorts and inns and campgrounds couldn't boast, then Freezeout Trail near Webster Stream would be perfect.

And it was, until Lena let her guard down.

From the moment their group set out from Church's Overlook, Jenny Curtis fit right in. She was the only other woman in their party, and she resembled a brittle tree with lean limbs and a mass of corkscrew hair that kept falling in her eyes. But nothing could stop Jenny from carrying more than her share of gear. She hiked out front, navi-gated maps, and when they arrived at the campground, she pitched in to set up the site. After Jenny and her husband, Eric, staked their tent, she moved right over to help Coop and the boys raise theirs.

On that first night, as Lena stirred the pot of beans, Jenny kneeled down beside her, grabbed the tongs, and started rotating the hot dogs over the fire.

"I love your boys, Mrs. Blackwell," Jenny said.

Lena looked over at the only tent that swayed and buckled. Luke and Jonah were horsing around inside it—an elbow here and a foot there; Lena half-expected the bulging canvas to expel the boys, one and then the other.

"I'm not married. You want 'em?" Lena asked, hoping Jenny recognized a joke when she heard one.

"Oh, sorry, I assumed you and Coop—" A wistful look flashed across Jenny's pretty face. "I'd take the boys off your hands in a heartbeat. Every fall, I get assigned a classroom of twenty-five children, and we become a kind of family. When all I want is one of my own."

Lena felt bad for Jenny, who, from the sound of it, was telling her she'd been having trouble conceiving. Still, there was no way Lena was having this conversation.

"Eric and I, we've been trying for a baby. We're starting IVF when we get back."

"Better take those off the flame," Lena said, pointing to the franks. "Beans are going to take longer than I thought." Not at all confident that talking about food would be enough to change the subject, Lena got up and started rummaging through her pack, making as much noise as she could, pulling out plates and cups and utensils. Creating distractions was something she was good at.

"Must be nice to have two," Jenny said. "How old are they?"

Lena closed her eyes before she turned around to answer. Not because she couldn't remember the story she'd been testing out for the last five years, but because she preferred to live the lie, not spend her time spewing it out on strangers.

"Luke's almost five. Jonah's six and a half."

"I thought they were much closer in age. My mother used to call my sister and me her Irish twins. I used to think having two kids born so close together would be awful. Now I'd give anything."

Lena remained silent. In her head, she searched for something, anything that would effectively end this discussion of babies and birthdays.

"Oh, now I get why Jonah's so annoyed Luke can read," Jenny said. "He can't yet, right?"

At the edge of the clearing, Coop nonchalantly picked up some brush and started making his way toward Lena. As if he sensed she needed to be set free from Jenny's interrogation, he locked eyes with her, and without words he told her to stay calm.

"I don't mean to pry," Jenny went on, "but what does Jonah's teacher say? Oftentimes kids his age just need a little help with phonemic awareness."

Lena stopped stirring. She had no idea how to answer.

"Teaching reading is my specialty," Jenny said. "I'd be happy to work with him while I'm here. I could make it fun for him."

"The boy's a good little reader," Coop said. "Self-conscious is all." After tucking twigs and sticks into the hot coals, flames shot up around the pot of beans. "Lena's doing a fine job homeschooling both boys."

"Oh," Jenny said with a critical tone. "They're homeschooled."

If all it took to silence the teacher was to admit that Lena taught Luke and Jonah, she would've said so much sooner. It wasn't the disapproval that bothered her, because she was neither a good mother nor a bad one for not enrolling her children in school. Lena simply had no other choice.

Aside from the occasional sour face Jenny wore when she saw Luke sounding out words and scribbling them on his list, while his brother with a jealous arm, threw rocks full force into the stream, the rest of the trip was uneventful.

Still, Lena breathed more freely at the end of the outing when, back at Church's Overlook, Jenny and Eric said their goodbyes; loaded their car with packs and suitcases; and pulled their vehicle out of sight.

Once again, Lena had a reprieve from her storytelling. Or so she thought.

"I sent the boys in to wash up for supper so we could have a word," Coop said.

They were standing at the bottom of the stairs leading up to the main inn. Lena steadied herself with one hand on the railing.

"I'm wondering if you might reconsider a few things," he said. "Like sending Luke and Jonah to school."

"You know that's impossible." Lena lowered her body onto the first step.

Coop sat down beside her and placed his hand on her knee. "What if it weren't?"

"What about the birth certificate problem?" Lena lowered her voice so the boys wouldn't overhear her. "You need proof to enroll. I checked."

"There's always a way around things. Up until now you've done right by those boys, but you can't run this place and keep teaching them too. Not for much longer anyway. Sooner or later, you're going to have to let them go. Maybe now's the time."

It didn't matter whether Lena agreed with Coop or not, she would never get over the fear that seized her when the boys were out of sight, playing in the woods or wading a stream.

"I would if I could. Without birth certificates, this discussion is moot." Lena stared toward the river, afraid to meet his kind gaze. Her resolve was known to falter in the face of Coop's compassion.

"You said a few things," she said. "What else do you need to say?"

"I can't help but think it might be time to tell those boys some version of the truth. It's only going to get harder to spin this tangled web of yours, the older they get."

"Absolutely not. They're too young to understand. It's not ideal, what I've told them, but it's worked so far."

Lena pushed off the step and took the stairs to the porch. Stopping at the threshold of the inn, she turned back to Coop. "You hear me? That door stays shut."

Two weeks later, Coop called her bluff. The boys had been in bed for over an hour, and with the kitchen clean and tidy, Lena moved toward the office to finish paying bills. He sat at the desk they shared; his hands were crossed atop a large envelope.

"Got something for you," he said. "A problem solved."

Lena had no idea how Coop had managed to do it, but she knew what was inside the envelope before she took it from him. The coarse, heavy documents she slid from it looked as official as any certificate she'd ever seen, except her boys' names were typed across the top.

Jonah Simon Blackwell, born March 7, 1992; adopted August 1, 1994.

Lucas James Blackwell, born January 4, 1994; adopted August 1, 1994.

On both documents, next to the word *mother* was her name: Lena Blackwell. The space next to the word *father* remained blank.

Thanks to Coop, Lena finally had proof that the story she'd told her boys was true.

eddy—*noun*. A pool of calm water at variance with the main current caused by rocks, obstructions, or the bends in a river or stream.

Millinocket, Maine—2012

LUKE

THOSE FIRST FEW days after Jonah left for school, Luke kept busy guiding hikes and showing guests how to respect the nature of things at Church's Overlook.

It was a relief, really, not to have to choose between satisfying his mother or his brother. Jonah could search for his birth parents from Bowdoin without any help from him, if that's what he wanted to do. Luke would chart his own course around Katahdin and the Penobscot.

He waited at the reception desk for Mr. and Mrs. Marshall and their kids, Alec and Kevin. They'd signed up for the Friday morning out-and-back hike of Little Abol Falls.

All the way into the lobby, the Marshall boys shoved each other over a single bag of trail mix.

"Hey, guys. Come here." Luke reached below the desk for a few more snacks and handed each boy enough so it would be even and fair. "Run into the kitchen and fill your water bottles, okay? Meet me at my truck."

As Luke and Mr. and Mrs. Marshall made their way outside, he gave them a little preview of the birds and trees they were likely to spot on the hike inland from the river.

His mother was outside and had her back to them, but at the sound of Luke's voice, she froze. Everything about her stillness reminded him of the way he felt at those times he'd nearly been caught in the act of pilfering.

Inside her truck bed was a duffle bag, some lanterns, and a heavy-duty cooler.

"Go on ahead. Hop in." Luke turned to the Marshalls and pointed in the direction of his truck. "I'll be right there."

Alec and Kevin came from behind and raced ahead of their parents, elbowing each other every step of the way. The last thing Luke heard out of Mrs. Marshall was a heavy sigh.

"Where are you going?" Luke asked his mother.

"Nowhere. Just packing up some things we don't need."

The Coleman LEDs weren't very old, and the duffle bag looked brand new.

"Have you heard from him?" she asked.

"Still no. Jonah's as pissed off at me for telling you about the search and his film as he is at you for practically ordering him to leave it alone."

"You didn't tell me. I overheard you two talking. He ought to know by now that not much gets by me. You should remind him of that."

One of the Marshall boys shouted from the end of the driveway, "Step on it, Luke."

Nice kid.

"Go on," she said, reaching into the truck bed to zip up the bag. "Not today, but maybe soon, I might need to get away from here for a few days. To clear my head." Her keys were out, and once again, without waiting for Luke to say anything, she started her truck, pulled around his, and was gone.

The Marshall kids bickered the entire drive to the trailhead. But their distraction wasn't the reason Luke couldn't call up a single time his mother had left Church's for an overnight. He knew the answer was *never* before he turned off Park Tote Road and pulled the keys from his truck's ignition.

While Mr. and Mrs. Marshall gathered their things out of the cab, the boys ran ahead. That's when Luke saw Sylvie leaning against the trail sign.

"Mind if I tag along?" she asked once he caught up to her. "I wanted to be sure you were okay."

"I'm fine. Happier now that I get to see you one more time before you go."

Sylvie locked step with him, looking as comfortable in khaki shorts and a threadbare T-shirt as she had when she had dressed up for Sunday supper.

"Alec, slow down," Mrs. Marshall called out. "Wait for us."

"No worries." Luke spoke loud enough for her to hear him. "They can't get into any trouble till we get closer to the log bridges."

"You don't know Alec," the boy's father said between gasps for air.

The Marshall kids were amped, full of never-ending energy, and their mother did a pretty good job of keeping up. But Mr. Marshall's belly hung so low, obscuring any evidence of a belt buckle, that Luke knew even this easy-enough-for-kids hike would tax this guy's abilities. He was what Luke called a lobby man: someone who preferred to spend his time reading field guides and marking maps, never really planning to use them.

"Alec, Kevin—see that boulder ahead, the one with the pointy top?" Luke asked. "Pick a rock around it, and sit. I've got a story to tell you."

"Speaking of stories," Sylvie said quietly, "that dinner was one for the books, huh?"

"Totally. At first I thought she was threatened because Jonah wanted to know his other mother. That she was jealous, you know? But after their fight, it feels like more than that."

"She looked afraid to me."

"When she first found out what he was doing, she told me someone was going to get hurt. I thought she was talking about her feelings, but now I don't know. Maybe she knows something. Something she doesn't want him to find out."

"His real parents could be terrible people. Last night my head was spinning, and I thought what if his birth mother is a criminal?" Sylvie asked.

"I hadn't thought of that. I'm stuck on why he needs to do this in the first place. Our life turned out fine. More than fine. Why does he need to screw everything up?"

"He says that because he's adopted, he has a soul wound."

It wasn't funny—what she said about Jonah—but Luke laughed anyway. "No wonder he's studying film. He's so dramatic."

Sylvie elbowed him the way she sometimes did Jonah. The direct hit to Luke's ribs was unexpected, but he wouldn't have minded if she did it again.

"Have you heard from him?" Luke asked. "He hasn't texted me in a couple of days."

Sylvie shoved both hands into her pockets. Pressing her lips together, she didn't say anything at first.

"What's the matter? Did he track something down?" he asked.

Before they caught up to the Marshalls, Sylvie came out with it. "I don't know, Luke. I thought he would've told you. We broke up."

He stared at Sylvie until the older kid, Alec, chucked a handful of small rocks at a nearby spruce, dinging the trunk with each pitch.

"Please don't," Luke said, loud and clear.

Then Alec threw another rock, bigger this time. The thwacking sound it made was so emphatic the little brother flinched.

"I said, *don't*." Luke's voice was sharp this time, letting the kid know he was pissed. But instead of the reprimand reining him in, Alec looked him right in the eye and did it again.

"Alec!" Close enough to his son now, Mr. Marshall grabbed the boy's arm and squeezed. Alec kept his mouth shut but shook his father off, practically sending the guy face-first into the rock pile. Father and son had done this before.

"What kind of Boy Scout behaves like that?" Alec's mother asked her son this question as if shame were a useful weapon against him. Mrs. Marshall righted her husband, then patted the back of the younger boy, Kevin, who looked like he was about to burst into tears. The little guy was the sensitive type.

"I do what I want," Alec said under his breath.

"That's exactly what Donn Fendler thought," Luke said. "And look what happened to him."

"Who's that?" Kevin asked, his stare fixed on Luke. Alec dropped the rock he'd been handling.

Luke knew he needed to strike the right balance between these boys. Cautionary tales had a way of scaring the wrong kid.

Sylvie sat on a rock and pulled her knees up to her chest, wrapping her arms around them. She acted as though she'd never heard this story before. Every single Marshall did the same. As Mr. Marshall laid down his load, Luke worried he wouldn't be able to get him back up when the time came to hike the falls.

"It was summer, 1939," Luke said. "Donn was twelve, and a Boy Scout from New York."

"Alec's twelve," Kevin said quietly to himself. "I'm only eight. We live in New Jersey."

"Donn was hiking with his brothers, his dad, and some friends. He'd run on ahead. Just crossed a part of the mountain called the massif, the plateau nearing the summit." Luke pointed in the direction of Katahdin; all eyes followed his hand.

"Fog rolled in. Sleet began to pelt him. He couldn't see where he was going."

"You said it was summer," Alec said with attitude.

"It gets cooler the higher you climb," Sylvie said. "It can be sunny and warm down here but something altogether different at the top of the mountain. Weather around here changes like that." She snapped her fingers.

The kid shut up.

It was nice having Sylvie play sidekick.

"Instead of waiting where his father told him to, Donn decided to head back down a different path, thinking he could meet up with them, cut them off at the pass. In just a few minutes, he knew he'd made a mistake. Donn was lost.

"He stumbled around rocky terrain that first night. Pitch-black, no stars; he heard sounds he'd never heard before. Donn thought he'd go crazy if he stayed still, so he kept moving. His plan was to find a tote road like that one we walked down. Or better yet, find water."

"By day two, he'd started to follow Wassataquoik Stream. He lost his sneakers, first one and then the other. The kid was eaten alive by bugs." Luke flashed his hand and both boys drew back.

"Brambles and branches grabbed at his pants until there was nothing left of the cloth."

By the time Luke got to this part of the story, he knew he had his audience if the kids didn't laugh at poor Donn lost in the woods with no pants.

"Shit, did the kid die?"

"Alec, language," his mother said. With her eyes she asked Luke, *"Well, did he?"*

"His legs were swollen to the size of tree trunks, covered with blood suckers. Donn lasted nine days by following that stream. He reached the East Branch of the Penobscot, and with all that was left of his breath, he called out: 'Help!'"

Every single Marshall jumped, and even Sylvie shook a little.

"Donn was found alive by the owner of a sporting camp two miles from here."

The Marshall boys breathed a collective sigh. And for the rest of the hike, Alec stayed on the trail. He didn't pick one flower or kick a single tree root. The ascent was gradual, which proved to be the right hike for Mr. Marshall. He was panting, leaning over, hands on his knees, now and then, but he made it. The reward for the climb—Little Abol Falls— had all the Marshalls proud of their accomplishment.

"Go ahead, boys. You can walk right into these falls," Luke said.

Kevin hesitated, but one nod from Luke, and Alec's shoes were off, and he was wading up to his thighs in the cool stream.

Mr. and Mrs. Marshall parked themselves on a rock. She whipped out a bag of trail mix, and he had his hand outstretched for the water bottle as if it were an emergency.

Sylvie leaned against a tree, watching the boys splash around in the falls.

"You're really great with kids," she said.

Luke stared at Sylvie fiddling with the drawstrings to her shorts. When she noticed him looking at her, he turned away and leaned against the same tree, bringing himself nearly back to back with her.

"Probably because deep down I still am one," he said.

"That's not true. You're a natural at guiding with kids and adults. Jonah thinks you'll never leave Church's. Do you think that's true?"

"My job makes me happy. It never feels like work. If you weren't here, I'd be right in there with them. Sometimes I think Jonah's just jealous because he hasn't really figured out what he loves."

Luke hadn't meant Sylvie, but he could tell from her silence that's how she took it.

"We weren't right together," she said. "And we're both okay with it. Breaking up, I mean. We're going to be friends."

"Everyone says that. But it's hard to stay friends."

If Sylvie hadn't come on this hike, right then Luke would've gotten the Marshall boys' attention to point out the red-winged blackbird perched on a limb above the falls. Instead, he turned toward her.

"I hope it doesn't wreck things between you and me," he said. "We were friends first."

"It won't. I promise."

The blackbird sang out his conk-a-ree call and went flying off above the trees. If Luke hadn't seen Alec with his own eyes, clutching his foot and hopping toward the bank of the stream, blood spilling on foam, he would've thought it was Kevin carrying on.

"Something bit me," Alec shouted.

In a handful of steps, Luke had him by the waist, plucked out of the stream, and planted on the ground.

"You probably cut it on a rock." Luke pulled a bandana from his back pocket and put pressure on the gash on

Alec's toe, assuring him that lots of blood can come from small injuries.

Mrs. Marshall was at his side in seconds. Sylvie tended to the father, yanking him up by the elbow. Kevin rocked and sobbed by the water's edge.

"It hurts like hell," the kid said, his voice shaky.

"You'll be fine," Luke said to Alec. "Hold this. And squeeze." He placed the boy's hand over the bandana-covered toe. Unlacing one of his boots and pulling off his sock, Luke lifted his foot, putting it in Alec's line of vision. "The spirit of Katahdin has marked you. Like me."

Alec's eyes bugged out when he saw the jagged scar that ran the length of Luke's heel.

"How'd you get that?"

Luke realized for the first time that he didn't have an actual answer. All he had to explain it was what his mother had told him over and over again when he was a boy. Did she use the captivating legend to evade the truth of what happened? Or as a proxy because she didn't know?

"That's not important," he said to Alec. "There's a legend having to do with this mountain. Few are marked by the spirit, but once you are, you'll always be safe in the wilderness. If you respect it."

Luke put his sock and boot back on and wrapped Alec's toe even tighter. After helping the kid hop on his back, Luke guided their party along a rock-strewn path, down the incline, walking Park Tote Road back the way they came.

*　*　*

Lena

She stood inside the old sporting cabin and looked out the window. With no higher hills to block the view of the river, it was easier to take in the landscape of stark colors—green forest and shelves of pink granite giving way to black water—than it was to turn around and confront a place she'd had no reason to step back inside for two decades.

Calling to mind how cold it could get in there without a fire going, Lena began to fight a nervous stomach. If she stood still much longer, remembering the rest of it, she might become immobilized. *Get moving,* she told herself. *You're not here to take a trip down memory lane.*

The only furniture that remained included the long pine table, a half-dozen wood chairs, and the floor-to-ceiling sideboard that she would use to hold supplies. Without beds or any other places to sit or sleep, she'd need to drop off a few camping cots and woolen blankets.

Lena lugged the cooler out of her truck, leaving it right inside the cabin door. By the time she'd hauled in the lanterns and bags, she felt a lot better. It had always been true that movement was her friend, purposeful action her kindling. Lena removed her jacket and began to empty the duffel bag into the sideboard, adding to her mental list as she went: *mess kit, canned goods, strike igniter.*

The knives she'd chosen to leave here—slip-joint, lock-back, reverse-edge—would serve all manner of utility. Lena felt nothing as she slid each one from the bag into the drawer. Until her cold fingers touched the switchblade, and Lena was reminded that the fragility that once owned her had a long shadow.

The easy thing to do would be to place this knife in the drawer beside the others. Instead, she trusted what life in the woods had taught her: Fear became small in the presence of bold action. Lena slipped the switchblade into her back pocket.

With the knife in contact with her body, she'd expected to feel stronger. Instead, the intensity of her agitation seemed only to heighten—telling her to put things away and get home.

She locked the cabin, as if that would deter anyone set upon entering it, and drove down the side hill along the rock cliff that dropped off in all directions.

On the ride back to Church's Overlook, Lena got her runaway thoughts under control, until a short distance from the main road she saw Luke's truck fly by, followed by Sylvie's.

Jonah. What did he do? How could he possibly have figured things out so quickly?

When all their vehicles were parked in tandem at Church's, Lena got out and ran toward Luke, who was shimmying one of the Marshall boys out of the jump seat.

"What happened?" Lena's question came out harsher than she'd meant it to. Where was her relief that Luke and Sylvie's urgency had nothing to do with her or Jonah? Luke was presenting her with a simple problem to fix, and she almost kissed him.

"He must've cut it on a piece of shale in the stream," Luke said.

"Where's your first aid kit?" she asked him.

"We only went up to Abol Falls."

"You know better," Lena said, her voice low enough to protect her son's reputation in front of guests. She cocked her head. "Get him inside."

Once Alec was in the lobby, Lena slowly peeled the bandana off his foot. She exchanged small talk with Mrs. Marshall about boys and the scrapes and scratches that came along with them.

Luke brought her his kit, and while she cleansed the cut, applied butterfly closures, and dressed it, he disappeared upstairs. She heard him in his room, and in no time he returned holding *The Legends and True Stories of Katahdin*.

Lena couldn't remember the last time she'd seen that book, though every word and picture was etched in her mind from having read those stories countless times to her boys at bedtime. In retrospect, protecting Luke and Jonah was so much easier to do when they were young and she could monitor their every move. When her children's incomprehensible questions could be answered with fanciful tales.

"Donn Fendler's story's in there," Luke said. "'The Spirit of Katahdin' too." As the book left his hands, her son looked over at her.

Lena didn't want to believe that this treasure of his childhood had lost its meaning. These stories that had shaped her son's love of her and of this place.

Lena felt her eyes well up seeing a stranger holding that gift from Coop. Luke asserting his independence inadvertently pained her. Something both her sons had been doing lately, whether intentionally or not.

Alec took it, but before he cracked the cover to start leafing through, Luke placed his hand on top of it as if he'd had a change of heart. "I expect you to return this to me before you leave Church's," he said. "In perfect condition."

8

Millinocket—1994

S HE WAITED UNTIL both babies were sound asleep in their car seats before driving the last stretch of deserted road. Perhaps it was the moonless sky or the cramped space she'd inhabited for nearly three days with two infants, but she felt ready. Or maybe she was willing to take this risk because she hadn't seen a single car or truck pass this way for the entire time she'd been parked there by the side of the road.

Since she'd left Boston, she'd tended to the boys in an endless cycle of feeding one then the other, changing their tiny diapers, and dressing the wound on James's foot—all from inside Marli's Audi. Whenever the boys had finally settled and she could no longer drive safely, she would pull over and sleep with her head down on the steering wheel.

Down the road, there was a promise of a bed in what appeared to be an abandoned cabin. Imagining a place where she could stretch out her weary body was a temptation impossible to ignore.

Slowing to a crawl, she backed into the space along the side of the blacked-out cabin, parking the vehicle in such a way that it was poised for a quick getaway, if it came to that. With the headlights switched off, but before she pulled the keys from the ignition, she turned to check once more on the babies before leaving to scout out potential lodging. She'd only be gone a minute, maybe two, to try the door, to peek inside. Still she feared leaving the children unattended in the car. She'd heard horror stories of other women foolish enough to do that, unaware of the perils. But rousing one meant potentially waking the other. She couldn't risk disturbing either of the boys by removing their car seats and taking them with her. Just look at Simon. He had to be dreaming, the way his eyes flickered under his smooth lids. One little fist rested on his cheek as if he were enjoying some kind of private movie. Right beside him, James slept soundly, his head tilted toward his brother, his perfect mouth open in the shape of an *O*. Flushed cheeks prompted her to press a palm to his forehead, checking for fever. His skin was cool to the touch. She loosened the sweater he wore, buttoned under the fold of his chin.

These two miraculous faces had kept her going these last few days. Running on remnants of fear, with only intermittent rays of hope, day and night blurred together. When they were awake, demanding her constant attention, she didn't believe she could do this, relying only on herself. Once asleep, their faces were so innocent, their expressions serene, and their collective silence spurred her on. She convinced herself she could do it. What other choice did she have?

Looking at them now, she couldn't remember the last time she'd felt tranquil.

Before slipping out the driver's side door, she whispered, "Mommy will be right back."

Finding her way with a flashlight, she found the cabin open, and though it could use a good cleaning, she didn't mind its rusticness. The furniture was limited, yet what there was of it was functional. Something about the cabin's simplicity soothed her. It was nothing like home. She was grateful for the unseasonable warmth and for the pile of quilts at the end of each bed, because the only way to heat the chilly space would be to light the fireplace. And she had no plans to send out smoke signals for anyone who might be looking for her.

It took her mere seconds to know this was where she would spend the night with her children. She grabbed two quilts from one bed. Her plan was to shake the dust off outdoors before bringing them inside.

Back at the car, the boys hadn't budged. Ready to chance moving them, as gingerly as she could, she unlocked one seat from its base, and then the other, lugging Simon and James into the cabin. Placing one car seat and then the other up on one bed, she hesitated. Should she take them out or let them sleep like that? God only knew how long it would be until one child woke the other for a feeding. *Leave them,* she thought. Never wake a sleeping baby. Let alone two.

She left everything else in the car for the time being. She needed to lie down for a minute, to rest her eyes.

And she slept.

When she woke to sunlight pouring in from the collection of windows lining the walls of the cabin, she felt an overwhelming sense of dread. Why hadn't the babies cried?

But there they were, still strapped in their seats, neither one the worse for it. Simon was making faces at James, who gestured wildly with his tiny hands. Like miniature mimes, they were playing a baby game, keeping each other company until she roused.

How long had she been out? It was after midnight when she'd last checked her watch. She'd been sleeping for nearly five hours, and now, with her feet firmly planted on the cabin floor and the children content in front of her, she felt better than she had in a long time.

The cabin looked shabbier in daylight. What was most pleasing to the eye was what lay beyond those windows. She had stumbled on one giant room with a view. Down the rocky hill from her hideaway ran the Penobscot River. She'd known it was there, of course. She'd seen it on her map. But to catch sight of it now, even through the grimy windows, it was stunning. The entire landscape around the cabin was striking.

Tempted to enjoy this unexpected find, she allowed herself another night. In this cabin in the woods with the boys, she began to feel safe.

On the next afternoon, when she was feeling particularly settled, the babies became fussy, and without a second thought, she wrestled them into a double sling and took them for a walk along a path high above the river. Simon fell asleep almost instantly, as if bored with his surroundings, while James could not have been more content to look around from inside his safe haven.

"You like it here, don't you?" she asked, rubbing his back.

Then, at the sound of birds chirping, his head snapped up, and she felt his whole body jostle against her own. James was giggling. She'd witnessed his first belly laugh. And with it came the sudden realization that she had not one single person in the world to share this marvel with.

She was a runaway woman alone in the woods with two babies, not nearly far enough away from where she'd taken them.

She needed to get going. She couldn't risk staying at the cabin another minute. Certainly the days she'd spent there were a welcome respite. Nature had tricked her into believing she had everything she needed right there. Until now.

Without a doubt she had enough food to last the entire trip to the Canadian border. But what she hadn't factored in was how long it took to meander side roads. Or the inaccessibility of gas and other necessities. She couldn't just pull into any parking lot driving a fancy car, carting around two babies. It would draw too much attention.

So there it was. The truth. She wasn't safe here either. People talked. For all she knew, she'd already made the local gossip circuit. People would be alert and on the look-out for her.

Quickening her pace, she turned around to head back to the cabin, careful not to trip or fall; she wouldn't do anything to hurt these children. She would collect what little she'd brought inside from the car and hit the road after she'd fed and changed the boys. Maybe she'd even risk taking the expressway for a few miles.

As she rounded the bend, nothing looked familiar. She was winded now. James had started to whimper and Simon stirred, either because of his brother's distress or in response to her jerky movements trying to navigate the narrow path.

Or maybe the babies could recognize fear. Two deep breaths and a full circle turn, and she began to trust once more in the direction she'd chosen to hike. With her heart-beat under control, she came front and center with the cabin.

There on the doorstep was a basket filled with a quart of milk, a loaf of bread, and an assortment of tomatoes. Between the ripe fruit someone had tucked a map, the words *"Penobscot Way"* in script printed across the top. Beside those words, handwritten in red ink, was a note clearly meant for her: *Stay as long as you like.*

As hard as she tried, she found it impossible to be frightened by a basket of tomatoes. She fed the boys and changed them, then placed them in the makeshift bed she'd made from a collection of pillows and quilts. Once they were asleep, her urge to flee had tempered. Maybe she could stay one more night.

For the next few days, gifts continued to show up outside her front door. Zucchini, native corn, and on the fourth day, a worn copy of Thoreau's *The Maine Woods*. Never were the items accompanied by footsteps on the path or a knock at the door. Their arrival had a mythical quality to them; they were merely generous offerings, no strings attached.

By day, she found herself imagining who her benefactor was. One night, she decided to stay awake, sitting in a chair off to the side of the front window, hoping to catch a glimpse of the gifter. By first light, having not seen anyone, her stiff neck and cramped legs told her to forget it, get some sleep while she still could. That's when she saw him.

The man's height was average. Shorter than Davis, but stockier than Nic. The closer he got to the cabin, the easier it was for her to figure his age. He couldn't have been more than a few years older than her.

If anyone had told her that she'd be helpless in a cabin in the woods with two babies, watching a complete stranger—a man—moving toward her and her children, and that she wouldn't be afraid, she would never have believed it.

Careful in the way he navigated the path, he didn't disturb a single blooming plant or flowering shrub—or perhaps he moved slowly because he didn't want to alarm her. Caught in the act of giving, there was nothing ominous about him. She could tell by the way he moved that he preferred to come and leave whatever it was he carried without fanfare.

However, this time, there was no basket in his arms. Instead, he held something large made of wood. All she could make out was what looked like lattice work or the pieces of a small ladder.

She ducked down at the window, hoping he hadn't seen her watching him approach. Unable to resist temptation, she peeked again to see what it was he was leaving her.

He took his time assembling the wooden structure, lightly tapping a few pieces into place. When she recognized what it was, she couldn't feel fright; she was downright excited.

A complete stranger had brought her some type of handmade crib and then positioned it near a tree under a canopy of leaves that would protect her babies from the sun.

She opened the door.

He didn't look up. "Hey," he said.

"Thank you," she said, her voice cracking from disuse. "Is this your cabin?"

He looked at her now, his eyes the warm brown of the earth. Certain features of his resembled the photos of native people on the map he had left her.

"It's kind of you to let me use it. I appreciate the food too. And that's amazing." She pointed to the crib. It was wide enough to hold both babies. Her thanks seemed inadequate in comparison to his gesture.

"I'm passing through," she said. "I won't be much longer."

"Like the note said, stay as long as you like. Cabins are all empty anyway. I don't let folks know the place is available like I should."

"Cabins? There are more?"

"Three. Plus the main house I live in about a mile downriver. You picked the best of the bunch up here. The whole lot was my grandfather's sporting camp. Only a handful of the old places like these left in these woods."

Wanting to get a better look at the assembled crib, she felt brave enough to step outside, to move closer to inspect it and the man. How could she be afraid of someone who loaned her Thoreau and then left a crib outside the cabin of a woman with no beds for her children?

"Name's Irving Cooper. Friends call me Coop." He dug both hands into his front pockets and rocked back on the heels of his boots.

She hadn't fully committed to choosing a new name for herself, so she didn't say anything.

"If you need something, don't hesitate," he said. "Leave a list of things tacked to your door. Must be hard taking care of two at the same time."

At the mention of the boys, her old friend fear crept back up behind her. As if Coop recognized the tension for what it was, he stopped talking and walked away.

She was filled with relief at this, his most generous gesture.

The boys loved their new bed. On the day it arrived, she let her babies spend the morning outside, staring at the sun flickering through the leaves above it. As the afternoon cooled, she moved it inside the cabin and positioned it next to her bed. While they napped, she spent her time reading *The Maine Woods* and searching the map Coop had given her for new names for her family.

South of Millinocket in a town called Madison, she noticed the words Blackwell Corner. Blackwell gave off a strong ring. Simon became Jonah. James became Luke. Her children would be known as the Blackwell boys. Away from her life in Boston, Lena Blackwell was born. The rest of the details of her story would come in time. For now, new names were enough.

In a matter of days, Lena allowed Coop entrance to the cabin, where she invited him to share the bounty of the late fall vegetables he continued to bring her. They ate companionable meals, and without prompting, once the dishes landed in the sink, and had been washed and dried, he would leave.

One night over dinner, she offered Luke to him, asking if he cared to rock the boy while she finished feeding his brother.

In all their time together, Coop never once asked what she was doing there. Why a woman with two infants would be hiding in the Maine woods, letting a complete stranger do her shopping, going to the store for her sundries. She wondered what the locals thought of Coop suddenly stopping in to buy diapers.

It wasn't until a month into her stay that Lena was sure Coop knew. Or at the very least suspected.

They were eating Sunday supper, and the boys were content to play their baby boy games in the crib positioned next to the table. "I've got a friend down in the Carolinas who might like to buy that Audi of yours," he said. "Should you be looking to sell it."

Her fork nearly to her lips, she held it in midair. Lena simply said, "That would be fine. I'd appreciate it."

"I could get you a fine truck with the money. Nothing fancy. Just something more useful in these parts." Coop leaned down and touched Luke's foot lightly, just the brush of a finger across the seam of his sock. "This here will need to be released from time to time as the boy grows."

Her new friend had a way of talking about something as clear as could be without using a word with the power to hurt her. Coop was talking about the scar—the violence made visible that ran the length of her son's tiny sole.

"There's a woman I know who does a fine job with medical things like this. I could introduce you."

All Lena could do was nod.

A week later, the Audi disappeared and Coop along with it. Days later, when he finally returned, he drove a used truck down the gravel path and parked it beside her cabin. He was accompanied by an elderly native woman.

When they entered the cabin, neither said much. The woman went straight for Luke as though she had sensed he was the one who needed her particular kind of attention. Coop didn't hand Lena the keys right away. Instead, he entertained both boys by jingling them the perfect distance from their little faces. The distraction he provided, as the woman inspected Luke's foot, was as skilled as that of any medical professional Lena had ever observed. The babies, all smiles, seemed happy to see Coop again.

And that's when Lena decided she would stay. For at least as long as it was safe to.

haystack—*noun*. A rhythmic series of waves caused by the meeting of currents, rising water, underwater obstacles or ledges, or an increasing river speed; may be fun to ride but large enough to swamp an open canoe.

9

Millinocket, Maine—2012

LUKE

WORD FINALLY CAME from Jonah the Saturday after he'd left for school. It was the longest the brothers had gone without talking. But he wasn't in touch to tell Luke about Sylvie. Jonah didn't ask about their mother or Coop, or even about him. What Jonah had to say shouldn't have surprised Luke, as he headed downstairs to the lobby reading those texts. Still it did. The search was on.

> Can't find my birth certificate
> Maine says I'm missing vital info
> No shit
>
> What are you missing?
>
> City/town where birth occurred
>
> Didn't we have to show birth certs to go to school?
> Or get our licenses? Maybe one of those places has a copy

You're a genius old man

Why didn't you tell me about Sylvie?

Needed time to wrap my head around it
What did she tell you?

Not much
You're going to be friends?

I guess. Can't deal with it now. Got a few things distracting me
Is Mom still acting weird?

I wouldn't know
I'm avoiding her
Gotta go. Work

With his mind on the day's business, Luke decided to take over the reception desk to check guests in. When his mother came into the lobby and saw him there, sorting information sheets into packets complete with maps for each registered party, she left unfazed, to take up the job of directing guests toward their cabins.

Through the picture window, Luke watched her wave a young couple driving a beat-up four-door into a parking spot along the circular drive. Then she did the same with two separate families in identical minivans. There was Coop, at the ready to take over for anyone struggling with bags and gear.

Nothing about the way his mother and Coop worked together looked any different than it had every other Saturday of his life. Luke hadn't given their partnership much thought till recently. Coop was always just there. A committed employee. A trusted friend. A member of the family.

They ran the inn together—each with his or her own responsibilities. So why lie about who owned the place?

Luckily, the rush of guests who landed in front of the reception desk after noon provided a welcome distraction. Luke passed out keys and packets, directed people to the restroom or back toward his mother and Coop for cabin particulars, all while he kept packs of kids from wreaking havoc in the lobby.

"Who wants a map of the mountain?" he asked. "Any of you ever hiked Katahdin?"

At the offer of a full-color foldout of the area, the kids stopped their games and crowded around him. Ten little hands reached out for his maps.

"I climbed Mount Washington with my daddy once," said a girl dressed in head-to-toe pink. The kid was so small Luke could barely imagine her climbing onto the lobby couch, never mind hiking Chimney Pond Trail to Katahdin.

In record time he had the lobby cleared, waiting on the last few check-ins. There were always those stragglers who took longer to show up, the ones who had a harder time making the shift from the overwhelming places they came from to their remote corner of peace and quiet.

With the rush over, his mother came back into the lobby. She didn't believe in wasting time standing still. "Let me take the bulk of cash and credit receipts and lock them up in the office," she said.

Luke wouldn't have compared his mother to a buzzing bee or a delicate hummingbird. Hers was more of a directed, cool kind of energy. Like a female marten, always with her head down, she paid attention to the work that needed to be done.

"I can do it," he said. Here was his chance to get into the safe. "What's the combination? Might as well learn the ropes. In case you need to take off."

"Not today," she said. "We're waiting on two more reservations, and then I've got to start supper."

"Three," Luke said.

"Three what?"

"Three more reservations. Noble. Thorne. And that last-minute booking." Luke looked down at the register. "I put the Winslows in Roosevelt."

"Can I see?" She reached for the reservation book, turning it upside down so she could read it. "Well, looks like we're full this week after all." Her voice struck a false cheery note as all the color drained from her face.

"Stay here," she said. "I'll let Coop know."

The downside to taking the reception job on Saturdays was being trapped there until the last guests showed up, when Luke would rather be outside.

To pass the time, he let his mind drift over to thoughts of Sylvie and how nice it had been to hike Little Abol Falls with her. When the lobby felt stuffy, and his face flushed, he moved toward the window overlooking the river, to throw it open and let in some fresh air.

Right then, a Range Rover and a Highlander pulled into the drive, followed seconds later by a Lexus, all three vehicles with a scramble of letters on Massachusetts plates.

Luke watched Coop direct the SUVs to nearby parking spaces but gesture for the Lexus to stop. He leaned down to talk to the driver through his window. Seconds later a woman got out of the passenger side. She moved toward the side entrance to the inn. Where his mother was standing.

Luke didn't know where to look. At his mother and the woman, or at Coop, who had directed the driver of the Lexus to park at the far end of the lot, when there were plenty of empty spaces up front.

Luke couldn't make out what his mother and the woman were saying because the kid from the Range Rover was leaning on the reception bell.

"Here's a list of things to do around here," Luke said to the dad. "Maps too. Some great hikes to take with kids." He ran through his spiel, tapping page after page of information, sliding everything into the packet so he could send the family on their way. All while he tried to keep his eyes on his mother.

The woman standing in front of her was dressed in faux fur and new boots; she carried an expensive bag. Oddly, she was doing most of the talking while she looked from the tall pines surrounding Church's Overlook, to the river, and back to his mother. It was as if she couldn't make sense of where she'd landed. Like the woods was goddamn Oz.

When the family in front of Luke headed out to their cabin, the outer door opened, and in walked his mother, side by side with their guest. The woman stared at him as his mother came around the reception desk to pull him into the hallway.

"She doesn't want to check in." His mother's voice was deep and low. "Call and get them a room up at Lakeside. When her husband comes in, I want you to tell him we double-booked their cabin by mistake and that the first night at Lakeside's on us."

"Why doesn't she want to stay?" Luke asked.

"Something about it being too rustic, too remote. Who knows. Just do it," she said, turning her back on him and disappearing into the office.

Back in the lobby, Luke took his spot behind the desk and made the reservation at the only competition within a few miles distance. The whole time the woman who hated their inn kept looking at him.

"Are you the one I spoke to when I made the reservation?" she asked after he'd hung up.

Luke nodded, and then she asked his name. After he told her, she reached out to shake his hand, holding on to it a little too long. "That suits you," she said, her smile warm and sincere.

She looked around the lobby like she was cataloguing things in her mind. "Your place is lovely, really," she said. "You don't know how much I wish I could stay." When she looked back at him, her stare was deep and piercing. "It's—"

"Marli. Are we all set?" The man who walked through the screen door, wearing well-worn clothing, had curly hair that reminded Luke of a gray jay. There was something familiar about the way he dropped his bags and marched up to the desk.

"Well, actually," the woman said, her voice cracking, "not really."

"Sorry, sir," Luke said. "There's been a mix-up. We double-booked the last cabin."

Luke's stomach flipped on itself when he lied. He was used to Jonah putting him up to no good, but now his mother was pulling his strings.

"You've got to be kidding," the man said.

"I got you five nights at Lakeside Inn. First night on Church's Overlook. You'll like it there. It's fancy."

The man sighed. "I don't care about that. We booked a week here. This is a major inconvenience," he said. "And why didn't you tell your man outside? He just had me park at the far end of the lot."

Luke didn't know what else to say, so he gave the man an area map with Lakeside Inn circled in pen. The guy huffed the entire time Luke gave directions. Then he picked up his bags and marched toward the front porch.

"Marli, let's go," he called through the screen.

"Be right there. I need to use the ladies' room."

When her husband had gone, hauling his heavy bags toward the edge of the parking lot, she leaned over reception and tucked a wad of hundred-dollar bills into the guest book.

"Use this to pay for the night at Lakeside. I don't want to be any trouble." She looked over her shoulder, then back at Luke. "Do you think I could see your mother for a minute? To thank her for doing me the favor."

Luke didn't need to answer. His mother was already in the doorway between the swinging kitchen doors and the breakfast room. The woman moved toward her, and without any words exchanged between them, the woman hugged her. Before they separated, his mother's hand landed firmly in the center of the woman's back.

Then the woman left. Out the door, down the steps, she walked toward the car near the road, her shoulders rigid. It was as if she was willing herself not to turn around.

When his mother finally spoke, she said, "Thank you for doing that. No one should make someone stay where they don't want to be."

Luke knew she was talking about the woman, but it made him think of Jonah. It felt like the right time to tell her he was going through with the search. But before Luke could say so, she'd slipped behind the reception desk and out the lobby door.

* * *

LENA

The innkeepers' office sat at the dead end of the hallway that led away from Reception. Prime real estate, the space was directly below the family quarters, in a part of the building that offered amazing views of the Penobscot, especially at night when the moon was lit half to full.

Lena kept the office dark as she made her way to the couch. With knees pulled tight to her chest, she gazed out the window, waiting. Despite having sat there hundreds of nights marking time, anticipating Coop's signal telling her everything was all right in and around Church's Overlook, Lena still worried that this would be the night the lights didn't flicker.

Sometimes she allowed herself to be distracted by the beauty she'd happened upon all those years ago when she'd pulled her best friend's car onto the road's shoulder, desperate for some sleep, a respite.

Tonight all she could think about was how that afternoon Marli Winslow had done the exact same thing. Without realizing it, her friend from all those years ago had stepped out of another expensive car and into Lena's secret life.

She stared across the expansive property toward Coop's cabin. When the lights went off and on—once, then twice—Lena took a deep breath. He'd been right. The sequence she knew so well was still a comfort. In a few minutes, Lena could expect to hear the familiar creaks and moans of old floorboards announcing Coop's arrival back at the inn.

If only Lena could lie down and close her eyes. Except every time she tried to, all she could see were Marli and Win. Not the middle-aged couple they'd become—but the faces of the friends she'd left behind in Boston.

"You want to talk?"

When Coop startled Lena, her whole body practically came straight off the couch.

"Sorry. I thought you heard me," he said, kneeling down in front of her.

"I can't believe they came here. What am I going to do?"

"Nothing," he said. "Nothing's changed."

"Are you serious? Jonah is probably searching for his birth parents right now. And then Marli and Win show up here out of the blue. It's a sign. A warning. How can you say nothing's changed?"

Coop sat next to her and turned her by the shoulders to face him. "Jonah isn't going to find anything. Marli is your friend and she's not going to tell anyone you're here."

"She's still married to Win. Her alliance will be with him."

"Look, she played along and left, didn't she?" Coop asked. "You can trust her."

Lena got off the couch and started pacing. "You want me to sit around and wait till this whole thing comes crashing down around me?"

Coop got up and stood by her. "Marli's up the road at Lakeside. She doesn't look like the hunting-fishing type, so why don't you meet up with her when the husband's off in the woods somewhere?"

Lena's head hurt from being so tense. Back when she was living the wrong life, she let herself have a good cry now and then. As much as she needed the release, she didn't know how to do that anymore.

"There are things she knows that might put your mind at ease," he said.

There was no need to admit to Coop that on occasion she did think about Davis. Marli would know how he was. Part of Lena also wanted to satisfy her curiosity about Nic. She could ask Marli about him too. Had he forgiven her for leaving?

"You don't have to do anything tonight," Coop said, taking her in his arms. "She's there for five days. Whatever you decide, Marli will go home, and everything will go back to normal."

Normal. Had Lena's life ever been normal?

She was so tired she closed her eyes, not caring if she fell asleep standing right there.

Coop guided her gently toward her room. "Things'll look better in the morning," he said. "With the sun."

10

Boston—1990

IT WAS THE first time she'd attended a fundraiser gala as Marli's guest and not as the event planner for the hospital auxiliary council. That didn't stop her from rearranging the remaining name cards more neatly on the welcome table or asking a staff member if the photographer had arrived yet.

"You don't have to do that. You're part of the VIP crowd tonight," Davis said. "Smile for a second. I think you have lipstick on your teeth."

Reflexively she covered her mouth. He reached out, bringing her hand to his lips to kiss it. "Never mind—you look amazing."

A handful of guests approached the welcome table for their seating assignment, and she could feel all eyes on her.

"Let me dash to the ladies' room to check. I'm feeling self-conscious," she whispered. "I'll be right back."

"I'll get us drinks," Davis said.

Out of the Grand Ballroom, she moved toward the lobby, with its ornate gold accents and marble columns.

The Copley Plaza was a lovely venue, the best of Boston, yet it felt altogether different walking through it as a patron and not as a hired hand. Invited guests started milling about, and as she passed, she nodded her hellos to recognizable lawyers, doctors, and local celebrities. She felt she needed to watch every move she made. Everyone was sure to be looking at her tonight, not as Miss Bennett, but as the next Mrs. Winslow.

"You beat us," Marli said, letting go of her husband's arm to give her a hug.

"You look lovely, Carolina," Win said. "Please don't tell me you've come here alone."

"No, no, Davis turned over his patients early and left the hospital right after you did. He's at the bar. I'm going to hide out in the ladies' room. To keep myself from telling everyone involved in planning this event what to do."

"I'll come with," Marli said. "I wouldn't want to disprove Win's theory that a woman can't go to the powder room without a friend."

Marli kissed him on the cheek, and the look he returned to his wife defied the urban legend about seven-year marriages.

Marli linked her arm with Carolina's. "I say we spend the whole night in here. Comfy chairs, best gossip in town. We'll pay the attendant to get us martinis. Our tip will be drinks for her too."

"Don't you want to see Win get his award?" Carolina asked.

"Of course. I'm just tired of having to tell people I recused myself from the board before they decided to give it to him."

"No one's going to challenge you. Everyone knows Win deserves it."

Carolina didn't add that this was true except for maybe Davis. While they had been dressing for the event, he'd been petty about being overlooked for the honor. Davis had run through a litany of comparable achievements to Win's. Carolina assured him that his day would come. And though she didn't share his sentiments, Carolina chalked Davis's diatribe up to what she'd heard about brothers being notoriously competitive. Growing up an only child, she had no firsthand experience with sibling rivalry in any form.

"Oh, come on," Marli said. "What everyone knows is that Win donates boatloads of cash. Only the board knows how often he volunteers."

You'd never know Win was a wealthy man if you saw him at the shelter. One Sunday afternoon, Carolina had stopped in to drop off some gently used clothing, and there her future brother-in-law was, dressed in old jeans and a worn sweater, sitting on the floor playing board games with the children. Which allowed the women who feared their husbands a chance to commiserate with each other out of earshot, over coffee and fresh pastries.

"The dress is spectacular, by the way," Marli said. "I can't see Win ever picking out something that fits me, never mind one so on trend."

"I told him not to, but you know Davis. He's so generous. And he had a point. I couldn't very well show up at an event like this wearing some old thing out of my closet."

The vintage floral gown was fantastic—form-fitting at the bust, a swirl of a skirt—and Carolina felt amazing in it. "I'd love to wear it again for the engagement party, but Davis said I deserve something even more lovely. And that some of these same people will be invited."

"You're gorgeous. You should do what you want. Tell Davis to worry about healing his patients and leave the party planning to us."

The ladies' room was empty except for the woman handing out cloth towels and keeping counters droplet free.

"I'm so happy it's official," Marli said. "You're going to be a Winslow. You've been great for Davis. He's never been so grounded, so happy."

"Sometimes it all seems too good to be true. Ever since you and I met, I've envied what you have with Win. Now here we are, Davis and me, about to start our life together."

"Speaking of that . . ." Marli finished touching up her blush, placing the compact back in her evening bag. Her almost giddy mood effectively replaced with a humorless one.

Outside the ladies' room, Marli led her in the opposite direction of the welcome table. "You should know, he's going to ask you to sign a prenup."

"He already has. Our appointment with the lawyer is on Tuesday. It doesn't bother me, Marli. It's not my money."

"It didn't bother me either when I was where you are, and it still doesn't. The Winslows are richer than God. It's completely de rigueur. I simply want to make sure you get your due. Win said he'd be happy to look over the agreement if you'd like him to."

"Are you saying you don't trust Davis to be fair?"

"No, it isn't that. You said it yourself—he's generous. But we both know how Davis can be when it comes to perceived slights. You don't have family looking out for your best interests. I care about you and wouldn't want to see you caught short if he starts espousing the thinking that *he who has the most toys wins.*"

Carolina wanted to be miffed with Marli for even considering the chance that her relationship would do anything but prosper. And for suggesting that Davis would be unfair to her if they ever parted. Except Marli's very frankness had always been her appeal. Carolina had to admit her friend wasn't completely off base. Even though he was magnanimous with her, Davis could be frugal with others. He was ambitious, with a taste for fine things that bordered on flaunting.

"There you are," he said. "It's not even Thanksgiving, and the two of you are already talking about the toy drive. Can we get through this shelter event before you start planning the next one?" His smile was arresting. Davis could melt the tallest New England snowbank.

Marli was a wonderful friend, always genuine, but in this she was dead wrong. If as a couple they were to lose everything tomorrow, Carolina and Davis would be fine. What they had ran deep and would be everlasting. A prenup was immaterial.

"I'm going to steal her from you, Marli," Davis said. "I have some people I'd like her to meet."

He handed her a drink and then waltzed her around the ballroom, introducing her to the attending physician he'd forewarned her he was out to impress. Her fiancé was smooth and engaging. He had the doctor and his wife laughing at every patient story he told. It became less easy to join in when their banter turned to talk of grand rounds and committee meetings. That's when Marli's words started niggling at her.

When the doctor and his wife excused themselves to go find their table, Davis suggested they go find theirs. "What were you and Marli talking about?" he asked.

"My gorgeous dress. She said you have impeccable taste."

With one arm around her waist, Davis pulled her close. "I do, don't I?" He bit her ear in an attempt to be playful.

"The photographer's here," she said, inching away. "Let me touch base with him to be sure he gets the right candids of Win. I'll be right back."

With his lips touching her ear, Davis lowered his voice. "I don't want people to see you working the event. You've got to get used to this. Your life is about to change."

She set her drink down on their perfect table with its towering centerpiece and elegant name cards placed in front of gold-leaf plates. Suddenly, looking down, she became hypnotized by the dizzying pattern of her gown. Davis was mistaken. Her life—she—had already been transformed.

"I've watched you do your thing before," Davis said. "I'll take care of the photographer. Wait here. Better yet, don't be a wallflower. Mingle."

As she watched him move across the room toward the photographer, part of her appreciated his generosity, doing what she had wanted done. Except making the shift from event planner to guest wasn't as easy as she'd thought it would be.

Carolina was one of them now, so she decided to do as Davis had suggested. She picked up her martini from the table of honor and tried to enjoy it going down cool and easy.

"We might as well say hello here as on Tuesday." A man about Davis's age, put his hand out to introduce himself. "Neil Holmes. Davis's lawyer?"

"Of course," she said. "Nice to meet you."

"How does it feel to be back at the scene of the crime?" he asked.

"I can't believe it's been a year since Davis and I met," she said. "In this very room. Marli hired me to plan the gala, and the rest is a fairytale."

"Yes, that's what Davis keeps saying." Neil's mouth puckered, making him look as though he'd swallowed something sour. He took a large swig of what looked to be good scotch. "It's not too late to change your mind about marrying him, you know. Davis can be quite a handful."

"Excuse me?"

"You seem like a nice girl. I'm only giving you a little friendly advice. Off the record of course." Neil had started to mumble. He gripped his glass with one hand, and with the other reached out for the back of a chair to steady himself.

She looked across the room toward her fiancé, annoyed with herself for not insisting she be the one to speak to the photographer. She didn't appreciate being left prey to this inebriated supposed ally. As if Davis sensed Neil had corralled her, he started walking in their direction.

"Don't tell me you haven't experienced the dark days of Davis?" Neil slurred.

"I don't know what you're talking about," Carolina said.

Before Neil could continue, Davis was by her side. "The photographer needs us," he said. "Family shots with the man of the hour. We'll see you Tuesday, Neil."

Working in hospitality, Carolina had seen all kinds of men behaving badly, and still the exchange was unnerving. The way Neil acted, three sheets to the wind before the party even started, that wasn't what struck her. It was what he'd said about Davis and dark days that was so unexpected, so cruel.

Unfazed, Davis took her hand, guiding her through the crowd. "There's no one better at what he does than Neil. During the day. Before cocktail hour."

"He's lit," she said. "Talking nonsense."

"If he said anything to upset you, I'm really sorry," Davis said. "Full disclosure. Our association is complicated. I went on exactly two dates with a girl he liked in college and it seems he'll never forgive me."

Davis waved at Marli from across the room, motioning for her to bring Win over.

"Bec was gorgeous," he said. "But she couldn't hold a candle to you."

"How gorgeous?"

"Ooh, jealous. I like it. But don't get those sexy panties in a twist. It's you. Only you." Davis pulled her close again; this time his grip was a little too tight around her waist.

When the two couples met near the photographer, Davis again took charge.

"We'll do one in front of the dais. Change it up. Instead of couples, let's have brother next to brother, and then our lovely ladies."

The photographer relinquished his role without resistance. Davis coordinated the shot, telling everyone where to stand, how to pose. What woman wouldn't want someone intent on taking care of her like this? Efficiently, effectively, effortlessly.

Carolina smiled exactly as her fiancé told her to, knowing before the shutter closed that he'd orchestrated the perfect picture.

slack—*noun.* Period between low and high tides when tidal currents reach their slowest rate and begin to reverse direction; the outgoing tide and its associated currents. See *ebb* and *flood*.

11

Millinocket, Maine—2012

LUKE

WILD AS IT was, Luke tried to tell himself that nothing had changed at Church's Overlook. Except at night, he stood in front of his collection, running his hand over the mural of worn book covers and scraps of paper he'd amassed, worrying about his family. Until now, Luke had never questioned why the odd lots of bird feathers, maps, and magazines had a calming influence on him, but they did. He flipped the pages of his dictionary open to the letter *S—sublimate, submit, suppress*. He tried to sleep.

Before long, he dreamed of hiking the Knife Edge Trail between South and Pamola Peaks. Bands of yellow and orange leaves marked the tree line. The only travel possible was forward, backward, or down. Luke passed where the ridge went narrow, and turned around to take in one of the best views of Chimney Pond and the Great Basin. He was lost in the landscape when he felt someone's hands on his back. The shove sent him straight off the mountain. In freefall, Luke's body jolted awake and nearly off the edge of his bed. He shook his head, trying to get the outline of Jonah's face out of his mind.

That's when he heard voices coming from one floor below him. It was after two in the morning.

Down three stairs, Luke hit a creaky step and froze. He'd never had reason to know the noisy ones so he could avoid them. It was Jonah who'd mastered the art of sneaking up and down those stairs in the middle of the night.

Luke heard Coop before he saw him.

"Take a load off. Have this." His raspy voice was kind of gruff when he was at full volume, but that night, speaking low, it sounded more like river water over smooth stone. "Let's be done now," Coop said.

The only way to get a glimpse of what was going on in the office was to whisk past the open door, hoping no one would see him. Or he could slip out the side door and peer in through the window.

As unkind as fall in the Maine woods could be, Luke chose outside. His breath hitting night air made him instantly regret what he'd worn to bed. Though his bare feet were an asset on the stairs, they were a liability on the ground, covered in twigs and rocks, sticks and stones.

When he got to the window, he saw cardboard boxes on the desk and floor. The bottom drawer was open, but the inside of the safe wasn't visible from where he crouched under the sill. His mother leaned back in her chair, shaking her head. Remnants of Jonah's Sunday supper contribution—the bottle of wine Luke got credit for bringing—was in Coop's hand. He topped off a glass, took a sip, and handed it to her. She closed her eyes for a second, then accepted it, her hands shaking as she brought it to her lips.

With the window closed, Luke couldn't make out what they were saying, so he risked trying to open the ancient thing a sliver crack from the outside. With the right amount of pressure against the sides and the top simultaneously, all he needed was enough space to allow sound to find him.

"Feel better now?" Coop pointed at one of the boxes on the floor. "We've gone through this place top to bottom. There's nothing here to give you away."

"Nothing else, you mean," his mother said.

"Come on. You know Luke was just poking around, looking to take things the way he does."

"No, this time Jonah put him up to it. He was angling to get into the safe."

Coop turned his back to the window, and Luke watched him massaging his mother's shoulders. "He can't connect those scraps to anything," Coop said. "You could explain it away if you had to."

Luke flipped his body around and sank to the ground. His back hurt for how hard he pressed it against the building. The last thing he heard was his mother's voice.

"Okay, so Luke isn't a problem. What about Jonah?"

What did it say about him that he pocketed stuff left behind by others, plus took little things he felt belonged to him, even though they didn't? And what did it say about Coop and his mother, that they knew Luke did it and talked about him behind his back?

They were ones to talk. Cleaning out the office in the middle of the night. Removing signs of something he could connect to something else. Talking about him and his brother like they were some kind of rock obstacle to row around.

Sleep didn't come for the rest of the night. By sunrise, Luke had convinced himself he could turn his back on everything and everyone by getting back outside.

He pushed his way through the kitchen without saying a word to his mother. After he filled a plate with eggs and hash and a big hunk of cornbread, he went to the breakfast room. With his pick of seats by the window, he put his plate down, and looked toward the Penobscot. His empty stomach rumbled, but his heart wasn't into eating.

Leaving his plate there, he ducked out the side door and moved down to the water.

The river looked like a mirror of broken glass—*"each fragment reflecting the full blaze of the sun"*—exactly as Thoreau had described it a hundred years ago.

Luke pulled a canoe from the bunk storage racks buried in the pine grove. In minutes, he'd pushed off, the dip and pull motion of his paddling laying down the rhythm for his day.

Out there, enclosed in the bend of a hook, riding with the current, everything was fine. He could erase his worries about the things his mother was keeping from him, how Coop colluded, and what Jonah might do. On the inky river, he told himself to stop perseverating over what he might be tempted to steal next. It was a harmless habit. At least Luke wasn't hurting anyone with his actions.

Instead, without a single field guide, Luke put a name to the family, genus, and species of the things that had never disappointed him. Peeking out from behind a white cedar, the American Marten: Mustelidae, *Martes, M. americana.* Jutting up from gray rock, scruffy colonies of Indian paintbrush: Orobanchaceae, *Castilleja, C. affinis.*

He spent the morning alternating between paddling to explore outlets and channels, and floating.

By afternoon everything changed. It wasn't just the wind gusts disturbing the peaceful flatwater. Or the heavy cloud cover obscuring his view of the mountain threatening to drench him. The blanket of denial he'd wrapped himself in began to unravel because Luke knew he couldn't stay out there forever. He had to admit, as much as he resented getting pulled into whatever was going on with his family, he needed to know at least a little bit more.

Resting the paddle on his lap, he dug deep into his pocket for his phone and texted Jonah.

I'll help you now

Holding out the phone, staring at the screen, he waited for his brother's reply. No sun, all clouds, Luke couldn't quite read the display, but he knew there was no message; there hadn't been a chime. After a few minutes, when Jonah didn't text back, Luke hit "Resend." The third time he got no response, a sick feeling washed over him.

Paddling toward home, Luke balanced the phone on his lap. Every few strokes, he rechecked it.

Canoe to shore and hauled up the incline, he didn't bother to put the boat back in the storage rack. He texted Jonah again.

One word to say you're okay would be nice

Chill old man
Major hangover
You got something for me??

FaceTime me

"Wanna see what you're missing?" Jonah angled his laptop to give Luke a three-sixty view of his room in Quinby House at Bowdoin. "You too could have had all this," he said.

The video tour showcased clothes piled so high on a bed there was barely enough room for a body. Four pizza boxes stacked on a desk and a waste can overflowing with empties, and Luke could almost smell the stench left over from the weekend.

"And I'm the neat one," Jonah said.

Luke heard the distinct flick of his brother's lighter, and smoke wafted over the scene.

"You're allowed to smoke in your room?" Luke asked.

"Of course not." Jonah laughed, and suddenly his wide smile filled the screen.

"Whatcha got?"

"I think a friend of Mom's showed up here."

"What the hell? Mom has a friend?"

"Her name's Mary or Molly, something that begins with *M*. Her Lexus has Mass plates: WINMD."

"You can remember her plates, but not her name? Anyone ever tell you you're weird?"

"I was bored waiting to register stragglers, so I played scramble with license plates. I had no idea what was about to happen."

Luke went on to tell Jonah about the lie he told to get the couple to leave Church's Overlook, about Coop playing along, and the strange hug between their mother and the woman who claimed she didn't want to stay there. Jonah sat up straighter and started scribbling notes.

"Then last night, Mom and Coop turned the office upside down. I heard her say, '*What do we do about Jonah?*'"

"You were in there the day before I left. I thought you didn't find anything."

"Nothing to do with this," Luke said.

Jonah stopped writing. The cigarette he'd set down on the desk burned closer and closer to the edge.

"Coop pays the mortgage on Church's Overlook," Luke said. "His name's on all the bills. Not Mom's. When I overheard them, they made it sound like there's something in the safe and some scrap in my collection that connects to whatever it is they don't want us to know. I just don't know what it is."

Now Jonah's notepad was front and center. "Stand in front of your goddamn mess of a mural and read me every name and place, every single detail that could mean something. Let's go."

Luke read from all four corners of his collection—a postcard signed Dolly, a random shopping list from a regular guest who summered in Emerson, a love letter written by someone named Davis. All kinds of maps—bits and scraps and notes. When he finished, they agreed none of it meant anything to them. That's when Jonah started grilling him about the woman who'd showed up at Church's. "What did she look like? What exactly did she say?"

The more he pressed Luke, the harder it got for him to trust his memory.

"Fine. Go get me her name and address from the registration book," Jonah said finally.

"Come on. Haven't I helped enough? I told you I didn't want to be part of this."

Luke still felt ambivalent about being involved, especially since whatever his mother was keeping from them felt more ominous now.

"Look, I've hit a brick wall on my birth certificate, and Mom won't talk to me. I need you to do this."

"I'm sick of you roping me in. All I want is to hike and guide and live here in peace. Doesn't what I want matter to anyone?"

"I had nothing to do with that lady showing up at Church's and you know it. Notice you're the one telling me things."

They stared at each other, neither of them talking. Jonah was right. Luke had been the one to give him information, not the other way around. Which made him *not* want to tell Jonah about their mother's truck filled with random supplies and headed to an unknown destination.

"Please get me the lady's info?" Jonah asked. "We can talk again after my meeting."

"What meeting?"

"I've got a call set up with the new director of Maine Child and Family Services."

When Luke didn't say anything, Jonah said, "I'm over twenty-one. They have to tell me whatever they've got in their files about me. I promise not to ask about you." Then he ended the call.

The registration book sat where it always did, but the couple's name, their address, and any trace that Luke had booked a cabin for them had been erased. Correct that— cut out.

There was a clean slice along the inner hinge of the book, where the page with their info should've been. The cut, disappearing into the spine, was so deep that if it weren't sharp and Luke hadn't seen the couple with his own eyes, he might've thought he'd imagined them here. All the other names were copied over one by one, on a new page, as if every reservation had been made on the same day by the same person. The handwriting was his mother's.

With the lobby empty, Luke stood at Reception and took a loose sheet of paper and a pencil tipped on its side; he rubbed the page below the one his mother had cut out, half-hoping it wouldn't reveal anything. When it didn't, he was disappointed. Again and again, he exercised the same precision his mother had used to cover it up, but it was no use. There was nothing to decipher.

Luke startled when he heard logs smack on top of logs. Coop was out front, loading wood onto his truck. He went to help.

"Hey," Coop said without stopping. "Haven't seen much of you lately."

"I've been guiding."

It was true Luke had hikes scheduled. Good, long ones. Cathedral Trail, Russell Pond, and Hunt. He had been dodging Coop too, and he knew as much.

"The couple in Scribner needs another rick."

"There was plenty in the stack at check-in. They're using a lot of wood," Luke said.

"They haven't left the cabin since they got here."

Luke had checked the Kirkwoods in last Saturday and had only seen them once since. At Sunday breakfast, the guy was all over the girl, and she giggled nonstop. Luke remembered being glad they kept to themselves.

"Anyone else need stacks?" he asked.

"A couple of bundles for my cabin oughta do it," Coop said.

Together they loaded the wood onto the truck. Coop worked up a sweat, and halfway through the job, he took off his field coat. He threw it over the side of the truck wall, and after wiping his brow with the sleeve of his shirt, he rolled both of them up and got back to work.

A piece of paper—some kind of receipt—poked out of the coat's pocket. Luke waited till Coop's back was to his, stacking wood on wood. Before he knew it, the paper was in his hand and then crammed deep into the pocket of his jeans.

"Did your brother start working on his film?"

"Working on his film" sounded like code for *"Has he started searching for his birth parents?"*

"He just started classes. I don't think so." Coop knew Luke better than almost anyone. He half expected him to call him a liar right then and there.

"Sylvie and Jonah broke up," Luke said, aiming to fill the silence.

"I didn't know that."

Though it was getting harder for Luke to believe anything Coop said, the older man looked genuinely disappointed to hear the news.

"She says they're going to stay friends. But I doubt it."

"You don't believe men and women can come to an understanding about things?"

"I guess," Luke said, tossing the logs, wishing he hadn't brought it up. He didn't want to talk to Coop about men and women and their understandings. He remembered Coop massaging his mother's shoulders the other night, and he was beginning to think there was something more between them. Things he wasn't interested to know.

Thankfully Coop changed the subject. "I offered to help Jonah with his documentary, but you know your brother. He's not much interested in my roots."

Jonah didn't have the same deep fondness for Coop that Luke did. The man was the closest thing either of them had to a father, but Jonah still kept him at arm's length.

"Not true," Luke said. "The other day he asked me if your family knew Mom's before she came here."

The way Coop loaded the truck, Luke couldn't see his face, but his body showed no change in rhythm; he kept loading wood.

"So do you know where Mom's from originally?"

"Couldn't say," he said. "Your mother's not the reminiscing type. You'd have to ask her yourself."

The muscles in Luke's arms and legs ached for how hard he tensed them. Tightening his grip on a load sent a sharp splinter of wood into his belly.

"All I know is the day she came to Church's Overlook was a damn fine one," Coop said. "Look around. This place would be nothing if it weren't for her."

"You work as hard as she does," Luke said. "Seems to me this place is as much yours as it is hers. The land belonged to your ancestors long before she showed up."

"That it did. Historically speaking, no matter what happens around here, it always will."

Coop tossed the last log on the pile. Out of his front pocket came his double-steel blade, inlaid with turquoise. After he wrapped an armful of kindling with twine, he cut the string with his knife. Finished with the task, he leaned against the tailgate, put the knife back in his pocket, and started rolling down his sleeves. When both cuffs were buttoned, he grabbed his field coat.

"It took me a while to learn you can appreciate things without knowing everything there is to know about them. Where people are concerned, there's no need to stake a claim," Coop said. "Your mother was the one who taught me that."

Luke didn't want to see the lines around Coop's mouth soften and the light in his eyes come on when he talked about her. He didn't need to be a genius to know their friendship ran deep. He'd just never stopped to think it might go further than that.

"Lena showed up here years ago with you boys in tow, stayed in one of the old cabins for some weeks, and that was it. She was here to stay. I was living alone, overseeing a run-down sporting camp built by my great-great-grandfather. Your mother saw what this place could be. What it could do for you boys. And I was happy to oblige."

"So Mom did buy Church's? Did she put up the money to overhaul it?" The way Coop told it, his mother's story could be true. "Does that make Church's Overlook hers or yours?"

"Why's it matter so much to you, Luke? Knowing that? I've heard stories my whole life about people turning themselves into knots over the people and things that can't be owned. I'm not saying there hasn't been a long history of wrongdoing where the land and my people are concerned. But your mother and me, we came to an agreement about this place. Formed a partnership around Church's and you boys."

Coop put his hand out, palm up, for Luke to slap it. He'd never offered him that gesture of solidarity before.

"I'll be needing that receipt now," he said. "First thing tomorrow, I've got to return a bag of hinges and fasteners. Turns out I already had everything I needed."

Luke could've denied that he'd taken that slip of paper from Coop's coat pocket. Or he could've said it fell to the ground when he tossed his coat over the side of the truck—that without thinking, Luke had picked it up and shoved it in his pocket, thinking it was trash.

"I don't know why I do that," Luke said, digging for the receipt.

"Nobody's perfect."

Coop clapped him on the back, leaving his hand there a second longer than usual. "I know you and Jonah like to stick together. But you owe your mother too. He could really hurt her with this, Luke. I'd put a stop to him if I were you."

Coop walked to the driver's side of the truck without asking Luke to hop in, to ride over to Scribner to unload the wood. Minus that paper in his pocket, Luke should've felt lighter, his habit of taking things out there in the open. Except now, thanks to Coop, he had a different kind of weight on him.

Watching the mist rise off the river, taking in the full expanse of Church's Overlook wasn't enough to calm him. For the first time in forever, being outside made him feel hemmed in.

Then Jonah's chime interrupted his attempts to feel sorry for himself.

Had the meeting
Last chance to tell me not to tell you stuff

Is it about me?

No . . . I don't know.
But it will knock you out
Up to you

Tell me.

I was never in foster care

* * *

LENA

Lakeside Resort was located ten miles upriver from Church's Overlook, yet Lena couldn't remember the last time she'd visited it. Her pride took a hit when she pulled into the circular drive and noted the main building's grandeur. Lined with rocking chairs, the wraparound porch alone was enough to add tens of dollars to room rates. Never mind what the owners could charge guests of the upper floors with private balconies. The views of the river they likely enjoyed had to be spectacular.

If only Lena had been able to let Marli stay at her inn. Under different circumstances, she would've relished cooking for her sister-in-law and showing her around the place she'd effectively built with her head, heart, and hands. But Lena could not do that. It was hard enough to trust that Marli would let her stay hidden and that she wouldn't confide her whereabouts to Win.

There was no way she could risk stirring things up where Luke or Jonah were concerned. With Marli gone, Luke might ask about the odd exchange on Saturday, but if Lena told the right story, he'd drop it. And Jonah didn't know anything about Marli and her accidental visit.

Once again, Coop was right. Lena was making a big deal out of nothing. If she wanted to, she could blow off this visit to Marli. No need to seek reassurance. Lena could turn the truck around and drive right back home.

Except it was too late. Marli was rushing down the inn's stairs, hustling toward Lena's truck before she was halfway around the horseshoe bend.

Lena had barely gotten out of the driver's seat before Marli embraced her. "I'm so glad you called," she said.

Lena hugged her back with matched ferocity. The memory of all the sisterly hugs they had shared flooded her with regret.

"Are you hungry?" Marli asked. "I told the kitchen we might like a late breakfast."

"Where's Win?" Lena asked, scanning the grounds.

"I told him to make the best of our last day. He took off before dawn to go fishing, and he won't be back until later this afternoon. I'm taking advantage of a kind innkeeper."

"If you don't mind, I've been feeding guests since six this morning. I'm breakfasted out," Lena said. "Plus, I can't stay long. I have to get back to work."

"Of course," Marli said.

Lena hadn't meant to be dismissive. She hadn't set out to draw a distinction between her reality and Marli's: that one of them had to work like a dog while the other one didn't. It was as though, in isolation, she'd forgotten the social graces involved in being a friend.

"We can take a walk or a drive," Marli said. "Or, to tell you the truth, I wouldn't care if we sat right here. It's so good to see you. I've missed you, Carolina."

"It's Lena now."

Without speaking, both women moved toward the porch. They took the steps side by side and claimed two rocking chairs angled away from the others.

"How is he?" Lena asked. Ever thankful for a view, she stared straight ahead. Or was she unable to look at Marli while she spoke about her husband?

"It's been up and down forever," she said. "He's been in and out of hospitals a few times over the years. The last time was about ten months ago. He's getting good care now. Win's working with a new psychiatrist, and they're pretty certain Davis is on the right medication. Finally."

"I'm not surprised Win's stuck by him. You married a good man."

"Win is one of a kind. He's even been okay with me staying completely out of it. Despite the fact that Davis is a shell of his former self and couldn't hurt a fly—and he is demonstrably ill now—I still can't bring myself to forgive him."

How many days and nights had these two women talked about the thin line between a very sick man who wasn't receiving the right treatment and someone who is a monster? As Marli talked, Lena experienced a sudden and painful clarity. Her sister-in-law didn't just look the same. Poised. Confident. Warm. After everything that had happened, Marli had remained true to her. She was still willing to put Lena's safety and that of her boys above her relationship with her own brother-in-law.

Only two states away, Marli must have been suffering right alongside Lena, losing her family too. Yet here these friends were, reunited in the Maine woods after all this time, and Lena was certain that Marli could be counted on to continue to protect them.

If only she could find the words to assure her that it had been worth it—that Marli had done the right thing by helping her.

"Simon is a senior at Bowdoin. Studying film," Lena said. "He's called Jonah now. That boy can test my patience, but he's a good kid. Smart. Funny. And a wonderful brother."

"It was unbelievable seeing James—I mean Luke—all grown up. I couldn't believe Win didn't notice how much he looks like you."

"I know. I worried he might. But so much time's gone by. He probably doesn't think about me much anymore. I'm just glad Jonah wasn't working the desk. It's remarkable how much he looks like Win did when he was young. Look." Lena showed Marli a few recent pictures of her sons. Marli's eyes widened at Jonah's resemblance to her husband.

"Where does Luke go to school?"

"He doesn't. Not right now anyway. He prefers nature over people. Working at the Inn suits him. He's a gentle soul. Very responsible. Coop and me, we plan to turn Church's over to him someday. When the time is right."

"I wish I could know them." Marli handed the phone back to Lena. "I'd give anything to spend time with those boys."

Lena got out of the rocker and put her back against the railing. She faced her and took her hands. "I wish things were different too. But I need you to promise me nothing will change now that you've found me."

Marli nodded, and as she did, she held tight to Lena's hands. "I knew you were going to say that. And as much as it kills me, I will keep your whereabouts to myself. But I need you to know, Davis can't hurt you now."

Lena wanted to believe her, but she would never again trust that her family was safe, that things were okay. Though well-intentioned, Marli had been devastatingly wrong before. And she hadn't been the only one who'd tried to convince her Davis could no longer hurt her.

"How's Nic?" Lena asked.

Marli pulled her hands free and fumbled with her phone case. Lena worried that she would think it was her turn to pull up pictures. This time of Nic, maybe with a wife and a family. Would Lena be comforted to see him again, smiling? With his arms around another woman, with different children? Or would she be crushed to learn that he'd been able to move on?

To Lena's surprise, no photos were forthcoming. Marli slipped a business card out of her case and held it up like a miniature sign. It had her name printed on it, under the logo for "*Nic's Italian*."

"After you left, he struggled mightily," she said. "I did my best to help him by taking over the receptions you'd already started planning. One thing led to another and Nic kept me on. He made me his event planner. I hope that doesn't upset you."

"Of course not," Lena said, taking the card.

"I learned from the best, by watching you," Marli said. "The place is busier than ever. Nic's won all kinds of awards. Best of Boston—that type of thing. He was nominated for a James Beard. Oh, listen to me. You don't give two hoots about that."

Lena's cheeks felt cool, as if the breeze coming off the river was there to remind her what it felt like to have tears on her face.

"No, I do. Of course I want him to be happy. I'm just sad it couldn't have been with me. Is he with anyone?"

"There's a woman he sees off and on," Marli said. "I've met her a handful of times. Neither of them wants anything serious. And no kids."

Lena slid the card into her jacket pocket. "I should go."

"I thought you'd want to know," Marli said.

Lena had wanted to know. Except finding out had been a bad idea. What good could possibly come from knowing about any of this? About Davis. Or Nic. Still, she thanked Marli for everything she'd done for her—then and now—and for renewing her promise to keep Lena's location a secret.

The women hugged one more time, holding each other for the longest time. As if they were trying to make up for all the years of affection Davis had stolen from them.

12

Boston—1990

CAROLINA BLEW OUT the candles, took one more sip of Merlot, and got up to go wash out the glasses. It wasn't as though Davis hadn't warned her. It was practically a given that they would miss the preconcert dinner at Symphony Hall, since a patient could always be counted on to spike a fever or drop his blood pressure at the precise time Davis needed to turn his patients over to interns so he could be someplace else. If he didn't make it home in the next ten minutes, they'd be cutting it too close and wouldn't be there in time for the start of the performance. Crosstown traffic on a weeknight was a bear.

It wasn't just the socializing with Marli and Win in the Beranek Room with cocktails or missing the Brahms and Dvořák that had her down. It was losing out on a night on the town with her husband. When she was dressed as she was now, in a golden sheath that hugged her curves and complimented her waistline—Davis noticed her. An evening like this had the power to distract him from his round-the-clock responsibilities at the hospital.

Amid good friends and family, surrounded by the beauty that was Symphony Hall and its music, she had the ability to take his mind off his persistent thoughts on how to get ahead. For three, maybe four hours, they'd be happy together, having fun. And she wouldn't have to listen to him perseverate over whether or not he would secure the right fellowship. She wouldn't need to keep reassuring him that someday soon he would be as successful as Win. They could stop talking about when she could quit her job at *Nic's*, when she had no plans to, ever. Carolina liked her work and she was good at planning parties, anticipating the needs of the people who enjoyed them.

When both wineglasses were rinsed and positioned upside down in the dish rack, she dried her hands on the kitchen towel and unzipped the back of her dress. He wasn't coming. Next time they had an evening out planned, she might as well stay in her robe until she was sure it was actually going to happen.

On her way to the bedroom to change, she heard the key in the lock. Oh good, they could still make it if Davis hurried. If he'd already taken a shower in the hospital's on-call room, he could throw on his suit, and they could fly.

"God, you look beautiful," Davis said. As he hung his coat by the door, he looked at her over his shoulder.

She ran to kiss him. "I'm glad you like it."

"I hope you got it on sale," Davis said, slipping his hand inside the open back of the dress, down the length of her spine. His cool hand against her warm skin made her shiver. "Well, how much?" he asked.

"It wasn't that expensive. I used my own money." Carolina wished she could take back the words as soon as she said them. Davis hated when she reminded him that she worked.

She kissed him again, this time on his neck in order to hide her face. Sometimes if she avoided his gaze, things went better for her.

"So were you getting into it or stepping out of it?" he asked.

There was no right way to answer this question. If she said "into it" Davis would wonder why she wasn't ready and waiting for him. If she said "out of it," he'd take it as an easy way to blow off the concert.

Instead, she ignored the question.

"Please tell me you were just trying it on," he said. "That Boston Symphony Orchestra thing isn't tonight, is it?"

"I reminded you this morning," she said. "I made you a sandwich to eat on the way over. If you're not too tired after the symphony, we can grab a late supper. Or if you have an appetite for something else, we can do that when we get home." She playfully squirmed out of Davis's embrace, backing away. In case seducing him to go out had the potential to backfire.

"Let's pretend we already heard the concert. And go straight to bed now," he said. "I'm exhausted."

"Please. It's been ages since we've done anything fun. We can still make it if you hurry. Plus, I promised Marli and Win."

"Look, I said I'm not up to it. The monkey suit. All that small talk. Jesus, Marli never shuts up."

"I picked up your suit at the dry cleaner's. The pinstripe shirt with the navy tie is plenty dressy enough. We already paid for the tickets."

"Do you even care about the day I had? It was one goddamned crisis after the other."

"Of course I do. That's why I think this will be good. A night out always takes your mind off work. You know once we're there, you'll be glad that we went."

"You're not listening to me. I spent the day in Win's shadow. I don't feel like seeing him tonight. Or anyone else from the hospital. I deserve a break from the bullshit, don't I? I'm sick of having to prove myself. Why can't you, of all people, understand?"

Davis stormed toward the bedroom; she followed him.

"What about what I need?" she asked. "You're never home. And when you are, you're either in a mood or sleeping."

"Are you kidding me?" Davis wrenched his shirt from his body with such force that buttons flew across the room and under the bed. When he whipped his belt from his pants with a violent snap, she knew there would be no sweet music tonight.

"Another woman would kill to have your life. Can't you see what I'm trying to build for you. For us?"

"You know I'm grateful," she said. "I just spend so much time alone."

Davis was pacing now. Shouting so loud, she worried neighbors would hear him.

"You think I don't want a day off? A week off? My shortest day is eighteen, twenty hours. Stupid interns fucking up left and right. If I don't follow them around all day, fixing everything they botch, it's my fault. It's my ass on the line."

Davis was right. The pressure was intense. Carolina moved toward him then, placing her hands on his beautiful shoulders. His muscles rigid, he was tense and uptight, and it was partly her fault. She'd been selfish. Insensitive. She'd contributed to his going off the rails by pushing him to go out when what he needed most was to rest. To sleep.

"You are working too hard. It's too much. I see that now. Please forgive me," she said.

He pushed her away roughly. "What, you think I can't hack it? That I don't have what it takes to be as successful as Win?"

With his arm, Davis swiped every pretty thing Carolina had off the top of their bureau and onto the floor. Perfume bottles shattered, flooding the air with a mix of flowery scents. A vanity mirror and their wedding picture—all glass—covered their bedroom corner to corner.

"Get out!" he shouted. "Go to the concert and then out to some overpriced bistro I bust my ass to pay for." Davis pushed Carolina again, yet she did not fear him now. As enraged as he was, he showed restraint. He seemed terrified that he was losing it, having some kind of breakdown. She knew he'd never hurt her. Still she backed out of the room, whispering, "I'm sorry."

If Davis didn't settle down by the time she got to the living room, what could she do? Marli and Win would be seated by now, listening to Brahms. Even if she could get word to his brother, it seemed Win was in some inadvertent way provoking Davis more than usual.

With her hand on the phone, wondering what to do next, suddenly the silence frightened her more than when Davis had been banging his fists on the wall.

Carolina tiptoed back to the bedroom, hoping with all her heart that when she peered into their room, she wouldn't set him off again. It was too quiet. Would Davis ever hurt himself? Carolina couldn't imagine him picking up a shard of glass and doing something impulsive and horrible with it. Or could she?

Then there he was, lying atop the duvet, subdued. Bare chested, with his pants and shoes still on, it was as though he'd used every last bit of energy to drop onto the mattress.

His chest rose and fell in a predictable rhythm. Her husband was somewhere between awake and asleep, and approachable now. The outburst over. The whole thing behind them. It had all been a fluke, she told herself.

Tenderly she removed his shoes and socks. With them placed on the floor beside the bed, she went on to unbutton his pants and work the fabric from his sturdy frame. Once undressed, the only movement Davis made was to roll away from her. He did not stir when she took off her pretty new dress and hung it in their closet. Or when she swept the glass that was strewn wall to wall across hardwood. Or when she finally slipped into bed beside him.

At first light, she turned toward her husband's side of the bed, reaching out for him, though Davis was no longer there. The bedroom looked exactly like it always did when she'd wake to find he'd already left for the hospital. Except for the empty bureau.

Before her feet hit the floor, the idea came to her that she should put slippers on in case she'd missed any glass in the cleanup.

When the smell of coffee reached her, she checked the clock. It was past ten, and Davis was in the kitchen, whistling.

"I took the day off," he said when she rounded the counter. "Screw them all if I can't take some time to spend with my bride. What's Win going to do—get me fired?"

Davis was upbeat, strangely cheery. "I didn't mean to scare you last night," he said, his voice suddenly low. "I was out of line. It'll never happen again."

"I shouldn't have pushed to go out," she said, rushing to him, letting him embrace her. "You were so tired. All I wanted was to spend time with you."

As they clung to each other, they wept. There was a hint of something fragile about his arms around her. How long they stood in their kitchen, Carolina did not know.

She wanted to hold Davis—and for him to hold her—for the rest of the day, for the rest of their lives.

"I love you so much," he said, running his hands through her hair.

She felt his tears on her neck.

"You know I would never hurt you." Davis pulled back abruptly, to look hard into her eyes. "You're everything to me. You know that, don't you?"

peel out—*verb*. To leave an eddy and enter the main current by leaning into it; see *eddy turn*.

Millinocket, Maine—2012

LUKE

I F HIS BROTHER had never been in foster care, then what about him? Jonah said this whole thing wouldn't affect Luke, but it already had. He stood in front of the inn, reading and rereading that message. His fingers locked on the sides of his phone, gripping it so tightly he couldn't move to text Jonah back.

Someone else would've gone into the kitchen and put his mother on blast. Demanding to know what was going on. Except working that out in his mind, Luke imagined her standing beyond those doors staring at him like he was making something out of nothing. After all, hadn't Coop said she was capable of explaining away anything? Even if Luke chose the perfect combination of words, his mother would not be convinced to answer a single question if she had no mind to. Or she'd make up some story.

Jonah was the one who got things done. He'd put it together with or without help, with or without interference. Luke should leave him to it.

When the river didn't work to settle him, he went to his room. Afraid to park himself in front of his collection, he didn't want to face the sheen of guilt that covered those scraps of abandoned things after what he'd heard his mother and Coop say about his predilection. Worse, he feared that among his found objects, hidden in plain sight, was something his mother didn't want him to have or to know was pinned there.

Instead, he sat in the dark by the window that looked down on the grounds. As he reread Jonah's message, a new text appeared from Sylvie.

How are things?

Jonah might not have been able to lean on her, but Luke could. He clicked on FaceTime. One ring, then two, and there she was, wearing a BU sweatshirt, a pencil tucked behind one ear.

"Hey," she said, using her fingers to brush her hair from her face. "I'm kind of a mess."

"It's only me." Luke didn't know what Sylvie was talking about; he thought she looked beautiful.

"I was just checking in," she said. "I haven't been here a week and already I'm buried. My pharmacology class sucks. I definitely should've taken Latin with you in high school."

Luke's room had a blue-black glow, courtesy of his phone. The dim light wasn't enough to block out the shadow moving outside his window. Coop was choring.

"You wouldn't believe everything I have to do before I start clinical. I got stuck in another surgical rotation. This time, cardiology. Last semester, whenever Jonah heard *gas-troenterology* he'd say, "the study of lips to assholes." Funny, now that he and I are done, it's hearts." Sylvie forced a smile, but she didn't laugh. Neither did Luke.

He hadn't called Sylvie to talk about Jonah. And he definitely didn't want to talk about their breakup. No matter what he did, Luke couldn't get away from his brother.

Or Coop.

Luke saw him walking the length of the parking lot, his head down and tipped sideways like he was scanning license plates.

"How is he?" Sylvie asked.

"Jonah? Fine, I guess. He's bugging me with all this digging around."

"Did he find anything yet?"

Luke heard Sylvie and he didn't. His attention was out the window now, on Coop taking a strange route back to his cabin, weaving in and out of the pine grove.

"You can tell me, you know," she said.

When Luke looked back at the screen, Sylvie had leaned in, her elbow on the desk, her head resting on one hand.

"Maybe staying here was a mistake," Luke said. Then, once the words were out, a kind of comfort washed over him. Because, when he said it, he knew it wasn't true. He belonged at Church's Overlook, and nothing Jonah could find out would change that.

"You could come here," she said. "If you got into Bowdoin, you can totally get into BU. I have friends you can crash with, even if you just want to take a class to see if you like it."

Sylvie acted excited, like she'd found the solution to his problems in one of the books on the edge of her desk, without consulting one page.

"I don't know. I'm only venting," he said.

Sylvie's phone played a handful of notes like waves. She looked at it and said, "I should take this. It's Jonah."

"I'll let you go then," Luke said, disappointed.

Seconds after ending the call, he saw Coop go inside his cabin at the farthest end of the property. One second, then two, he flashed the light. Flick, flick, pause. Flick, again, the light stayed on.

At first Luke sat there, lost out the window, the moon and stars his only confidants. He wondered how he could've missed his mother and Coop acting so strangely. Had they always been so sly? Like the people Luke guided through the woods who'd ask about those delicate rills cut into the soil of a stream or the way tree roots burst through the ground overtaking a trail, there was no going back. Once you noticed something's true nature, you saw it everywhere you looked; you couldn't unsee it if you tried.

His mother had no friends. Then along came that *M* woman.

His mother and Coop never let anyone near the office, and supposedly there was something in the safe, or in his collection, that raised a red flag but could be explained away if need be.

Why was Coop flashing his cabin lights like that? Had Luke ever noticed him do it before?

And why was Jonah still calling Sylvie when they were broken up?

Luke replayed his one-sided conversation until night became morning. When he finally checked his phone, there was a text from Jonah that changed everything.

I love you, brother
So I've decided to leave you out of it
Also can't risk Mom cross-examining you
I am going to find them

It was Jonah's act of excluding Luke that pushed him to want to be all in on the search. Who was he kidding? There was no way this didn't affect him.

Luke dialed his brother, but the outgoing message came on after one ring. Jonah had either turned off his phone or he'd gone dark on him.

Outside the window, storm clouds broke over the river. Rain pelted the glass as Luke grabbed his laptop and shoved a handful of clothes into his backpack.

The last thing he did before leaving his room was stand in front of his dictionary and flip its pages. Like a prophecy, they fluttered and landed open on *C*—and the word *confluence* captured his attention.

portage—*noun*. The carrying of a canoe and its gear across a stretch of land between two bodies of water; a solid reason to reduce gear to the lightest load possible.

14

Millinocket, Maine—2012

LUKE

H E DIDN'T MAKE like he was sneaking off as he came down the stairs into the lobby. Luke didn't try to cover his footfalls, the sound of hiking boots against plank floors. At the reception desk, he stopped to say goodbye to his mother.

"I'm spending the weekend with Jonah." He expected her to come up with a litany of reasons he couldn't or shouldn't, having no idea what he'd do if she did.

His mother smiled. "You deserve some time to yourself. Coop and I can handle changeover. It's not going to be that busy."

Up till now, all Luke had wanted was to go back to a time when everyone was happy at Church's. And now that his mother seemed suddenly grounded, why was he leaving?

Outside, despite the rain, Coop was parked on the ladder, diligently removing debris from the downspouts. Without taking a break, he called out from above. "Where you headed, son?"

Luke pretended not to hear him over the scraping sounds he made. He hopped in his truck, tossed his backpack into the passenger seat, and pulled out of the driveway before he could change his mind about what he was doing.

What exactly am I doing? Luke had no idea. The only thing he knew for sure was that he felt certain Jonah needed him.

Ice had left its signature along the roads he drove south to Bowdoin. To his right, tumbles of rocks were deposited unsorted by the road's shoulder. Hundreds of years ago, runoff had created winding ridges, reaming out valleys only now interrupted by stretches of highway. Smooth granite here, a cleft in a surface there, the glacial boulders lining the corridor he made his way down were as unique as the faces of his family.

Regret traveled the road with him. Luke should have helped Jonah the first time he'd asked him to. Every time he thought about those unanswered texts, he felt dread in his gut. It reminded him too much of another time he'd been cut off from his brother without warning.

It was early November, three days after Jonah had turned ten. The combination of fresh powder and bright sunshine had prompted Coop to take the afternoon off to go touring. He didn't outright ask Jonah or Luke to get their backcountry boots on, to layer up and meet him outside to help load skis and poles into his truck. It was their mother who let them know they were going by handing out insulated gloves and holding up last year's ski pants to see which ones might still fit.

"Lace those boots tighter," she said to Jonah. "And Luke, please keep your hat down over your ears. I don't want a repeat of Thursday. If I never again hear you complain about tingling and numbness, it'll be too soon."

His mother didn't need to remind him. Luke had paid a price for leaving his hat on the bus. By the time he'd made it back to Church's Overlook, his ears were frost nipped, the tips the color of milk.

"Got everything in the truck," Coop said, stopping short on the threshold to the lobby, careful to stomp his boots on the mat before moving in.

"Can we do the trails over near Black Cat?" Jonah asked. His head was down, and he struggled to pull his bunched-up sweater from the zipper of his ski pants.

Luke was relieved when Coop said, "Too many tourists." At eight years old, he'd already come to prefer the rugged natural look of the open wilderness.

Jonah filled the silence the entire way to the back gate of Baxter State Park. Coop mostly nodded as he drove, occasionally saying, *"Uh-huh"* in response to Jonah's nonstop yakking. Luke looked out the window of Coop's truck, trying to work out how the snow had done its magic. Outlining the length of branches short and long was easy enough to figure. When the snow fell, it simply took its rest there. But how it chalked the trunks up and down, Luke couldn't wrap his mind around that.

"You remember how to snap your boots into the bindings?" Coop asked. Luke knew he was talking to him because Jonah had his skis out of the truck bed and clipped onto his boots before he could get out of the cab.

Luke said, "You go on with Jonah. I'll be right behind."

Coop pushed off on his skis, whoosh, whoosh. *Great,* Luke thought. He could pull up to the rear and take his time. The farther he was from Jonah's mouth, the more likely he'd be able to listen for winter birds; the husky, rolling rattle of snow buntings or, if he was lucky, the low trill of Bohemian waxwings.

Halfway between Jonah and him, Coop stopped. "Get a move on," he said. "I promised your mother we'd stick together."

It was Luke's habit to obey his mother out of fear of getting in trouble, but right then it was impossible to follow the rules. Jonah was bigger and faster than he was, and before Luke knew it, he was at least a quarter mile ahead. Poor Coop. The trip couldn't have been much fun for him since he had to keep speeding up to tell Jonah to slow down and then wait for Luke to catch up.

It got more difficult to play their little game of tag when the open field closed in around the ragged outline of spruce tops. When the trail sloped down some miles to the West Branch of the Penobscot, that's when they lost sight of Jonah.

"Luke, you gotta step on the gas. Hop to," Coop said. "It's too cold to be dawdling like you're on some springtime hike in the woods."

"Shh," Luke said, pointing to a cluster of snow-veiled brush, his ski pole dangling from his wrist.

Not twenty yards from where they stood, the head of a baby moose peeked out. The little guy didn't move, but Coop extended his arm across Luke's chest as if they were still driving and he'd been forced to come to a quick stop, like an automatic attempt to keep him from lurching into an imaginary dashboard. That's when Luke got the feeling. The prickliness on his skin despite layers of outdoor gear. The agitation that stole his focus away from the calf and onto his out-of-sight brother. As if Luke's own life depended on it, he had the sudden urge to get to Jonah.

He backed away from Coop's arm, disregarding his clear message not to move for fear of spooking the moose. Or worse, bringing the calf's mother out of hiding. Luke's thighs burned from pushing off and breaking free; no time to enjoy the glide.

He didn't see Jonah at first. He'd been looking left, right, and straight ahead. Then he saw the one ski planted in the ground like an arrow showing him the incline his brother had fallen down.

Seeing Jonah at the bottom and the scrub brush dotting the slope, Luke knew there was no way to get to him without kicking off his skis. Using one pole, Luke slowed his slide down to meet him. There was a brief moment when Luke didn't think Jonah was breathing, but that was because his own lungs refused to inflate. And his brother was quiet. No cry. No moan.

Lying there so still, Jonah looked like he was taking a break to make a snow angel. Luke half expected his eyes to fly open and for him to say, "Tricked ya."

Then Coop was beside Luke. Whipping off his gloves, he ran his hands up and down one of Jonah's legs and then the other. His touch was tender. But Jonah let loose a sound so disturbing it sent the birds from the trees.

"It's his ankle," Luke said.

"I think it's broken." Jonah gulped air in between each word.

"You stay here. I'm going for help," Coop said. His gloves were back on and he was halfway up the incline.

"I'll help you carry him. Don't leave us here," Luke said.

Coop pointed to Jonah. "We can't take any chances it's his neck or back."

"It's just his ankle. I'm sure of it," Luke said again. Why didn't Coop believe him? He could feel it. He was certain.

When Coop was gone, Jonah had found Luke's arm and squeezed it. In between biting his lower lip, he spoke.

Of course he did. Jonah was never quiet for long. "Tell me one of your stories," he said. "The scarier the better."

Turned out Jonah's ankle was broken, a boot-top fracture the doctor called it. The way his brother told it, he'd been looking behind him to see where Coop and Luke were when he came too close to the edge of that ravine. Next thing he knew he was flying down the incline, calling out his brother's name as he went.

The following day, sitting in the breakfast room, going back over it, Coop said Luke must have the hearing of a collie to have heard Jonah from that far away. Luke looked at his brother parked in a chair, the broken leg casted and propped up on a pile of pillows, and he didn't say a word. He didn't tell his mother and Coop that he hadn't heard Jonah call him. Luke just knew he needed help. And he didn't tell them that since his brother's accident, sharp pains came and went from his own leg too.

A siren brought Luke back to Route 95 in the present and his mission to pursue his brother once again. Sure enough, the cop was pulling him over.

"Dude, you were flying. Clocked you at ninety," the statey said.

"Timmy Ellis. I see you still like to exaggerate." Luke felt relief at recognizing Sylvie's cousin, not just because he liked Timmy but because he knew he could get out of a ticket.

"Lead foot runs in the family," Timmy said, laughing. Everyone within thirty miles of Millinocket knew that speeding tickets with the Blackwell name on them usually belonged to his brother.

"Where you headed?" Timmy asked.

"Going to visit Jonah. Then I thought I'd swing down to Boston to say hey to Sylvie."

"I heard they broke up," Timmy said. "Which is a damn shame for me because your brother used to let me stay gratis in one of your old cabins so I could get my fishing fix on."

"Give me your number. I can hook you up," Luke said.

"Great," Timmy said. "But slow down, you hear?"

After he and Timmy exchanged numbers, Luke drove paranoid all the way to Brunswick.

When he got to Bowdoin, it was weird walking around the campus. The last two times Luke had been there, it had been all about him figuring out if he could see himself going there. A year ago, he'd toured the school undecided, and then last March as part of a group of accepted students to get a feel for the place.

Even with all the times Luke had visited Jonah, by no means did he have his bearings. The buildings were massive and all spread out, and there were too many people coming and going for him to know where to turn. Luke needed a map.

A granite slab with a campus plan etched in white was easy enough to follow, and it put Luke at ease. He found Quinby House, a stone's throw from where he stood. Its peaked roof and clapboard sides made it look like an ordinary home, not anyone's idea of a dorm. The entrance reminded Luke of the main inn at Church's Overlook, except the great room was much nicer. Newer hardwood and the heady smell of fresh paint.

Disinterested kids blew past him, some with armloads of books, others hugging six packs. A friend of his brother's leaned against the inside stairs, swilling a giant coffee.

"Mark," Luke said. "Know where I can find Jonah?"

Jonah's roommate for the last two years put his hand out to shake his. "You changed your mind. That's awesome."

"Actually, no. I'm just crashing for a few days. Where's Jonah?"

"J took off early. Can you believe he's started researching his film project before everyone else? I don't even have a topic yet." Mark moved up the stairs, motioning for Luke to follow. "I've got senior seminar now. But if you're expecting him back, you can wait in our room."

Mark swiped his pass card and pushed open the door. Seeing Jonah's things brought that awful feeling back in full force.

"Did he tell you where he was going?" Luke asked. "Maybe he mentioned who he was going to see?"

"Sorry, no." Mark slurped the dregs of his coffee. "I gotta go to class. If you take off, pull the door tight, okay?"

Blame it on his collection, but Luke had known for a long time that the way to get inside someone's head was as easy as looking at his stuff. Jonah was no exception. When Luke flipped open the lid of his brother's computer and typed *BlackwellBoys,* the screen came to life.

Looking for his brother turned up more than Luke wanted to know. The laptop was bogged down with emails, bookmarked web pages, and internet searches, all having to do with adoption. The name and number of a woman from Child and Family Services of Maine—likely the one who'd told Jonah he'd never been in foster care—was on a desktop note.

For a second, Luke thought about calling her. To ask about him.

Then he scrolled down Jonah's search history, and his mood went right along with it. Jonah had googled fake birth certificates, missing children, how to do criminal background checks. There were their names: Irving Orono Cooper | Lena Blackwell.

Then a message from Sylvie flashed on the screen.

I can't believe I missed you.
But I go to class. Ha.
I'm back in my room now if you want to talk

She must've seen Luke online and thought Jonah was free. With every blink of the cursor, he got more stressed out. What did she mean, *I can't believe I missed you?* Had Jonah gone to BU?

Luke imagined Sylvie propped against that stack of purple pillows she had arranged on her bed, waiting for Jonah to answer. Loyal Sylvie. He should've known that even though they weren't dating anymore, she'd still help him. Maybe they could stay friends. Or maybe they were back together.

Luke was about to tell her it was him there, not Jonah, when she messaged again.

I promise not to tell Luke
You can trust me

Luke shut the laptop and tucked it under his arm, somehow feeling justified in taking it. If Jonah went to Sylvie, so would he. Next stop, Boston.

* * *

LENA

Back to work at Church's Overlook, Lena felt unexpected pride. After spending time with Marli at Lakeside, she was seeing her inn anew. Though her lobby was more shabby chic than well designed, the views from its windows rivaled the ones at the resort up the road. And this place was all hers.

Lena hadn't anticipated being okay with Luke leaving to spend the weekend with Jonah. Her time with Marli had offered her some peace she hadn't known she needed. Luke had never been this agitated with his brother, so he must be making the trip to Bowdoin to pressure him to side with her. Coupled with Coop's insistence that there was nothing that could lead Jonah and Luke to Davis, Lena relaxed and turned her attention to the night ahead.

She pulled the old dress from deep within her closet. When the iron was hot, she pressed out the wrinkles, forcing them to let go of the hold they had on the fabric. Here she was, ready to try again to make a special dinner. This time for Coop.

The meal idea shaken from her memory after seeing Marli was simple and savory. Spinach ricotta gnudi, a dish she'd recreated hundreds of times on a restaurant stove back in Boston, and in her mind when she dared to reminisce.

While Lena had always imagined her story would end in some horrible way, what she'd failed to consider was an opposing view. That this was not a secondary life, some poor substitute of another. It was the one she was meant to live.

Lena was not confined to Church's Overlook, like dark roots planted beyond the shadows of her past. Looked at another way, she was as free as ever. New shoots stretched into her future.

Tomorrow, she'd come up with a script more truth than lies, and give the boys some details they would appreciate. Kidnapping was the act of knowingly and secretly using power, trickery, or enticement to hold another person against his will, and Lena's actions couldn't be said to satisfy the elements of that crime. She had every right to steal the boys away from an unpredictable life to keep them safe. The story she had crafted all those years ago had allowed Luke and Jonah a healthy, normal childhood. She would tell them this, finally, with only enough specifics so that the most horrific details need never be shared.

Thanks to Marli, Lena was reminded that she was strong. Having already handled so much. Couldn't she trust, at least for one night, that she could cope with all of this too?

Tonight, she would concentrate on Coop. After all, he'd been the one who rose every morning to silently work with her. At night, he was the person who calmed the fears that could run in her like turbulent water. Rare were the instances of friction or upset between them. He never pushed for what he wanted or asked for more than she was willing to give. Because of this, she had the deepest need to let him know that she was exactly where she wanted to be, and that if it weren't for him, would not be.

The debt she owed Coop for his nearly constant reassurance could not be repaid with a single gesture. He would appreciate the dinner all the same.

CHAPTER

15

Boston—1993

You would think that the safest place to be in your own home would be in your bed. Still, Carolina woke to her heart racing, her nightgown sweat drenched and clinging to her skin despite the open window beyond her nightstand.

Her body knew before her mind registered it. Davis was home.

Her head pounded with more force than it had when the migraine had arrived mid-afternoon, forcing her to lie down. To lose track of time. She hadn't meant to sleep for nearly four hours. All she'd wanted was a short nap—long enough to lessen the throbbing.

She heard glass shatter. Kitchen cabinets slam. Her name attached to a string of expletives. Carolina wondered if Davis even knew she was there. She was always to be home, regardless of when he got off shift. A meal was to be made, parked in the oven warming, a martini chilling—and Carolina looking pretty for him after his long day at the hospital.

As she threw her legs off the side of the bed and grabbed her robe, Carolina had a momentary wish—albeit a sick one—that she would inch down the hallway, round the corner, only to find it wasn't Davis making a racket, but an intruder. Someone whose choice to target her, to strike terror in her—perhaps tonight to hurt her—had been random. Not evidence of pure hatred emanating from the man she loved, who said he loved her too.

"I'm here," she whispered. Not at all sure it was the right thing to do to announce her presence, she froze on the threshold to the kitchen. Carolina tried not to react to the mess strewn from one end of the ceramic tile to the other.

Davis turned to her. Once upon a time the sudden appearance of that face would have delighted her. His perfect mouth, his sea-blue eyes. Now his mouth twitched; his look was ice.

"Where the hell were you? Sleeping?"

"I had a headache. Still do."

"Isn't that convenient. I wish every time I didn't feel like doing something, I could pretend to be sick. Come here."

Carolina didn't move. Her stomach churned at the mounds of food, fresh and cooked, rank and sour, all over the floor.

The way Davis reached his hand out to her, she had no choice but to take it. Once clasped, he pulled her arm, nearly dislocating it. He coerced her to squat, then kneel, and finally to come face-to-face with the tile, her arm wrenched behind her back.

"What's for dinner? Huh?"

"I can make you whatever you want. You can go read or something while I clean up."

"Bet your ass you will. What about you? You must be hungry. Nothing like sleeping the day away to make a person ravenous, am I right?"

Davis grabbed a handful of cold leftovers from the floor and smashed them into her face. Carolina pursed her lips, rejecting his effort to force the slimy angel hair into her mouth. She should've known it would not pay to spurn him.

When she wouldn't comply, he yanked her by the hair and slammed her face down hard on the tile. A scorching heat burned the length of one cheek, up and out the top of her head effectively eliminating her headache. Replacing it with shooting stars. Carolina retched at the mélange of smells. "Please stop," she whispered.

Davis ended his torment not because his wife had asked him nicely, but because the ringing phone split the air. The answering machine kicked on.

Carolina's taped voice lied when she said she and Davis were not home and that one of them would return the call as soon as they were able. It certainly would not be her, because the new rule was that she couldn't use the phone without his expressed permission.

Marli's friendly cadence filled the brownstone.

"I hope you're finally getting some sleep," her sister-in-law said. "Hopefully you took my advice and turned the volume down on the machine before you napped. I just wanted to let you know that I made an appointment for you for tomorrow. A week of migraines isn't anything to fool around with. I won't take no for an answer. I'll pick you up at nine. Sweet dreams."

Click.

"I told you to stop talking to that bitch. No more calls. Absolutely no more girl time. It's bad enough you spend time with her whenever I'm with Win."

Davis got up and climbed over her curled-up body, leaving Carolina in a heap on the floor, surrounded by a line of broken plates.

"Get out of going with her. Tell her I said you're fine."

If only Carolina could have enjoyed the relief that came with Davis's departure from the kitchen. But he wasn't even out of the room when she felt it. A wetness seeped out between her legs. And later, when she dared to look at the sticky dampness, there was blood. Too much blood.

Carolina did not tell anyone—then or ever—that she'd lost the baby. There was no need to, since she'd never confided in anyone that she'd been eight weeks along.

What she did do was get up the next morning, as she always did, to tend to her husband. It had been three years since Davis had stopped making reference to any events of the night before. Flowers and apologies were a distant memory.

This morning, though it was impossible not to notice, he didn't comment on the blood vessels that had burst in both her eyes as a result of his latest rage.

Faking a cheerful attitude, Carolina went about making a hearty breakfast, served piping hot and on time. The morning newspaper was folded thrice and placed to the left of her husband's steaming cup of coffee. Exactly as he liked it. She even kissed Davis goodbye. "Have a great day!"

Once she was sure his car had pulled away from the curb, she blatantly disobeyed him. Carolina got dressed and was ready when Marli arrived to escort her to the appointment, though despite her miscarriage, Carolina had no intention of going to a doctor's office. She had a different clandestine meeting in mind.

"Oh my God. What happened?" Not one foot inside the house, Marli placed a hand on Carolina's shoulder and with the other, gently took hold of her chin, lifting it, staring at her friend's blood-streaked eyes and purple cheek.

"I can't do this anymore." Carolina brushed Marli off. She stooped down to pick up the one small suitcase she'd dared to pack after he'd left. "He needs serious help. But not from me. I'm done."

"Oh, honey, I am so sorry. I knew things were rocky, but how long has it been this bad?"

"Up and down and off and on for months. I can usually calm him and then he's fine for a while. Lately he's volatile all the time. And he refuses to get help. He says everything's my fault. That I bring out the worst in him."

"That's not true. This has gone too far. Win will drag him to a psychiatrist whether Davis likes it or not."

While Marli surely knew that at times things were contentious between the young couple, Carolina hadn't dared tell her the extent of the horrors she'd been forced to suffer at the hands of Davis.

In the beginning, trying to be a good wife, Carolina made excuses for her overworked, stressed-out husband. His mood swings scared her certainly, but he never went so far as to hurt her. Not in the beginning.

She told herself if only she weren't his trigger. Or hadn't provoked him. By never being home. Spending too much money. Not caring how she looked. Becoming a messy homemaker. A horrible cook. Being lousy in bed. Blaming herself was easy because Davis was so good at it.

These last few months, awash in the shame that there was little she could get right no matter how hard she tried, Carolina became as masterful at covering for Davis as he had been at torturing her without leaving marks.

She'd only been to the emergency room twice. The first time, when Davis himself had become worried about her mental confusion, the result of a concussion he'd inflicted by smashing her head into the passenger seat window when she'd wondered out loud if he was too tired to drive. The other time, after the couple took a Sunday stroll on the Esplanade with Win and Marli. Carolina had had a hard time concealing a limp, the result of a bruised and swollen knee. Her brother-in-law had insisted the injury be checked out by a specialist. Davis was quick to make up an elaborate story about how it had happened, when in actuality he'd kicked her over something trivial she couldn't recollect. He'd almost had her believing that she'd been mugged on Huntington Avenue while going to meet him in the hospital cafeteria for a bite to eat between patients.

Once, and only once, had she dared to called 911.

"I'm locked in the bathroom," she'd whispered.

"Speak up, kiddo," the male operator said. "I can't hear you."

"My husband had too much to drink, and now he's threatening to strangle me. Please, can you send someone? He's having some kind of breakdown."

"If I had a dime for all the drunk husbands who say things they shouldn't. You got a family member you can call? Maybe a sister or a girlfriend you can crash with until he sleeps it off?"

The operator could not be convinced that Davis was a menace, not a garden-variety drunk, but a very ill man. No officer was ever dispatched to the brownstone on Beacon Street. Davis, however, never let her forget the mistake she'd made in making that call.

"Why didn't you tell me?" Marli moved into the kitchen, toward the fridge. While spilling ice cubes into a dish towel, she kept turning back to look at Carolina as though she needed to keep her eyes on the injuries to believe they were real. "I'm on the board of a women's shelter for God's sake. How could I have missed that things were this horrible?"

"We see what we want to see," Carolina said. "Believe what we want to believe about a person. It isn't anyone's fault but my own. I stayed. Until now. Just tell me you'll help me get out of here. Today. I need a lawyer. Not Neil. Someone who isn't beholden to the Winslows."

"Of course, I will. But, honey, you're not going any- where. This brownstone is as much your home as his. You haven't done anything wrong. We'll get him a psychiatrist. And you a restraining order. Regardless of what's going on with him, that will shame Davis into submission. I'll stay here with you for as long as you want me to."

Despite Carolina's taking issue with staying in the brownstone, and her protests about relying on an order of protection to keep her safe notwithstanding, she did finally acquiesce to her sister-in-law. Marli was able to con- vince her that law enforcement was now seeing the light on domestic issues, siding with women who suffered at the hands of their husbands. She insisted that Carolina's lone call for help that never came had been a fluke. Marli implored her to trust in all that she and Win had learned about keeping women in exactly the same position safe. Marli promised that Win would handle Davis from this point forward.

So four days after Carolina lost her secret baby and then cast her troubled husband out of his house—after nights of Marli sleeping on the couch—Carolina held the restraining order in her hands. Case No: 48231. Like a middle name you've never cared for, the number would forever identify her.

Ordered by a judge, and served less than a day later, Davis agreed to keep his distance and get psychiatric help. If he came within fifty feet of her, or anywhere near the brownstone, he'd be considered in violation of the injunc- tion. And he did indeed stay away.

Marli had been right. Shame was a powerful weapon against Davis Winslow. He didn't phone her. He didn't drop by. Davis went so far as to arrange to take his things from the house on an afternoon when Carolina was at work at Nic's North End restaurant. Win had agreed to be the arbiter.

Yet for all the hoops Carolina had jumped through— the lawyer meetings, the appearances in front of a family court judge, the utterances of hollow apologies she'd been subjected to coming from Davis—both behind a defense table and via his attorney in writing—for all the hours she'd fretted, Carolina still worried that what she'd done would only make things worse for her.

Subsequent mornings, she woke with a start, comforted only because she could add one more count to the days she'd spent without Davis. When she was good and ready, she got out of bed, and without anyone telling her what to do, she moved through the house at will. Into the kitchen, her eyes fixed on the spot where the man she had trusted with her heart—the man she once believed she could fix—had taken her baby.

More than once, Carolina had run her hand over the single sheet of paper lying on the countertop. Black type on white paper, the order a promise to protect her. It was all she had.

Carolina believed it would be enough.

pry—*noun*. A canoeist's short, quick, powerful turning stroke; the forward sweep draw for turning in turbulent water.

16

Boston—2012

Luke

Nothing short of a miracle, Luke found on-street parking outside Sylvie's BU apartment, a high-rise not two miles out of Kenmore Square. It took him three times around the circles of hell created by Storrow Drive before he found a spot.

The plants and trees and wild creatures known to calm him in the Maine woods were nowhere to be found. Sitting in his truck, shielded from the noise the cars made running east to west on the Pike, he finally understood the words *concrete jungle*. Luke took one deep breath after another, trying to lift the heaviness in his chest.

Or maybe he was stalling. Jonah might be inside, and here he was, about to learn things he had never wanted to study. Except he was there to finish what he'd started: find Jonah. If he could see for himself that his brother was okay, he could be back to Church's Overlook by nightfall.

Luke could've texted Sylvie to tell her he was outside her dorm, but after she'd agreed with Jonah not to tell him things, he decided to go with the element of surprise. He got out of his truck and went straight for her building.

A girl who looked more like a high school kid than a college student stood at the door to the dorm. Before swiping her pass card, she glanced over her shoulder, staring at Luke a little too long.

"My friend lives here," he said. "You can trust me."

"I'm not worried," she said offhandedly. The gym bag she swung higher on her shoulder was almost as big as she was. "But you won't get past her." The girl tipped her head and made a mock scary face at the woman in uniform sitting behind the desk inside the glass. The security guard had her feet up on the desk, reading a paperback.

"Right. Didn't plan on that," he said.

"I'm Daphne. Who's your friend?" the girl asked. "Can't you text her?"

"Sylvie Ellis. I want to surprise her."

"Come on, then," Daphne said.

It was hard to believe someone so small could push through the heavy doors the way she did, holding it open for him. When they made it up to the security guard, Daphne asked, "Do you need my friend to sign in?"

The guard's feet came down, and she shoved a clipboard in Luke's direction; the woman never lifted her eyes from her book.

Daphne flashed Luke a "watch-this" kind of smile. "Can you look up what suite my friend Sylvie Ellis is in?"

The guard turned to her computer and tapped a few keys, then handed Daphne a slip of paper with Sylvie's suite number on it. Two minutes later, Daphne and Luke were standing by the elevator.

"Thanks. That was nice of you," Luke said.

"No worries. You don't look so scary." Daphne was the definition of cute the way she smiled, owning the gap between her teeth. "Plus, I could take you down," she said. "I'm stronger than I look." When she flexed her biceps and laughed at herself, it dawned on Luke that she was the kind of girl Jonah would flirt with.

After Daphne deposited him outside Sylvie's door, he braced himself for a confrontation. He'd shot the rapids without a paddle before, he could do this, he told himself. But Sylvie wasn't there and neither was Jonah. Not one of Sylvie's roommates knew where she was, and no one could remember the last time they'd seen his brother.

When he asked if he could wait for Sylvie in her room, no one objected, and still it took him a few seconds to work up the nerve to go in. There was something different about being in Sylvie's space alone without her permission. Back at Jonah's, he didn't feel like an intruder. He'd even swiped his laptop. But being in her room got him wondering if they'd ever talked about his penchant for stealing things. Sylvie had seen his collection.

Standing there, surrounded by her art posters on the wall, the books stacked neatly on the edge of her desk, it felt like he'd blown past a no-trespassing sign.

He opened a desk drawer anyway.

Like his mother's desk, Sylvie's was ordinary and organized. She had highlighters bundled in elastics and neon rainbows of Post-it Notes in big blocks. Luke wasn't sure what he'd expected to find, or if he even thought there'd be something in there worth seeing. Until he found something worth taking.

The stack of Polaroids she took last summer were various combinations of Luke, Jonah, and Sylvie with a trio of kayaks. They'd ridden the Penobscot South and stopped at an inlet Luke had only recently discovered. In the first few pictures, Jonah and his then-girlfriend were playful, wasting the instant film with ridiculous faces. Luke had taken care to position the pair off to the left of the hulls wedged into a sandy patch at the water's edge, so Katahdin was front and center.

Sitting at her desk, shuffling through the batch, Luke stopped on a picture of him and Sylvie. What made him flip the photo over, he couldn't say. But there on the back of it was Sylvie's script: *June 25th | Luke's Cove | My favorite.*

Usually the connection he felt to inanimate things was obvious. He would know exactly when something wanted to be taken. The photo would have been simple enough to lift. There wasn't anyone there to stop him. Sylvie had left the pictures tucked in a desk drawer, and his guess was that she probably didn't look at them for days, even weeks at a time. Maybe never.

Still Luke couldn't bring himself to steal from Sylvie. He put the stack back in the same order and placed them inside her drawer, right before she flipped on the light in her room.

"Oh my God, Luke," Sylvie shouted. "You scared me to death. What are you doing here?"

"I need to talk to Jonah."

"Why didn't you text or call? You guys are freaking me out," she said. "First Jonah doesn't show up when he says he will, and now I find you hiding in the dark in my room. What the hell is going on with you two?"

Her nervousness gave way to anger. Sylvie yanked at the sleeves of her sweater, fighting to get the thing off, then she tossed it like a ball on top of her bed.

"So he *was* here," Luke said.

"He texted. Said he was in Boston and wanted to meet me after class. Then he never showed."

Sylvie talked slowly, like she was working hard to choose her words.

"I know Jonah wasn't in foster care," Luke said. "I don't care what else the two of you are keeping from me. I just want to make sure he's okay. Then I'm going back home."

Luke dropped into Sylvie's desk chair and slid his backpack across the floor, anchoring it between both feet. The way she looked from his eyes to Jonah's laptop and back again, he knew she recognized it.

"I was online when you messaged him. I don't care what you promised, Sylvie. Just tell me enough to find him," he said.

Sylvie kicked her shoes off and dropped down on her bed. Her movements were sharp and exaggerated as she curled her legs under her, making a tent over her knees with her dress.

"He was coming to Boston to talk to a friend of your mother's."

"The woman who showed up at Church's?" Luke asked. "How did he find her?"

"He looked up the license plate you gave him," she said. "The car belongs to Winfred Winslow. He's a doctor at Brigham and Women's. And he's married to Marli. She's an event planner at a restaurant in the North End. When Jonah called me last night—when I was online with you—it was to ask if I knew the doctor from any of my rotations at the hospital. If I could, he wanted me to get his phone number or an address. I haven't heard from him since."

Sylvie pointed at the laptop. "Why do you have that?"

"I went to Bowdoin. He left it out, and this is just one of the pages he bookmarked." Luke turned the laptop around so Sylvie could see the endless list of names of missing children. She didn't flinch.

"You're not surprised to see this." Luke flicked the screen with his finger then put the laptop on her desk.

"When he first told me, I thought maybe he made up this elaborate story as an excuse to call me or get back with me. But he really believes your mother is covering something up. That the lack of records in Maine means he was abducted."

Sylvie's head was down. Luke wheeled the desk chair over so he was right in front of her, their knees almost touching. "Look, I don't care if you think you're protecting me. You have to tell me. I have a feeling he's in trouble."

The air between them was charged with something; neither of them moved. Sylvie didn't look up when she said, "He did a criminal background check on Coop and your mother. Coop's came back clean. He is who he says he is."

Luke lifted Sylvie's chin to make her look at him when she said whatever it was she and Jonah had been keeping from him.

"Your mother's didn't come up at all. There's no one who fits her description anywhere in Maine or New England. There is no Lena Blackwell."

"That can't be," Luke said. "What about Church's? How did she get a driver's license?" Before a half-dozen questions were out of his mouth, Luke remembered Coop's name on all those bills. His mother was a liar; her license could be fake.

Sylvie put a hand on his shoulder, and Luke wanted her gesture to settle him, but instead, the heat from her hand made everything more confusing. Thoughts came to him like broken glass. Pieces of information that didn't fit together.

"Jonah thinks she stole him from some family?" he asked.

"He doesn't know what to think, but he wanted to go to the Winslows to talk to her friend."

Luke got up and tried to pace the room. But Sylvie's space was nothing more than a cement box. No room to move. No air to breathe.

"Did you text him an address?" Luke asked.

"Yes. I have it." Sylvie got off her bed and reached for her shoes. "I'm coming with you."

She moved past Luke to open her desk drawer. "I have a bunch of pictures of him on my phone, but this'll be better. It'll appeal to her conscience."

Sylvie pulled out the batch of photos Luke had just gone through. She chose a posed shot of Jonah standing alone at the edge of the Penobscot—a place he claimed to never belong. Maybe he really didn't.

Walking to his truck with Sylvie, Luke searched his body for any feeling, some tangible sign Jonah was okay. He registered only a kind of numbness. His instincts were dulled in this land not his own.

The hardest thing about sitting in front of the Winslows' house on that wealthy street on the Brookline–Boston line was wrapping his head around how his mother could ever have been friends with a woman who lived in such a showy place. Three stories, not counting the sunken garage and what looked like a garret, it was at least twice the size of the main inn of Church's Overlook. The Winslows would need twelve kids to justify living in something so huge, but according to Sylvie's digging, Marli and her husband didn't have any.

Anyone who'd ever spent time with Lena Blackwell— or whatever her name really was—would find it impossible to believe that she and Marli had a single thing in common. From the time Luke had spotted her at the inn until he sat outside her house lurking, it had been less than a week, and in that short time everything seemed different.

"Guess I have to marry a doctor, huh?" Sylvie asked, poking his arm.

"I don't see that for you," Luke said without thinking. He hoped she wouldn't want to know how he did picture her life—back when he spent time pondering nice things.

"Me either. I was trying to bring you out of your funk. Ready?"

Seconds before Luke and Sylvie got out of his truck, the garage door began to rise. When it cleared the back of the Lexus, out rolled WINMD.

Luke had seen the guy only once for a short time, but he didn't doubt it was him driving past them. It was the first lucky break he'd gotten since he'd started trailing Jonah.

"Good, it'll be easier to talk to her alone," he said.

When Marli opened the door, he could tell she recognized him immediately. With panicky hands, she hurried them inside. Luke got the feeling Jonah had been in that house before he crossed the threshold.

The three of them stood inside her foyer. Marli wrapped her sweater tight, cinching it at the waist with her arms. Sylvie stood next to Luke, her messenger bag poking him in the side.

"This is my friend Sylvie. We're looking for my brother. We haven't heard from him in almost two days."

"Jonah isn't here."

The minute his name was out of her mouth, Sylvie let loose a wisp of air. Not quite a gasp, but still he could feel the breeze on his neck.

"How do you know my mother?" he asked.

"We were—friends. Another lifetime ago," she said. The warmth her voice carried back in Maine when she'd introduced herself was missing now, but the tone wasn't mean or demanding. She was strangely controlled, on guard, afraid of giving something up. Marli didn't seem scared or surprised to see him either. He didn't know what to make of the way she acted, but it reminded him a little too much of his mother.

"You had to ask my name when you were in Maine. But you know my brother's. How's that?"

"I can't talk right now. I'm sorry. I have somewhere I need to be." Marli looked away toward the massive clock standing sentry in the hallway.

"Why did you come to Church's and then leave? Is it because you didn't want your husband to see my mother?"

"Both of you boys need to go home. Talk to her."

When Marli said *"both of you,"* Luke got the sudden urge to search the house.

"Just tell me if my brother's here."

A row of lines appeared on Marli's forehead. She started talking fast. "No. He isn't. Now you really need to go. I'm late."

Sylvie leaned in, talking directly to Marli like she was taking her side against Jonah and Luke. "I think they should leave their mother alone about the adoptions. So what if she doesn't want to go back over it. Not *everything* needs to be talked about, you know what I mean?"

Luke could tell by the way Marli nodded that she had no idea what Sylvie was talking about. She might know they existed, but that didn't mean she knew the particulars of their mother's lies.

"Can I at least leave you my number in case Jonah does show up?" Luke asked.

"Sure, fine." Marli reluctantly walked toward the back of her house into a giant kitchen. Luke followed right behind her. A collection of menus and seating charts from a place called *Nic's Italian* covered the counter. Like a kid caught with candy, Marli acted fast, opening a drawer and swiping the lot of it on top of the forks, knives, and spoons.

But not before Luke saw a notepad with his mother's phone number scribbled in Sharpie.

"Sorry for the mess," she said picking up a pen. "Go ahead."

Luke gave her his cell number, and then Sylvie gave her hers.

"Mind if I use a bathroom before we head out?" he asked.

"Me too," Sylvie said.

"All right, but please make it quick," Marli said. "There's one right through there. And another off the living room to the left of the front door as you came in."

Sylvie caught his vibe and moved toward the closest one. He trusted that she'd do her part to hurry back to keep Marli occupied, buying him time to look around.

To satisfy his curiosity, he ducked into a room, off the hallway, that screamed Marli's name. It had lace curtains and pretty furniture. Bookshelves lined the walls, floor to ceiling, holding as many photos in frames as hardcover books. In every one, Marli wore a cheery smile and formal clothes. Luke had never seen so many tuxes and gowns and diamonds. And then another face jumped out at him.

A man who looked like Jonah stunned Luke so completely that he almost missed his mother staring out from inside one of those frames. All dressed up, she had her arm linked with Marli's.

Minutes later, Luke and Sylvie walked away from the Winslow house, down the brick path. He felt Marli watching them go, but he didn't turn to look. He didn't want her to see the outline of a frame under his coat, tucked into the front of his jeans.

"Drive to the end of the street," he said, tossing the keys to Sylvie. "Take a left and pull over on Cypress."

"What did you do?"

"You would've taken it too if you'd seen it." Luke waited till Sylvie took the corner before pulling it out of his jeans. "It's my mother," he said, tapping the glass.

Sylvie pulled over, and together they stared at a younger version of the woman who called herself Lena Blackwell. In the photo, she wore a long flowery dress, pretty jewelry, and makeup, but there was no camouflaging the angles of her face.

"It's her."

Marli was in the posed shot too. And another man Luke didn't recognize. The shocker was recognizing a younger version of the man who'd tried to check into the inn. In the way his eyes were bright and his smile broad, he looked exactly like Jonah.

"Jonah is a Winslow?" Sylvie asked.

"This was tucked behind a bunch of pictures on a shelf. I saw Jonah in this guy before I recognized my mother. You see it too?"

Sylvie ran a finger over the glass. Luke couldn't tell what she was thinking.

"When I saw him at the inn, I didn't see the resemblance," Luke said. "But I wasn't looking for it, and he's older now. There's no doubt, right?"

"If Winslow is Jonah's father, who's his mother? Your mother or Marli?"

"If it's Marli, why isn't she acting angry? You'd expect her to be railing against my mother for stealing her kid, not keeping her secret. Unless she wanted my mother to take him. Is that why she held on to this picture for all these years? It doesn't make sense."

"None of it does," Sylvie said. "If your mother and the doctor had a child, your mother doesn't seem like the type to accept being paid off to leave town."

"Or to make up some lame story with fake birth certificates." Luke surprised himself with the word *certificates—plural*. He hadn't come there to find out about himself.

"So, what do we really know then?" Sylvie asked. "Jonah looks like the doctor. Your mother knows the Winslows. But who's this guy?"

Luke pulled out his phone and typed in every combination of *Winslow* and *Marli* he could think of. Galas and fundraisers and gallery exhibits were listed for pages. Nothing else worth mentioning popped up.

Sylvie reached over and clicked on Google images. "Look," she said.

Among the photos that appeared on the screen was the same one staring up at Luke and Sylvie from the dashboard.

The sick feeling that Jonah was in danger kept getting stronger. As reluctant as Luke was, he clicked the image.

It linked to an old article about some organization's award ceremony. The caption listed four names: Winfred Winslow, Davis Winslow, Marli Winslow, and there she was—his mother—Carolina Bennett.

Luke didn't know which face to look at. Or what to think. Maybe Winfred was Jonah's father. Or maybe Davis Winslow was.

Davis. Luke remembered. His collection. The name of the person who'd written the letter he'd found in his mother's field guide to birds back when he was a boy, now pinned to his wall. The one he'd read to Jonah a few nights ago.

Luke texted his brother.

I found your mother
Your father too

I'm in Boston
Call me

*   *   *

LENA

The meals her guests had come to expect were easy to prepare and left Lena time to tend to other chores. The predictable offerings featured meaty stews and chowders, plates of rustic American. Never Italian.

Tonight, with the radio at low volume, the intricacies of the recipe came back to her without hesitation. Her hands performed the task without conscious effort. It was hard to come by good-quality ricotta in Millinocket, so Lena worked the dumplings with the ingredients she'd been able to find. The prospect of doing something nice for Coop filled her with a puffed-up pride. He deserved her appreciation. Lena knew when she plated the gnudi in brown butter, it would taste good.

When Coop came into the kitchen, the first thing he did was move toward the stove and shut down every burner. Everything about the way he held his body told Lena something was terribly wrong.

She should not have put so much effort into trying to be happy. It was always when she let her guard down that she was blindsided.

"There's a call. It's Marli."

Lena wiped her hands on her apron, then ripped it from her neck, exposing the old dress. What had she been thinking taking a second chance on this embodiment of bad luck? She should've known better than to pull the threads of her past life in Boston, as if she were yanking all of it forward into the present.

Or was it that Lena dared to share Nic's recipe with someone else? The sweet smell of sage and bitter onion like a song meant only for him.

"Are the boys okay?" Lena asked Coop as she moved toward the office. When he didn't know the answer, she repeated the question to Marli on the phone.

"They came here," she said. "First Jonah, then Luke and his friend."

"Sylvie's with Luke?"

"They wanted to know if we'd been friends. If I knew anything about their adoptions."

"What did you say?"

"I didn't tell either of them anything. All I said was that we knew each other a long time ago but hadn't kept in touch."

There was a hesitation in Marli's voice that even after all these years Lena recognized as wariness.

"What did you do?"

"I told Win. He's my husband, and I knew he'd be relieved to hear you and the boys are well. Win promised not to tell anyone. Especially not Davis."

"And not Nic?" Lena asked, looking away from Coop. "Please tell me you haven't told Nic any of this."

"No. Of course not, no."

Even with Coop's arm around her, and Marli's reassurance, the sound of his name sent a twisting pain through Lena's body.

"I mean it, Lena," Marli said. "Win would never say anything to Davis. You're fine."

When Lena ended the call, she looked up at Coop. "What am I going to do?"

"What we're not going to do is jump to conclusions." He took the phone from her and punched in some numbers. "You'll call Luke. Check up on Jonah. Play it cool about Marli. Offer to give them what they want. It's time to tell them, Lena. It'll be better for everyone. You'll see."

Coop handed her the phone and gestured for them to move to the couch. Sitting by him, Lena gripped his hand. They'd been thrown together all those years ago. And now all she could do was whisper, *"I'm sorry."*

She took a breath when Luke picked up, hoping her voice wouldn't betray her. "I'm checking in to make sure you got to Bowdoin safe and sound."

"Yeah, I made it fine," he said.

His voice sounded different over the phone, but then she and Luke mostly spoke face to face.

"How's Jonah?"

"He's okay, I guess."

"Then he's there with you?"

There was a pause on Luke's end, and Lena could hear conspiratorial whispers, but she couldn't make out who was talking. Were they going to come clean about being in Boston with Sylvie?

"Can you put him on?" Lena asked.

"He's in the bathroom."

"I don't mind waiting."

"He doesn't want to talk to you. And you know what? I'm sick of being in the middle of this. Call him yourself."

"I'm really sorry. About everything. But please, I need you to ask Jonah to call me. I'm ready to tell you both what you've been wanting to know."

There was another break in the conversation. This time only silence between them.

"I gotta go," he said.

When Luke hung up, Lena should have felt better knowing her boys were together. But paralyzing emotion would not lift from her body.

During the next hour, waiting for Jonah to call, Lena and Coop didn't speak. She ran through all the worst-case scenarios multiple times in her mind. He sat next to her without moving.

By the time Coop did speak, she'd almost forgotten he was there.

"I'm going to call all of tomorrow's guests to cancel. Claim a force majeure," he said. "In the morning, once checkout is done, I'll go to Boston and bring back the boys."

She'd lived around Coop long enough to know the nuances of his moods. Still she couldn't read him.

"If you think things are that bad, we should go now, not wait until the morning," she said.

"I didn't say things were bad. But this has to end. If I'm the one who has to make that happen, so be it."

For all their midnight conversations and the closeness they shared, Lena could see she hadn't only hurt her sons with her deception. Coop had every right to call it quits on protecting her.

She thought about the safe and the gun she had hidden inside it. "Okay," she said. "Cancel the guests. You go get the boys tomorrow, and I'll head up to the old cabin to wait for you."

"Excellent." Coop pulled her close and hugged her. "You think that meal of yours is salvageable?" he asked.

Lena nodded, glad he couldn't see the slack expression on her face. Her trembling chin and wet eyes. That Coop believed she would do as she said broke her heart. Of all people, he should've known not to trust her.

17

Boston—1993

Nɪᴄ's ʟᴏꜰᴛ ᴡᴀѕ directly above the dining room of his eponymous restaurant. It was almost as big as the brownstone Carolina once shared with Davis, but it was warm in a way the Beacon Street apartment never had been—even with her husband out of there for over six months.

Red brick outlined her lover's place. Antique maps hung on walls. Low bookcases—filled to brimming with art and history and travel books—separated Nic's space into quadrants. Cozy coves for reading, an island for cooking, his bed positioned like a raft in the middle of the section facing the windows that showcased Boston's bustling North End neighborhood.

Carolina slipped from under Nic's arm and repositioned herself at the bottom of the bed, pulling a tangle of sheets around her as she moved. As Nic slept, the smell of garlic and oregano began to fill the loft. Chef and sous chef had begun prep for dinner service, which meant she should wake Nic. *A few more minutes,* she thought. He'd be needed downstairs soon enough.

As reluctant as Carolina had been to enter into a relationship with Nic, there was nothing like being with him. Lying there, she recognized a long-ago feeling, a peace that had been stolen from her bit by bit, day by day, stripped from her night after night by Davis.

At Nic's, the feeling of safety was slowly being returned to her.

As charming as the loft was, so too was the city visible out his window. From this side of the four-story walk-up, Carolina could make out the golden belfry of Saint Stephen Church. The narrow, curvy roads carved out a path leading to the sanctuary. Old-fashioned street lamps were already lit and decked out with Christmas wreathes, though it wasn't yet Thanksgiving.

"Penny for your thoughts, *Cara mia*." Nic climbed partially on top of her, his chest against her back, the only thing separating their bodies a thin sheet. His sweet breath made her want to kiss him, except that she didn't want to move, didn't want the memory of cold to find her.

"I love it here," she said. "I'll never tire of this view."

"Then move in. I'll make room for your things. I promise never to turn the bed away from the window."

With his cheek next to hers, Carolina could feel Nic smile. Without turning to look at him, she knew his eyes would be hopeful. It hadn't been her intent to lead the conversation in this direction. To bring up talk of doling out spaces and dividing up chores, or of sharing more than a piece of her life with him. They'd only been together three months, and Carolina wasn't ready.

She didn't know if she ever would be.

"What about the brownstone?" she asked as a means to evade.

"Rent it. Anyone but you would jump at the chance to live there. When things get sorted out, you can sell it."

By "sorted out," Nic meant when her divorce was final. The prenup she'd signed long ago would officially hand the property to her outright. Back then she hadn't cared what Davis wanted her to agree to, but Win did. Carolina had never fathomed things would end this way, though Marli clearly had an inkling. Davis becoming so possessive, trying—and at times succeeding—to isolate her from everyone, including her best friend. How her husband had spiraled down, ultimately transformed into a heartless, hurtful stranger.

Nic rolled off her, keeping his body close at her side, his heat still surrounding her. With his hand he cupped her chin, gently turning her face to meet his.

"Never mind," he said. "No pressure. When you're ready, you will know. I will wait."

With one finger, Nic outlined her lips before he kissed them, softly, tenderly. Carolina knew Nic wasn't just savoring their time together. Sometimes it was as if he saw her as a thoroughbred conditioned to be spooked. He'd told her before the first time they made love, on an afternoon like this, that he never wanted her to mistake him for Davis.

Carolina had reassured him that that would be impossible. Nic's every touch—every time they'd been together in the loft above his restaurant—he had been gentle. Patient.

Though she wasn't ready to surrender her life to him completely, she could let Nic touch her. Carolina could at least give him that.

As if he read her mind, Nic began to stroke her, caressing her breast, moving his hand down the length of her hip. Carolina let her mind slip away, imagining the two of them together years from now, maybe with a family. Her fantasy, a fresh start, an altogether different story than the one she was in the process of closing the book on.

After Nic left the bed to shower and change, after he kissed her goodbye and dashed downstairs to greet the early-bird crowd who loved him, Carolina slid on her own clothes and set out to hail a cab.

The pleasurable feelings that marked her time with Nic began to fade as night fell. Walking down Beacon Street toward the brownstone, uneasiness washed over her. Carolina found her body tense against the cool air. She buttoned up her coat and adjusted the briskness of her step.

On the way up the stairs, she checked over one shoulder and then the other, to be sure she wasn't being followed.

Key in the lock, quick turn, quick turn, and she was inside a space she would forever associate with her marriage. She tried to take a deep breath, desperate to call up the warm feelings that had enveloped her only moments ago. The goodness that was Nic.

Carolina leaned against the heavy oak door, telling herself to calm down. *Everything is fine. More than fine. Going to be fine.* She could almost hear Nic whisper softly, *"Relax, Cara mia—a hot bath is all you need."*

drop—*noun*. A steep, sudden vertical change in the riverbed; see *waterfall* or *pitch*.

CHAPTER

18

Boston—2012

LUKE

HE IMAGINED HIS mother in the office at Church's Overlook, holding the phone so that Coop could listen in. When she said she was ready to tell them things they'd been wanting to know, he wanted to correct her. To remind her that he had never wanted to know any of this. His mind formed the string of words. *What things? Why now?* But not one question came out of his mouth.

Sitting in his truck next to Sylvie, he should've felt worse for being mean to his mother and for lying about Jonah. Except the photograph of her with the Winslows, staring back at him from the dashboard, and her voice on the line—it was all so disorienting.

One of the things he loved about the Penobscot was that it had no predetermined shape of its own. In constant movement, the current could be defined by a rock or a stone; even a pebble could interrupt its course, ensuring that the river in any two flashes of time would never be the same. The mysteries below its surface intrigued. The weather above it—with the power to change its direction on a whim—never frightened him.

So when Sylvie put her hand on his arm and asked if he wanted to go home, she inadvertently loosened a memory. Right then, Luke recognized a shift in his thinking, wishing he had appreciated the day Jonah first let him know how he felt about family in general and theirs in particular.

"Do you remember when you and your cousin Timmy came with Jonah and me on a river run with that bratty kid and his sister from the Cape?"

Sylvie nodded. "What about it?"

They'd been playing *Simon Says* on a section of camouflaged shoreline locals called Maliseet Deadwater. Near the oldest and uninhabited cabins of Church's Overlook. At the water's edge, where they'd lodged their canoe, Jonah stood on a salt-and-pepper rock that jutted over the river, his loyal subjects below. His brother loved that platform almost as much as the one it resembled near the main inn.

"Jonah wouldn't let anyone else be Simon," Luke continued. "Timmy kept going on about rules and that everyone should get a turn."

Sylvie's cousin Timmy was the conscience of their group, and Luke secretly liked when he kept Jonah in check. It meant for once, he didn't have to do it.

Luke could tell by Sylvie's expression that she remembered the rest of the day too.

How Jonah had jumped off that rock and offered an alternative game.

Truth or Dare.

The bratty kid, Bobby, from Scribner muttered under his breath, "Thinks he's the boss cuz he lives here."

The sister tugged on his shirtsleeve. "Come on, Bobby. Let's go back to the cabin. It's hot. And I'm hungry."

"I'm playing. You go," Bobby said, as if his sister could hop in the canoe and paddle back to Church's without the rest of them having to go with her.

The girl crossed her arms across her chest and huffed at her brother. Then she stormed toward the water.

Jonah kicked a fallen tree that divided the spot, testing it with his boot before he sat on it to be sure the decaying limb could hold his weight.

Bobby knelt down on the ground across from Jonah. "I get to go first," he said, crossing his arms like his sister.

Timmy pointed to them one by one, ending with Jonah. "You go last," he said. "It's only right."

Luke sat by Jonah, having learned the hard way that it was better to stay out of his line of vision when they played games like these. The less anyone paid attention to him, the better.

"Truth or dare?" Bobby said, staring right at Jonah.

"Truth," Jonah said without missing a beat.

"That Indian you got working here—tell us how many white men he's scalped."

As if a storm moved in off the river, the air changed in their little circle.

"Native Penobscot," Luke said.

Bobby ignored Luke and locked eyes with Jonah. "How many people know the Indian is your dad?"

Jonah threw himself straight across the divide, landing on Bobby's chest. "He's not my father."

He had the kid by the shirt, grabbing fistfuls of cloth so tight that Jonah nearly cut off Bobby's air. Sylvie screamed, *"Stop!"* but it took both Luke and Timmy to pull Jonah off the kid. Luke got an elbow in the head for his trouble.

He knew without Jonah telling him that he didn't deck the kid because of the way he'd referred to Coop and his people—the very thing that upset Luke. No. Jonah flew off that log and into Bobby's face because he had said the unspeakable word *father*.

Timmy took Bobby by the arm and hauled him toward the canoe, away from Jonah and Luke. No matter how much he struggled to break free, Bobby couldn't shake Timmy's grip.

"Calm down," Timmy shouted. "Jonah, head up to the old cabin and wait there. I'll come back for you after I drop these guys back at Church's."

Sylvie helped the little girl into the canoe, looking over her shoulder to make sure Jonah and Luke were okay.

"After you left that day," Luke said to Sylvie, "Jonah told me his father would *never* live here. And that he wasn't gonna rot in a place called freakin' deadwater either. 'Someday, I am going to find him,' Jonah said."

The way he spit out those words, it was as if he hated those woods, the river, and everything to do with Church's Overlook and their family. "He's out there somewhere, Sylvie. He's doing what he promised he would do."

"Marli is definitely protecting your mother," Sylvie said. "She said she didn't tell Jonah anything, but I think he figured out on his own where to find Dr. Winslow."

Sylvie had to be right. All rivers have a source, a starting place, an origin. If Jonah was one step ahead of them, he'd be at the hospital.

At first, tracking down Winfred Winslow started off easy. Sylvie was positive that as an attending physician at the hospital, he'd have an office there. According to the staff directory in the lobby of Brigham and Women's, his suite was outside Surgical Specialties, a few floors up.

They entered the flow of traffic behind a guy, a little older than Luke, gripping a metal pole with both hands. He wasn't pushing it forward as much as using it to hold himself up. A milky bag of liquid hung suspended from it, connected to a tube that disappeared inside the folds of his hospital bathrobe.

A crowd had gathered outside the tower elevators. At the front of the line, waiting for the next car, was a man in a motorized wheelchair, his back so rounded and his neck so crooked it hurt Luke to look too long in his direction.

The nausea hit when it was their turn to board the elevator. Everyone squeezed into the car, and once the door had closed, Sylvie leaned against Luke to make room.

The enclosed space took his breath away, and he was grateful when the door opened up again and Sylvie tapped his arm to let him know this was their floor.

"Give me a minute," he said, taking deep breaths and trying to call up images of Maine.

Sylvie rummaged the depths of her bag and pulled out her student ID. "I'll go see if he's here," she said. "I'll be right back." In one smooth motion, she slipped the lanyard over her head and took off down the hall like she knew exactly where she was going.

Once he was able to will the panic away, Luke followed the signs to Winslow's office. Right turn after right turn, straight, and then left. Despite being aboveground, the place reminded him of a warren. No matter how much money Winslow got paid, Luke couldn't imagine himself walking these halls, day in and day out, when what he needed was air.

The lights were on in Surgical Specialties, but when Luke peered through the glass, row after row of waiting room chairs sat empty. Only random magazines scattered about gave evidence that they'd ever been occupied. No one sat behind the reception desk. He didn't see Sylvie either.

The door was unlocked and the strong need for some kind of explanation propelled Luke forward through that maze of offices. He wondered if this was what his brother was also feeling.

A woman in blue scrubs rounded the corner, practically slamming into Luke.

"Can I help you?" she asked, startled to find someone there. The laptop perched on her hip sent an unhealthy roll of flesh tumbling off one side of her body. An ID, similar to the one Sylvie had, dangled around her neck.

"He's with me."

Luke heard Sylvie before he saw her coming out of one of the offices.

"I'm a BU nursing student and this is my first surgical rotation. I'm trying to find the mailbox my instructor left for us to turn in our presurgical assessments." Sylvie waved a folder he hadn't seen her carrying before. "Due yesterday. My bad."

"You should check with your teacher," the woman said. "There's no one here to ask. The clinic's closed today."

Her phone rang and without looking at the number, she answered. "Olson." She pointed them back in the direction of the waiting room. Then she disappeared out the side door to the stairs, leaving the office the way only insiders were allowed to.

"He isn't here," Sylvie whispered. "What do we do now?"

"I still want to look around," Luke said.

Dr. Winslow likely spent more time in his hospital office than he did at home, so it was weird how the place was all function, standard-issue stuff, no frills. It was nothing like what he'd seen of the house he shared with Marli. The doctor's desk faced the door and was flanked by two nondescript guest chairs. How much bad news had been delivered here, Luke didn't want to know. The place was dim and depressing, maybe more so because all the lights were fluorescent. The lone window on the short wall faced another building blocking the promise of sun. The majority of light in the office came from the computer Luke was drawn to.

After he sat in the doctor's chair, he realized that for the fourth time in as many days he was invading someone's privacy, pawing through desk drawers without permission.

"What are you doing?" Sylvie asked.

"Maybe there's something here that will help me find Jonah." Even as he pulled open another drawer, he registered his disappointment that the unlocked office contained nothing of value. Until the ping of an email arriving notified him that someone was still logged on to the desktop computer. It turned out that someone was careless. That someone was Winslow.

"You can't do that," Sylvia said. "Come on, don't."

Scrolling through Winslow's inbox, the addresses contained random names, medical societies, and countless foundations. Nothing meant anything to Luke. Until he saw Davis's name.

He knew before he clicked on the email that of all the hundreds of things he'd clipped and lifted—what he was about to steal a look at now was about to change everything.

From: Anthony Walters <A.Walters@McLean
.Harvard.Edu>
Date: Friday, Sept 5, at 3:58 PM
Subject: Re: Davis Winslow
To: Winfred Winslow <W.Winslow@BWH.Harvard
.Edu.com>

Hi Win,

Sorry I missed your call. Between rounds and clinic, I've been out straight. I'm going to try you on your cell, but in the event we miss each other again, I'll outline a few things here.

Staff reports say that yesterday when Davis got back to the group home after work, he seemed more scattered than usual, and when they tried to redirect him, he became agitated. This morning he picked a fight with a new resident who apparently took something of his, and Davis threatened to call police. After he calmed down, Davis admitted he isn't taking his meds.

As you know, we don't force residents of Waverley to take their medications. We will certainly encourage Davis to do so, and we've offered him additional one-on-one counseling sessions to support him to make that decision. In the meantime, he's been upped to 30-minute checks when he's in-house, and it was suggested that he take a personal day off from work. Davis refused and is presently at the job site. Staff tell me that he had calmed down substantially by the time he left.

Sadly, we've been down this road before. As you well know, it isn't always clear what triggers a relapse of psychotic depression. Regardless, if Davis continues to refuse his meds and there's any increase in hostility, specifically any questionable threats of violence to himself or others, we will have no choice but to proceed with involuntary commitment. I do have a bed available in The Appleton Residence, should it come to that this weekend. It goes without saying that his move to the apartment is on hold for the time being.

I'll remain in close touch with the staff at Waverley, and suggest you stop over to the worksite to check in on Davis. As always, I welcome your insights. See what you can do, specifically around the meds.

Let's be in touch later today.

Best, Tony
Anthony Walters, MD
Director of Clinical Medical Programs, McLean Hospital
Director Outpatient Psychiatry, The Waverley House
(617) 565-6565

Luke grew detached reading about all of this, as if it had nothing to do with him. As if these brothers—Win and Davis—were characters in some story. "Is this why my mother wouldn't tell Jonah about his father? Because it's Davis and he's mentally ill? Potentially violent?"

Sylvie was behind him now, leaning over his shoulder. When she caught up with Luke's reading, she sighed and a strand of her hair fell forward; it swung inches from his face. The fresh scent of white aster—either her perfume or his imagination—had him wishing they were anywhere but in yet another concrete container.

"Would Dr. Winslow be able to access anybody's medical records from here?" Luke asked.

"Yes, but the electronic medical record requires a separate username and password. We don't have his." Then Sylvie motioned for Luke to get out of the chair. After she'd taken his place, she clicked on the EMR icon.

"We can use mine," she said.

"I can't let you do that. You could get in trouble for opening things you have no business reading. Right?"

He didn't trust himself to move closer to her, to get near enough to her sweet scent. Luke didn't expect her body to throw heat like sparks off a campfire. He closed the gap between them anyway, but the closer he got to Sylvie, the smaller the office felt.

"No one will find out. And if they do, I can say I opened the wrong patient record by mistake." Sylvie logged into medical records and started typing *Davis* in the search field.

"Wait," Luke said. While he'd never agreed to take a detour from the life he loved on the river, here he was. "No, put in Carolina Bennett."

When Sylvie stared at him, he nodded, and she typed his mother's name and hit "Enter."

There were lots of Carolinas and even more Bennetts, but there was only one Carolina Bennett Winslow.

Sylvie clicked on her name and Luke began reading. She'd lived in Boston. With her husband—Davis Winslow.

The first entry was an Emergency Room record, dated March 1992, for a concussion she'd suffered in a fender bender on Storrow Drive. There was another emergency visit in August 1992, for contusions to the left knee after being kicked during a mugging on Huntington Avenue.

There was nothing else in the record from that set of notes in 1992, until December of the following year.

All Luke could do was read it, and reread it, and as he did, he told himself this was just another story. Carolina Bennett Winslow's pregnancy had nothing to do with him.

December 22, 1993

OB Practice Admit Note

First visit for this 26-year-old primigravida. Note: husband, Davis Winslow MD, currently third-year resident in general surgery; brother-in-law, Winfred Winslow MD, Chief of Surgery.

Past Medical History:

Unremarkable. See notes of two ER visits for minor injuries.
Last menstrual period 10/30/1993. Cycles regular, Q28 x 5.
Estimated date of confinement (EDC): 8/30/1994 by dates
Blood type: A+
Meds: none
Allergies: Amoxicillin (rash)

Habits: No smoking, social alcohol, no illicit drugs

Physical Exam:

VS: Temp: 97.6, P80, R16, BP 120/70, Wt 115
Heart: normal sinus rhythm, no murmur
Lungs: clear
Extremities: no edema, normal reflexes
Breasts: no masses
Abd: normal, no masses
Pelvic: pelvis measures adequate for EDC
Urine: negative for protein and glucose

Assessment:

1. First trimester, approximately 3–4 weeks, EDC 8/30/1994 by dates, to be confirmed by 1st trimester ultrasound

Plan:

1. Monthly prenatal visits
2. Start multivitamin, folic acid, standard
3. Routine ultrasound at eight weeks (schedule for end January)

Hugh Michelson, MD

February 3, 1994

OB Practice Progress Note

Patient is aware of twin pregnancy per results of first trimester ultrasound. Patient discloses having been the victim of violent rape around the time of conception. Requesting options for determining paternity.

Note: Patient becomes agitated as information is entered into medical record. Requests careful attention be paid to confidentiality because of family on staff at BWH. Asks that progress notes re: paternity conversations contained within medical record be expunged.

Assessment:

1. EDC 8/30/1994 by dates, confirmed by 1st trimester ultrasound, approximately 10 wks
2. Question: paternity

Plan:

1. Schedule amniocentesis with DNA testing ASAP (before week 12).
2. Patient to obtain testing samples from husband (nurse to provide instructions for specimen collection).
3. Continue monthly prenatal visits.

Reviewed medical options pending paternity results:

1. Carry twin pregnancy to term.
2. Terminate twin pregnancy, which would need to be done prior to week 15.

Mother states unequivocally that termination of pregnancy is not an option.

Hugh Michelson, MD

February 17, 1994

OB Practice Progress Note

Social worker on hand to assist in the delivery of amniocentesis results and to help patient process options. Confirmed by amnio, patient is carrying dizygotic (fraternal) twins (two male fetuses).

Baby A and baby B have confirmed DNA match with mother and confirmed DNA match with sample.

Plan:

1. Per patient—Carry pregnancy to term.
2. Continue monthly prenatal visits.

Hugh Michelson, MD

Scrolling through subsequent doctor's visits, the only thing Luke could see written on imaginary lines above and below every other entry were the words *rape* and *twin*.

He skipped to the labor and delivery notes, knowing full well how it ended; with the birth of healthy boys. Their birthday wasn't either of the ones Jonah or Luke thought was theirs; still their date of birth had significance.

According to their fake certificates, August 1, 1994, was their supposed adoption day. The only day of the year they celebrated, with a shared cake tricked out with the number of candles that matched their mother's story.

"Now that I have answers, why don't I feel any better?" Luke asked.

Sylvie didn't say anything; she didn't need to. Once the words were out, Luke knew exactly why. He'd gotten what Jonah came for; this wasn't at all what he wanted.

All Luke ever needed was for things to stay the same.

19

Boston—1993

Carolina didn't go to the hospital after Davis raped her; she didn't report him to police. When he left her shattered and nearly drowned in that tub, Carolina lay there for many minutes, perhaps hours. When she'd finally convinced herself Davis was gone, and she dared to drag her bruised body from the water, blood-tinged and icy, she could not feel her limbs.

At first moving through the brownstone, she was cold, so cold. Then, without warning, every nerve ending in her body caught fire. Her hair and her skin, her body inside and out, burned as it never had before.

Still she was methodical. Carolina fixed her hair. She put on makeup. The way she packed her clothes was neat and tidy. The attention she paid to choosing the belongings she would take to Nic's was careful. It was as though when she stepped out of that tub, she'd become someone else entirely. Someone restrained, apathetic. Certain violations were too terrible to dwell on.

So with suitcase in hand, Carolina arrived at Nic's restaurant as the last patron was leaving the bar.

"I've had a change of heart about moving in," she said.

Nic hugged her and began to spin her around his empty dining room. Carolina stifled the electric pain she felt throughout her body, but the dizziness was harder to mask. When Nic dashed behind the bar to grab a bottle of chilled champagne, she gripped the back of a barstool to steady herself.

"Let's toast," Nic said. He popped the cork and poured two flutes of Moët, handing her one. "To our new beginning!"

Carolina smiled the best she could; she raised her glass as best she could. Tentatively taking the first sip, she willed her stomach not to reject it. As she continued to act as if all was right and well, Nic continued to effervesce. As he talked of their future, she became fixated on an odd thought. Would she ever enjoy alcohol again? Or would the sound of a cork bursting free from a bottle always remind her that this was what she'd been drinking when she became an expert liar?

"Listen to me rambling on," Nic said. "Are you all right? You look unwell suddenly. It's late. You must be exhausted. Let's get you to bed."

"I'm fine," she said. "But I am tired. I've been thinking of you since you offered to let me move in. I want you to know I'm ready."

And Carolina had been ready when she made it out of the brownstone and over to Nic's. By keeping her focus on taking her next step. Except when she heard the word *bed*, it was as if the walls of the restaurant began to close in on her. What was she thinking? How long could she pretend everything was as it had been between them?

As it turned out, quite a while. Nic's *Cara mia* was a clever storyteller.

In the ensuing afternoons and late at night when Nic wanted to make love, Carolina exhausted a litany of physical complaints. She had her period, the flu, a cluster of headaches. Whenever she could, she blamed Davis. "I still need time. Be patient with me," she said. "It's not easy to start over."

Nic was a saint, and his love for her never wavered, which only helped her to keep lying.

During the day, working beside him at the restaurant, intrusive thoughts urged her to tell Nic the truth. Shouldn't law enforcement also know, so Davis would have to pay for what he'd done? At the very least, shouldn't Carolina come forward so that he couldn't ever do this again to anyone else?

But like a cautionary tale, second thoughts came when she would look up at the TV over the bar and catch coverage of the trial of William Kennedy Smith, the privileged man accused of sexual assault of a woman at the Palm Beach compound of America's royal family.

Day and night, Nic's patrons weighed in. *"What kind of woman stays out that late at night?"* *"Who goes back to the guy's house without knowing what could happen to her?"* *"No question about it—she's after his money."*

Watching and listening for weeks, Carolina was unsurprised by the not-guilty verdict. Who would believe the woman over the upstanding, powerful man? And in her case, who would believe a married woman had the right to claim to have been raped by her husband?

Carolina worried about confiding in Nic too. How could he fully love someone who'd been so violently attacked—once by the man she had trusted—and then, if she had the courage to come forward, by the system supposedly meant to protect her?

So off went the TV and on went Carolina's life. Despite November giving way to December, each day seemed a little brighter than the last. She had survived Davis. And she convinced herself that he wouldn't hurt anyone else because it was she whom he despised.

Life with Nic, and his devotion to her, made it easier to look ahead, to believe that the worst was behind her.

Until she didn't get her period.

The fictional fatigue she'd manufactured in order to stave off sex with Nic had become a reality. Her queasiness had nothing to do with living a lie. When her breasts became tender, the constellation of other physical ailments suddenly made sense. She had felt this way once before.

Carolina didn't need to go to her gynecologist to confirm her pregnancy. The appointment was made and the paper gown donned in order to determine her child's true father.

Except when she hoisted herself up on that exam table, she couldn't do it. Carolina could not ask the doctor to do the definitive test. She didn't want a stranger to be the first to know something so personal about her life.

Instead, later that day, Carolina asked Nic to take the night off. In his loft above the restaurant, in his home kitchen, she set out his favorite meal.

When at last they were seated, she said, "I have something to tell you. I need you to listen to the whole thing. Please don't react until I'm finished."

Nic reached for her hand across the table. Carolina pulled back. Until he heard the whole story, she would remain alone with it.

"The night I came here—to move in with you. It was after Davis raped me."

"Oh, *Cara*. Why didn't you tell me? Are you okay?"

"I was numb. I needed to be someplace safe, so of course I came to you. But I couldn't talk about it. I couldn't tell you."

"How could I not have seen you were hurt? How could I not have known?"

"You were happy I'd come around to the idea of moving in with you. And I didn't want you to know. Not then anyway. But I want you to know now."

"I'm going to kill him." Nic got up from the table and started pacing.

Carolina couldn't bear to see him act this way. She pushed her chair back and went to stand in front of him. "Stop. You're not going to do that. You are nothing like him."

Nic put his hand out to take hers. The gesture was gentle. She let him pull her in. With her head against his chest, she let him stroke her hair.

"I'm so sorry, *Cara*. I'll never let him hurt you again."

Carolina slipped from his embrace. Backing up to the bank of windows, she purposely put a few feet between them, because she wasn't finished.

"I'm pregnant."

Nic didn't speak. He simply looked at her with such sadness in his eyes.

"It's your baby. I know it," she said. "I don't need some test to tell me it's yours."

Carolina started to cry. Not in an attempt to get Nic to sign on to be a family with her, though this was what she wanted most deeply. She simply couldn't hold back the flood of emotion a second longer.

When she told Nic that the child had to be his, she'd reasoned it would be easier for both of them not to know. Everything would be fine if he was the father. If anyone could carry the burden of this unforeseen circumstance, it was Nic. Steady, loving Nic.

Though she didn't say so to him, Carolina wasn't sure she could handle it if every time she looked at her baby she was reminded of Davis. The child who was the result of his rage.

"Of course it is." He walked toward her again, taking her in his arms. "We'll move. I'll take you anywhere you want to go. We'll start over together, away from all of this."

"I can't let you give up the restaurant. I will not let Davis win. He may think he broke me, but he only made me stronger."

"The baby is mine," Nic said, as if this were a fact. The vehemence in his voice, a desire to convince himself as much as her.

"I will love you both with everything I've got," Nic continued.

When his face softened as he talked of their imagined child, Carolina wished she could join in to the sweet talk of babies and plans for their future. Except hope was not safe territory for her yet.

"We won't do anything to provoke Davis. I'll let him have the brownstone," she said. "My lawyer can handle the divorce on his timeline, and he will eventually move on."

To all these conditions, Nic agreed. For several weeks everything went ahead in dreamlike fashion.

Then Carolina gave in to curiosity and consented to an ultrasound. Never in her wildest imagination did she expect it would reveal she was carrying twins. Not one child, but two boys whose father could be Davis Winslow.

berry break—*noun*, slang phrase for taking a rest on a long and difficult portage.

CHAPTER

20

Boston—2012

Luke

No part of him wanted to go back to Church's Overlook to confront his mother. Luke had lost the urge to search for his brother too.

Where words had once been a game to him, Luke couldn't come up with anything to say to Sylvie. So he closed off his heart and crawled into his head by going back to her dorm and throwing himself on her bed. He flipped through television channels at a rate of one per second. Despite how high he raised the volume, he couldn't get the word *rape* out of his head.

Parked at her desk, Sylvie treated him like he was a bomb with a fuse so short and chemicals so unstable that Luke could explode or implode without warning. But he felt strangely calm. Jonah was the twin with the temper.

His brother. His blood. The way they could read each other's minds. The times Luke had felt Jonah was close to danger. Those feelings didn't come because the Maine

woods forced a bond between them. Their connection
came by way of a different definition of nature.

Luke wished then that he'd gone with his original
instinct not to help Jonah. If he had found all of this out
from his brother, and he'd been back in his room with the
door locked against the world, at least he could have looked
over his collection. He could have flipped and turned the
pages of his dictionary to look up words that made sense.
Without hesitation, he would have unpinned Davis's letter
from his wall because Luke wanted nothing to do with
someone so cruel.

"I have so many questions," Sylvie said, her voice
almost a whisper.

Luke shut off the TV. "I know. I do too."

Sylvie opened the mini-fridge and pulled out two
beers.

Luke wasn't a big drinker, not because he was too afraid
to party or too uptight to have fun, but more because he
hated the way Jonah looked when he had one too many. He'd
get all angry and easy to provoke. Still, Luke took the Sam
Adams Sylvie offered and swigged the contents down to half.

"None of this explains why she took us away from
Boston, went into hiding at Church's, and then lied to us,
telling us we were adopted." Luke said. "Who does that?"

"Wow. Are you kidding me?" Sylvie asked. "She was
sexually assaulted. Then she's pregnant with twins, by
a husband who's mentally ill and abusive. Imagine how
freaked out she must have been."

"So she makes up stories and fakes birth certificates?

"It didn't happen to you. You have no idea what you'd
do in her situation," Sylvie said.

"I can't do this right now." In one long pull off the
bottle, Luke finished the beer. "I've got to get out of here.
Let's go to a bar," he said.

Sylvie didn't have a chance to protest. Just then, one of her roommates knocked on her door.

"Someone's here for you," the girl said, pointing at Luke.

As they walked toward the living room, he was half hoping that the someone was Jonah, except it wasn't his brother standing there. It was Daphne, the sweet girl who'd help him find Sylvie's place.

Sylvie gave him a look.

"Hey, Luke," Daphne said. "If you and your friend aren't doing anything, I thought maybe you'd want to come to a party."

As Daphne talked, her cheeks flushed pink.

"Sure," he said. "We were just saying we wanted to go out."

"What about Jonah?" Sylvie asked. Like out of the blue, after blowing them off, he would show up and ask where they'd been.

"My brother," Luke explained to Daphne.

"He can come too," she said, flashing her gap-toothed smile.

"He can text us or call," Luke said. "Come on, Sylvie. Let's go."

Daphne seemed nice and clever, easy to talk to, but if Sylvie didn't want to go, Luke wouldn't go without her. One beer does not a brave man make.

"Let me grab my stuff." Sylvie let loose a huge sigh.

The three of them weren't halfway through the sea of red Solo cups when Luke regretted agreeing to go. He wanted out of that room. But he grabbed another beer and parked himself on a couch between the girls. Daphne tried to make small talk, pointing out her friends from the gym. That's when Luke learned she'd been hauling that huge athletic bag when he met her because she was a star on the BU gymnastics team, and this crowd was celebrating a successful meet.

The pounding backbeat had Daphne yelling in his ear, and still he only caught every other word. At first Sylvie sat stone-still next to him. He could tell she was pissed at him for bringing her here. If she'd had her way, they'd be back in her room, fretting about Jonah and planning their next moves with notepad and pen.

Luke was relieved when Sylvie caught sight of someone she knew and left her helicopter pad to go talk to the guy.

"Come dance. It'll be fun," Daphne shouted, her cheek nearly touching Luke's ear.

"Go ahead. I'm good." He kept swilling his beer. Sitting that close to Daphne, Luke felt like a giant; she was so tiny. Everything about being here felt exaggerated and sensational.

To his left, two guys had lifted a girl by the arms, tipping her upside down so she could do a kegstand. All giggles and shrieks, she used one hand to keep her skirt from bunching up at her waist and with the other she found her balance and drank. Directly in front of Luke, a guy was feeling more than the music, grinding his crotch into another girl from behind.

There was no safe place to look.

Chugging his beer now, all Luke could think about was the last time he'd been to a party like this. He'd been with his brother. Jonah had started college and Luke had been a senior in high school, visiting Bowdoin for the weekend, right around the time Jonah launched his campaign to convince him to follow him there. Maybe—without him even knowing they were twins—he had some need to have Luke nearby, taking classes right alongside him.

Luke wondered suddenly why their mother had pretended they were different ages. How exactly did it serve her story to push Jonah ahead in grades and hold him back?

The party he went to with Jonah had started out exactly like the one he was stuck in the middle of now. If Luke had to guess, that was the beginning of him not really wanting to go to Bowdoin—or any other college, truth be told. A packed schedule of courses, studying all night, writing research papers—none of those things fazed him. It was the social terrain that proved most treacherous.

The Bowdoin party had happened before Jonah started dating Sylvie. Luke agreed to tag along with him and a senior named Phoebe. The plan was to meet her at one of the upperclassmen social houses, where reportedly the booze was plentiful and the girls fine. Jonah's words, not Luke's.

"Brother, you are seriously fun-deprived," Jonah said tapping the top of a backup cooler he carried. "Tonight, we're gonna drown your inhibitions."

Jonah tossed back a forty-ounce beer before they made it to the parking lot. Luke got to the driver's side of the truck before him, blocking the door, his hand outstretched for the keys.

"Don't get hammered." Luke said. "I'm not here to clean up your puke."

"No worries, man. I'm still trying to make an impression on Phoebe. I'll be good. Promise."

Baxter House was tucked away on an isolated part of campus. By the time they'd parked Jonah's truck and followed the foot traffic to the basement, Luke was already wanting to call it a night. Four kegs squared off the room, and there was some asshole handing out condoms. There were no windows and even less air. Luke would be lucky to last an hour in that sweaty cellar.

Before Luke met Phoebe, he couldn't get the image of the bird of the same name out of his head. The Eastern Phoebe liked people, and one could nearly always be found by the water. After Luke met Jonah's Phoebe, he couldn't help but think she shared her namesake's habits. The girl loved a good party, and the entire time Luke spent with her, she had her hand on the keg faucet.

The more Phoebe drank, the more she flirted—with everyone who entered her vortex except Jonah. At first his brother kept his promise to limit the beers. He played along with Phoebe's attempts to make him jealous, being a good sport, laughing things off.

"Want to meet my ex?" Phoebe asked. "Blake! Come here, honey."

A guy wearing pressed jeans and a dress shirt with the sleeves rolled up made his way through the crowd. Blake had *trust fund* written all over him, and he traveled the room with a full bottle of Patrón in one hand and a shot glass in the other. He flashed Phoebe a lime smile, and the two of them howled as if no one had ever done that before. After spitting the rind into the glass, he pressed the chilled tequila bottle to Phoebe's bare back, causing her to arch her breasts in his direction. Then Blake kissed her right in front of Jonah, all tongue.

"Hey, hey, hey," Jonah said. "Keep your hands off the merchandise."

"Excuse me." In an exaggerated move that challenged her balance, Phoebe placed her hand on her hip. "Merchandise?"

"It's an expression. I didn't mean it that way." Jonah took another swig of liquid courage. "I was kidding. And I was just letting Mr. Patrón in on our secret."

"Which is what, exactly?" Phoebe leaned toward Blake, who was simultaneously pouring a shot and looking Jonah up and down. The kid didn't spill a drop.

"That we have a thing." Jonah pointed at Phoebe and then back at himself.

"Oh my God, Pheebs," Blake said. "This is the guy who grew up in the woods? I thought Bowdoin was the boondocks. But raised by wolves?"

Blake was drunk, just fooling around, like Jonah was. Except little did he know he'd picked the wrong minefield to strut around in. He held his brother back by the arm, knowing full well that if Jonah wanted to break free and smash Blake's face in, Luke would be no match for him. Jonah pressed forward with his shoulder, bringing Luke into the mix against his will. The only thing between these two idiots was Luke's head.

"Don't," Luke said to Jonah, dropping his voice low to make himself sound threatening.

When he saw the veins in his brother's neck pulse and watched him toss back the dregs of his beer, Luke knew he was gearing up to blow.

"Jonah, I'm gonna be sick," he said, loud enough to get above the music. So of course, the whole party turned in his direction. Embarrassed as he was, Luke said it again. Anything to get them out of there.

"Outside. Now."

Jonah took Luke's cup, and together with his, clapped them both right in front of Blake's face, letting the dripping broken plastic land in shards at the kid's feet.

"Luke, you're scaring me. Are you all right?" Sylvie was in front of him now; her palms placed firmly on his knees. She took the red cup Luke had just crushed from his hand. "This was a bad idea," she said, pulling on his arm. "Come on. Let's go for a walk."

Once, Luke had read in one of his guidebooks that it was next to impossible to make a city man completely at ease in the woods. He knew that to be true, having worked his whole life at Church's Overlook watching those types. By the same token, the book said, a Maine woodsman, if left to his own devices, could get lost on a city street in less than five minutes. That, together with the fact that he was buzzed, was why he let Sylvie lead him away from Daphne's party and back to her dorm.

Hyperalert to the sights and sounds of the city, all of them foreign and displeasing, Luke walked the Boston streets beside Sylvie. Cars whizzed past, the drivers loose with their horns. College kids stumbled out of bars, either singing or arguing, their mood not as much a choice as dependent upon the way beer mixed with their personality.

Even with the path unrecognizable and his sense of direction compromised, Luke realized early on that Sylvie wasn't leading him back the way they'd come.

"Where are we going? Luke asked.

"You'll see."

Sylvie had been quieter than usual with him since being in Winslow's office. After reading those emails and health records, and learning the truth about him and Jonah. A more confident person would have taken her hand and asked if she was okay. Did she want him to get in his truck and take off? Would she rather he bring his messy family problems back to Maine and out of her life?

Block by block, it became more residential, until the air became clean and the trees began to cluster, and Luke figured out where Sylvie was taking him.

As they neared the Charles River, she moved with purpose, leading him down a footbridge and along a trail designed for runners and bikers. Looking across the water in the direction of Cambridge, Luke could finally appreciate how picturesque Boston was from this vantage point.

Minutes later, Sylvie stopped at a stately maple planted on a piece of land that jutted out away from the path.

"It's always so peaceful here. You can almost convince yourself you're not in the city. It's such a nice night, I can't believe no one's claimed this spot already," she said.

"Do you come here often?" Luke was relieved when Sylvie laughed.

"During the day, I do," she said. "The Esplanade's a mixed bag at night. It's not a good idea to come alone."

He sat on the ground and leaned against the tree trunk, comforted by the familiar grooves of bark pressing into his back. Years of heaving themselves aboveground, the maple's roots had done him a favor, forcing Sylvie to choose a spot close to him. She lay down on her side and rested her head in her hand.

"Thanks," Luke said.

"For what?"

"For bringing me here. Leave it to you to know I could use being by a river."

She smoothed out her dress, positioning her arm over the curve of her hip.

"You scared me back there," she said. "It was like you disappeared or something."

There was a special tenderness in the way Sylvie tilted her head and looked at him. It was in simple gestures like these that she got him to open up to her, to say things he could never say to anyone else.

"Were you ever afraid of him?" Luke asked. "Did Jonah ever hurt you?"

"No. God, no," she said. "He never would. You know, hit me or anything like that."

Luke wanted to believe her, but there was something unspoken in her denial. Sylvie plucked out pieces of grass sprouting up in front of her. He covered her hand.

"You don't have to hide things from me. Is that why you broke up with him?"

"He really didn't talk to you about us, did he?"

When Sylvie paused, Luke braced for another revelation having to do with his screwed-up family.

"I didn't break up with Jonah," she said. "He broke up with me."

Luke heard her, but what she said made no sense. He knew Jonah loved her. How could he not? What reason would he have had to end it with her? As close as Luke was to Jonah, and to Sylvie, how come neither of them had confided in him?

"He was obsessed with this thing about our parents," Luke said. "It didn't have to do with you."

"It had nothing to do with his search."

"What then?"

"It was you."

"What do I have to do with it?"

"It had everything to do with you. He knows I have feelings for you."

Jolted out of his buzz, Luke opened his mouth, intent on asking Sylvie a thousand questions, but nothing came out. All at once, he remembered the picture she kept in her drawer back at her dorm: *Luke's Cove | My favorite.*

"Jonah broke up with you because of me?"

A collection of shadows moved at the edge of the Charles, stealing his attention for a second. When Luke looked back at Sylvie, her eyes were closed against him. Was she also trying to think of what to say next? Or did she worry he didn't care for her?

Luke didn't wait for her to speak. He wanted her to know he felt the same way about her and had for a long time. When he placed his finger gently on her lips, her eyes flew open. When his mouth found hers, he could tell by the way she leaned into him that she wanted him to press his body against hers—something he also wanted.

With the sound of ripple waves against shoreline, and firm ground beneath them, the moment should have been perfect. But with everything Luke had recently learned about his family, he couldn't ignore the pull of a distant river.

Jonah was his brother. All of a sudden his *twin*. Luke had no idea how long Sylvie had been conflicted about them, or how hard it was for her to own up to Jonah about her feelings for him. Still, the totality of it overwhelmed Luke.

"There's a secluded bay in the North Wilderness with unreal views of Katahdin," he said. "I want to show it to you. Be with you there. Make it our place."

Sylvie nodded, and she kissed him again, this time so deep and long he almost gave in to what his body needed.

His old life in the Maine woods could not have seemed farther away. With Sylvie beside him, holding his hand, his decision to leave Church's Overlook seemed prescient now. Though never once had he believed that his search for his brother would lead him to her.

"First we need to find Jonah," she said finally. "You need to talk to him about your parents."

Luke loved her even more then, for reading his mind and not being swayed by what the rest of him wanted.

For things between them to start off right, he needed to hear Jonah say it was okay for them to be together.

This moment called for him to find his brother and face whatever else there was to know about their family.

It could have been the sound the river made or Sylvie's touch or the word *parents,* but all of a sudden Luke knew where to find Jonah. He would be wherever Davis Winslow was. Jonah would have found their father.

reversal—*noun*. When the current curls back on itself; usually treacherous. May be caused by large obstructions, either on the surface or underwater.

Millinocket, Maine—2012

LENA

OVER THE YEARS, she had adjusted her response to danger considerably. When she'd been living with Davis, her fallback position had always been to freeze. *Careful. Don't provoke. You can make things better, or you can make things much, much worse.* Words to live by.

Then, of course, she chose flight. After losing her baby, when Davis's cruelty reigned supreme, she attempted to end her marriage, and when that didn't work to thwart him, and her beautiful sons were in harm's way, she'd made a break for it. She'd been willing to sacrifice everything, including Nic, to save her children from their father.

So when Marli called Lena again, this time to say that Davis had never returned to his group home and that now Win couldn't find him, Lena knew this moment called for her to fight for Luke and Jonah.

An expert at controlling her mind by controlling her body, Lena got dressed, and without alerting Coop, raced to the office.

Hours ago, she'd thoroughly convinced herself she didn't need to remove the gun from the safe. All she had to do was drive to Boston, find the boys, and explain most of what she'd done back then and why. She'd used the lie to keep the boys from Davis for so long; it was time to use the truth.

Marli said he was harmless now. *"A shell of his former self"* were her exact words. But Lena had been right not to believe that. The gun would give her a sense of safety if she had to face him—though she hoped with all her heart she wouldn't.

As Lena crossed the threshold of the office and moved toward the desk, she texted her boys identical urgent messages. She pleaded with them to call her or come home. She covered her bases by texting Sylvie too.

Lena barely had the safe open when Luke called.

"Are you okay?" she asked.

"I think Jonah found Davis."

When her son said that name, it took her breath away. Luke didn't give her the chance to ask how much more he knew.

"I'm going to his halfway house or whatever the place is," he said.

"You don't need to. Win and Marli already checked. He's not there."

"Where could they be then?"

"I don't know. But I'm sure Win will find them. Luke—listen to me, please. Davis can be violent. I need you to promise me you'll wait this out at Sylvie's."

"Yeah, sure. I'm here now," Luke said. "But you need to call the police. Or at least call Timmy Ellis, okay? In case they're headed to Church's."

When Coop came into the office, Lena put a finger to her lips.

"Mom, you need to call Timmy or I will," Luke said.

"Okay, I will. But they're not coming here. Davis doesn't know where I am," she said. "Honey, I'm sorry about everything. I was going to tell you—"

She didn't have a chance to make any more promises. Luke ended the call.

"You weren't planning to go downstate without me, were you?" Coop asked.

Lena's urge was to say, "No, I came in here to grab cash," but she was weary from all the lying. She nodded.

"Something has you riled," he said. "What's changed?"

"They know," she said. "I don't know how they found out, but they know Davis is their father."

Coop had always been kind, and lately they'd grown less hesitant about expressing their affection for each other. When he moved toward her, he would embrace her. And once on the other side of their shared desk, he would see the open safe.

Lena raised her hand like a stop sign. "I'm sorry. I'm grateful for everything you've ever done for me. But I need to do this by myself."

She didn't tell Coop that Luke had been lying earlier when he'd said Jonah was with him. Or that Marli had called again to say Win couldn't find Davis.

Without any trace of emotion, Coop spoke as if she were one of their guests. "I appreciate that. But Luke and Jonah are like sons to me. I won't take no for an answer. It's eleven now. I've got one more cabin to clear. Give me a few minutes, and I'll meet you by my truck."

Lena watched him go, and at first her limbs were too heavy to move. The sight of the gun lying in the safe at the bottom of that drawer flooded her with terror. The barrel of it pointed at her like an accusation, questioning the lengths she was willing to go for her children.

She picked it up, once again surprised by its light weight. Lena tucked it into the back of her jeans and pocketed some of the cash. She closed the drawer, without locking it. No point to that now.

Lena had no intention of waiting for Coop. Just as she had no plans to call Sylvie's statey cousin, Timmy. Neither the police nor the courts could be counted on to take her side—and she'd felt that way since before she'd fled with her children.

Convinced that no one could help her—not even Coop—she would find the boys on her own and make them see she was justified in what she'd done. Lena would beg them not to invite Davis back into their lives.

Heavy footfalls sounded against creaky floors. Apparently Coop had finally learned not to trust her to follow through on what she'd promised to do. He'd come for her.

With only seconds to decide whether to ditch Coop by slipping out the side door and taking a circuitous path to her truck, or to give in and let him help her, she pulled her shirt down to cover the gun and stepped quietly toward the outside door.

That's when she heard Jonah.

He burst into the office as if in some kind of stupor, Davis right behind him.

At a distance, her husband looked nothing like he had all those years ago. The man she had loved in another lifetime had become haggard, his face and neck gone doughy. Hollow-eyed and otherwise thin, his abdomen was the only thing round and taut.

"Practically in my backyard, Carolina?" he asked. "You've been here all along?"

Lena wanted to feel sympathy for him—like she had in the beginning. To remember he was sick. But Davis's twitchy mouth and the way he squinted those queer translucent eyes were enough to convince her, to remind her, he was exactly the same man.

Lena went to Jonah to guide him to the couch, all without taking her eyes off Davis.

Jonah sounded completely out of it. His singsong sentences were clipped and slurred.

"Something. In coffee," he said.

"You're okay," she whispered. "Rest here."

Lena eased Jonah back against the pillows, all her movements slow and careful. Her son's efforts were sluggish, his reflexes off.

Davis circled the desk. He mumbled something over and over, but Lena couldn't hear it. She didn't dare speak. Or run for Coop. Lena wouldn't leave Jonah alone with him.

The more agitated Davis got, the louder Jonah spoke. He babbled on about finding him at a worksite, grabbing coffee with him, passing out in the front seat of his truck, and waking up home.

"You took my kids," Davis shouted. "All this time they were right here."

With every sentence, he turned a deeper shade of red. His neck veins pulsed.

"Let's let Jonah sleep it off," she whispered. "Come talk with me in the lobby."

"His name is Simon." With a clenched fist, Davis struck himself repeatedly in the face. On his cheek. Near his mouth. Over one ear. Every punch exaggerated the marks on his skin. His shouting got louder with each blow. "Where's James?"

At the sound of her other son's name, Lena heard someone approaching the office. She'd never been so happy to see Coop step across that threshold. Of course, he'd been right. Lena did need him. Desperately. He took a quick glance at her standing above Jonah, and turned to face Davis.

"Who the hell are you?" Davis asked.

"Irving Cooper. I run the place."

Coop stood still at first. Then, when Davis seemed to calm down, he dared to walk slowly toward him with his hand outstretched. It was as if he instinctively knew Davis could be settled by merely blocking his ability to see Lena.

"She was my wife," Davis said. "All she ever did was tell lies about me. My own brother believed her. She took my kids." At first, when he backed away from Coop, his unsteady gait made it look like he needed to lean up against something. Until in quick time, he kicked away the doorstop and shut and locked the office door.

There he was, as capable and dangerous as he'd always been. When he glared at her, there was nothing but hate in his eyes.

Being trapped in a room with Davis brought everything back. The familiar splinter in the way her mind processed information had her focused on only one thing now: getting him away from Jonah.

"I can take you to James," she said. "He's staying in a cabin upriver. He'll want to meet you. We can bring him back here so we can talk. As a family."

Coop shook his head so only she could see. He didn't understand that Lena had no intention of taking Davis to the safe house. All she wanted was to move him out of the office, away from her son. She wouldn't hesitate to overtake Davis once she was alone with him, outside. No matter how violent his outbursts could be—how brutal he was, how strong. She was strong now too.

"I have a better idea." Coop said. "I never knew she took your sons away from you. She should have to pay for that. We'll call the police."

Everything happened at once. Davis bent down for the heavy doorstop. Lena had no time to put herself between the two men before Davis turned on unsuspecting Coop and brought the iron down on his head.

He collapsed to the floor, and Lena ran to him. With both hands she gently rolled him on his back, positioning his body so she could feel for a pulse and check for breathing. Then Jonah screamed, "Mom!"

Davis put a choke hold on her from behind. Oddly, for a brief moment, Lena relished being proven right about her reason to run with the boys all those years ago: Davis still had an unending desire to squeeze every last bit of life out of her.

Then he abruptly let go. Right after he'd reached into the back of her jeans to pull out the gun.

launch—*verb*. To enter the water in a boat, to set a thing in motion.

22

Millinocket, Maine—2012

LUKE

E VERY OTHER TIME he arrived home from a getaway weekend, he'd been happy to see the cedar sign that read: "Welcome to Church's Overlook." Approaching it now, he wished the burnished wood staked to an oversized oak wasn't so prominent. If they'd gotten this far, there would be no way for Jonah to steer Davis clear of their place and their mother.

His brother's truck wasn't in the drive when Luke pulled in front of the main inn. Coop's was. His mother's too. There was no sign of Timmy Ellis or his cruiser. And not a single guest vehicle. On a Saturday.

Luke hopped out of his truck and ran full speed into the inn. The lobby was empty, which it never was this time of year. He flipped through the registration book, counting reservations—Scribner, Roosevelt, Emerson, Thoreau—every cabin was supposed to be full.

Luke called out for Coop and his mother as he made his way to the back of the inn. The office door was closed, and he couldn't hear any voices coming from inside. He tried the knob; it was locked.

Luke took the side door to get a look inside the office from outside, as he had the night he'd eavesdropped on Coop and his mother through the sliver of a crack in the window while they disposed of some kind of evidence.

Through the panes, he saw Coop sprawled on the floor, his unmoving body next to the old desk. Luke scanned the place, dreading the possibility that his mother and brother were in similar positions in far-off corners of the room. They weren't there.

Luke fought the window, damning the swollen wood as he jimmied it. No matter how much weight he threw against it, he couldn't get it all the way up. He was about to break the glass when the ancient thing gave a little. With the window halfway open, Luke forced his body through the small space, scraping his back and nicking his arms on the way in.

"Coop," Luke yelled, but there was no response. He knelt beside him, pushing the heavy doorstop away from his head. Coop was still breathing. Shallow, quick wisps of wind. Nothing deep. But breaths were breaths as far as he was concerned. Coop would be okay, he told himself. The bleeding he could see around his head wasn't anything dramatic, and it seemed to have stopped.

If Coop's hands weren't gripping his chest, it might've looked like he'd been so desperate to take a load off that he'd chosen the floor as the place to lie down instead of the couch.

"Come on," Luke said. "Wake up. Talk to me." His hands trembled as he shook Coop's shoulder and urged him to come around. When he stirred and moaned, Luke wanted to hug him.

As relieved as he was that Coop was conscious, he needed to find his brother and his mother. "Where are they?"

Luke loosened the collar of Coop's work shirt with one hand, and still he struggled for air. With his other hand, Luke pulled his phone out. "You're okay. I'm calling 911."

At the sound of those numbers, Coop's hand jack-knifed like a primitive reflex. He gripped Luke's arm and squeezed it. "No."

"We need to get you checked out. It could be bad."

"Four-seven-two-zero-one." Coop chanted a number with each brusque puff of breath.

"Slow down," Luke said.

Coop repeated the numbers.

"The safe?" Luke asked. "Is that the combination?"

He left Coop's side and pulled open the bottom drawer of his mother's desk about to come face-to-face with what Coop and his mother had been hiding in there.

Except the safe was already open. Luke shuffled papers left and right. Pushed around ledgers and passbooks and disturbed boxes of checks.

"What am I looking for?" he asked.

"Gun."

Luke stopped rummaging because he thought he'd misheard him.

Coop rolled on to his side, drawing together what little strength he could muster to get up.

His breathing was deeper now, his words guttural. "Take. The. Gun."

"I don't know what you're talking about," Luke said. "There isn't one here."

Luke watched Coop sit half upright, leaning against the front of the couch for support.

"She kept one here because of Davis?" Luke asked.

Coop nodded and then shut his eyes, as if everything hurt when he moved. When he brought his hand up to touch the back of his head, he winced.

"I have to find them."

Coop nodded again.

"Do you know who has the gun?"

Even before Coop could get anything out, Luke knew he couldn't know. He thought the safe was locked when he wasted his breath huffing out the combination.

"Here," Coop said.

It was hard to watch this ordinarily strong man struggle to straighten his legs. Luke went to help him sit up.

"Take." Coop stretched one leg out and tapped his pants pocket.

"No," Luke said. "I'm not taking your knife."

Coop's voice got softer with each word he forced out. "Cabin."

As much as Luke didn't want to take it, he appeased him by reaching into his front pocket for the double-steel blade. After he shoved it in his own jeans, he handed Coop the office phone.

"Don't be stupid. Call for help. If Mom is in trouble with the police and that's why you're being reckless about involving them, make up a story. You're both really good at that."

Coop took the phone from him, but he didn't let go of his hand. Luke thought he was going to pat it or squeeze it or use some other gesture to say he was sorry.

Instead, he puffed out, "Dead—"

Luke couldn't believe it. He didn't let Coop finish. Taking off through the lobby, down the steps of the main inn, toward the cabins nestled between the Penobscot and the Maine woods, he could not acknowledge what Coop had just given him permission to do.

* * *

LENA

It was one thing to imagine taking on Davis in the abstract; it was a different thing altogether when he was standing in front of her.

Hours ago, he'd taken advantage of Jonah's dulled reflexes—and everything Lena had ever been in fear of—by putting the gun to her son's head and walking him over Coop's body and out the office door.

There was a moment in the lobby when Lena had almost convinced him to leave Jonah behind and let her take him to the imaginary James downriver. "He's groggy and clumsy," she argued. "He'll only slow us down."

True to form, Jonah didn't take to being left out. "I'm coming," he said. "She doesn't know the fastest way to get there. I do."

At first Lena felt betrayed by Jonah. But when Davis started roaming the lobby, walking in circles around him, brandishing the gun, one quick look from her son told Lena he wanted to come to protect her.

"Let's go," Jonah said. "The cabin isn't far."

Lena didn't know what his plan was, but minutes into the walk she figured he was moving them toward the cabin farthest from the main inn. Only she couldn't figure out why.

To the left and right of the tunnel of trees, Jonah's truck came into view. Both doors were wide open and the overhead lights were on; the keys dangling from the ignition sang out their whereabouts like a warning.

"We'll go inside. You can have something to eat and then rest until he shows up. He's due back any minute." His movements still clumsy, Jonah took his backpack out of the truck but didn't bother to slam the door; he left the chimes ringing. Unsteady on his feet, he lurched forward and swayed sideways; he kept moving toward the cabin.

"We're not driving there?" Walking next to Jonah, Davis fell into a rhythm despite his erratic gait. He seemed calm in his presence.

Counter to the way Davis was with her, the more Jonah talked, the more cogent Davis seemed. Once inside, Jonah pulled a box of saltines and a jar of peanut butter from the stocked staples cabinet located in each cabin above the stove. It didn't take much coaxing for him to convince Davis to sit down and take what was being offered to him.

In that cabin, Jonah resembled a snake charmer. One story after another poured out of him about his childhood. And he invited Davis to do the same.

In the years Lena had known Davis, she'd tried every tactic her brain could come up with for dealing with him. And here Jonah was, barreling ahead, solving the Davis problem by ignoring his derangement and acting like the situation was normal. An ordinary Saturday catch-up between father and son.

Had it not been for the gun in Davis's hand, Lena might have simply gotten up and walked out, leaving them to tell the stories of their lives. But Davis was Davis, and he was aiming the pistol at her child.

So while they traded anecdotes, her mind raced with possible endings to this pretense.

Could Jonah talk Davis into a stupor? Would he eventually be able to convince him to give up the gun?

Or maybe Jonah was buying time because he expected Coop to regain consciousness and come to their rescue, as he was known to do.

All obvious possibilities—except the only option that resonated with Lena was that Jonah was counting on Luke to find them. He was waiting for his brother.

Not long after they had entered Emerson—as minutes ticked by and the stories remained uncomplicated—Davis appeared so rational that Lena was lured into speaking.

"Can I get you something to drink?"

Her well-intentioned attempt to be reasonable, to accept what was before her eyes, to believe what Marli had told her about him being seriously ill, to give Davis the benefit of the doubt—all of it was doomed ultimately. The sound of her voice, which had always been a siren, precipitated further escalation.

"What's taking so long? When is he coming?" Davis stood, and his movements went back to being fitful.

"Wait," he said. "You lied. You said James was in a cabin upriver. Get up," he said to Jonah, grabbing his arm. "Move."

Lena got up too and she stiffened as Davis brushed by her. With no warning, he shoved her back against the log wall, sending a sharp pain across her shoulders.

"Do you really think I won't hurt him?" Davis pushed her again, this time with less force.

All these years later, this strange pair stood together in the same room, but they were changed. Where Davis was still hateful, she'd become more cunning. Where he had bursts of energy, she had endurance. Lena could best him. She would take him deeper into the woods until he was zapped of whatever strength he had left, and it would be effortless to take the gun from him then. Or perhaps she'd wait until the inevitable moment when he would look away long enough for her to slip out of sight. There would be unconscionable satisfaction in leaving him in the dark woods to fend for himself.

"I know where he is," she said. "I'll take you to him. But put the gun down, or at least point it at me."

dead reckoning—*noun*. The method of determining the position of a boat by charting its course from a previously known position.

23

Millinocket, Maine—2012

LUKE

THE BLUNT EDGE of Coop's knife handle pressed against his thigh as he moved across the expanse of Church's Overlook toward the cabins. Unnerved as he was, Luke couldn't help but notice the afternoon light refracting off the Penobscot in a way that was known to lure him. Early September was a month like no other in the Maine woods, when warmth lingers and wind conditions remain favorable, so it was rare for him to resist the pull of the current.

In that moment, he would've given anything to ignore the foreboding deep in his chest, to make a U-turn and head down the path toward the bunk storage units that housed their boats. With every footfall, it was as though he was breaking in two. His body lurched forward over land it had memorized while his mind worked with a different map, going in the opposite direction. Luke could almost see himself turning his back on them, dropping a kayak at the shoreline, and paddling away from it all.

His mother and brother proved to be the stronger draw.

Each of the cabins had a front entrance flanked by side-by-side double-hung windows. Roosevelt was dark. But this particular cabin faced away from the river, making it easy for him to slip around back, where he could get a better glimpse inside without risking Davis seeing his approach. If that's where he had barricaded his family.

There were no fresh footprints leading up to or around the small building. No voices drifted toward him. Luke's instincts told him they weren't there, and he was right. Through the window, he could see that the place was Saturday-clean and it looked like no one had been in there since checkout.

Scribner was a different story, the way it was set further back off the trail. Looking at it with fresh eyes, it was the first time Luke noticed how overgrown the foliage around the foundation had become. The front door faced the path, and to get a closer look without anyone seeing him, he'd have to bushwhack the trail from the opposite side of the cabin. The side that abutted Emerson. He'd start there first.

To the guests of Church's Overlook, Emerson's appeal was that it was closest to the water, though it was the oldest and farthest away from the main inn, and a good fifteen-minute hike to get to breakfast. First-time visitors would complain on their way from lobby to cabin, until they saw the views.

From a distance, owing to the angle of the late-afternoon sun, it had been easy to miss the soft glow emanating from the cabin. Someone had left all the lights on in this one. Luke circled Emerson, advancing toward it like he had with Roosevelt, from the rear of the building.

Jonah's truck was parked along the east side of the cabin, the doors still open.

With each snap of a twig, each boot tip hitting stone, Luke wondered if he should lose his shoes, taking his chances by moving closer in bare feet. But what if he needed to run?

Debating what to do, his hand found its way into his pocket. He gripped the knife before it dawned on him what he was about to do. *What was he about to do?*

Luke withdrew the knife and extended the blade.

Crouching down, he used Jonah's truck for cover. Once fully shielded, he reached up to place his hand on the hood. It was cool to the touch.

He left the truck as it was, and weighing his options, moved to the back of the cabin. Since the master key made noise in the old lock, he wouldn't be able to sneak in. If he did enter that way, once inside he'd have to play dumb, pretending he'd expected Emerson to be empty. But someone in there had a gun, and if his mother and brother weren't making their way back to Coop, it had to be Davis.

As he stood there, about to enter a kind of standoff, it was the first time Luke wondered about the gun and why his mother felt the need to keep it buried in the safe. Had she always been this afraid? Or had Davis ever been good or kind?

Sweaty as he was, winded as he was, uncertain as he was about what to do, Luke chose to barge in.

Emerson was empty. Of people. But not of things that gave away that at least Jonah had been there.

His backpack sat unzipped on the couch. A sleeve of saltines, trailing crumbs, made a ring around an open jar of peanut butter on the coffee table. Whether or not their mother had been there could not be confirmed. Nothing that specifically belonged to her littered the cabin's main space. But if she had been there, and if she'd been in charge, she never would have left food out to attract creatures great and small. Or left the lights on. And the front door open.

Luke closed Coop's knife and went back outside, coming face-to-face with the river. It would be futile to go in the direction of the main inn. Though it wasn't visible from where he stood, he would've crossed paths with them if they'd gone back that way.

Even at this distance, he should've heard an ambulance by now too. Unless Coop hadn't called one. Luke had to believe he was feeling better since he'd left. And that Coop could take care of himself.

Thinking of him, Luke was reminded of the last time they had talked. They'd been tossing wood onto Coop's truck bed, collecting a rick for guests in Scribner. He'd said something about his mother showing up at Church's with him and Jonah, staying at one of the old cabins. But which one? The handful of rundown places left over from that time were scattered throughout acres of woods.

Luke felt himself give in to the sway the river had over him. On his way down the embankment, he began to notice small things that held meaning. Footprints the approximate size and shape of a woman's boots planted firmly in the dirt *off* the trail. The stems of tender meadow rues snapped in two, creating haphazard angles, the heads of the flowers sacrificed and wilting. Luke suspected his mother was responsible for the damage, since she'd left her favorite, the Linnaea undisturbed. As if her destructive efforts weren't enough to point the way, Luke had Jonah to thank for confirming their party of three had left the property in this direction. Quarter-inch pieces of unsmoked cigarettes—tobacco bread crumbs—were dropped every few feet down the hill, ending at the shoreline.

At the river's edge, Luke realized these signs meant Davis wasn't the one directing Jonah and his mother. Somehow they were leading him away from Church's

Overlook. But why? And if he had the gun, how were they able to get away with leaving clues?

If they left by waterway—and Luke was certain now that they had—they'd likely start out traveling with the current, which meant his mother and brother were bringing Davis deep into the woods.

It wouldn't be long before night closed in on him, so he doubled back to Emerson to grab Jonah's backpack, stuffing it with a flashlight, a jacket, and whatever else he thought to shove inside it.

By the time he ran back down the hill and hauled a kayak toward the shoreline, he felt certain he could find them. As three people traveling together, they would have been forced to take a canoe. With their much slower glide, hampered by the size of the boat and the weight of their load, Luke had the speed advantage.

No matter when they left, catching up with them on the water would be tough, even though he was better off than if they'd taken off in Jonah's truck toward Baxter State Park. If they'd done that, finding them would've been impossible.

Torn between rowing into the middle of the river or hugging the shoreline, Luke's paddle fought to find its rhythm. If he hung back, it increased the odds that he could sneak up on them undetected. But if he could find a haystack to ride, he could run the river faster, and he'd be able to see much farther ahead.

Surrendering to the current, he took the risk and paddled into the flow.

With every forward sweep of his paddle, Luke tried to guess where his mother and brother would be bringing an untested city man, and this one in particular, into the wilderness.

With his body hunkered down deep inside his kayak, he leaned all of his weight into the tide. His mind was far ahead of him. Busy checking rock outcroppings and lean-to shelters, Luke scanned favored campsites and abandoned sporting camps along this stretch. His strokes kept pace with his breakneck thoughts as he paddled by the hide-and-seek places of his childhood.

Luke couldn't tell if it was because the wind had shifted and the temperature dropped ten degrees since he'd peeled out, or if the chill that grabbed hold of him had something to do with Jonah and his mother being in trouble.

He tried to imagine her, quietly but completely in control of their excursion. She would play reserved to Davis's daring, acting deferential, letting Jonah row. Without his brother even realizing it, she would be doing what she always did. Telling Jonah with a blink of her eyes or the twitch of her lips what she wanted him to do. Where to point the bow. In which direction to take the trip.

His duplicitous mother and all her secrets—two lives, two stories, twin sons. Things she'd done in the last few days started to make sense. Her truck bed full of supplies on her way out of Church's and, in a matter of hours, empty without explanation. Luke wouldn't put it past her to have a covert hideaway where she went when he wasn't paying attention. Because until lately, what reason did he have for being suspicious of her?

Luke kept paddling, forcing himself to conjure a map in his head. He called up the river runs they'd taken as a family, camping together along the Penobscot. He brought to mind the day trips and overnights they'd taken up and down these tributaries to places as varied as the trails laid out on Katahdin. With each spot, Luke mulled over the likelihood they had gone there.

He ruled out Freezeout Trail near Webster Stream because they couldn't get there from here without having to portage.

Russell Pond Campground had too many hikers populating that campsite.

They would've needed a vehicle to get a boat to launch at Turner Deadwater. And his family's trucks were all still parked at Church's.

As Luke rejected each site, he became lost on the water. There were an infinite number of places they could've stepped off. Still, something told him he could figure this out.

To track them down, he needed to put himself inside the mindset of the one making the decisions. His mother was the enigma. It was easier to start with Jonah's favorite places since he didn't have that many.

Luke remembered the story he and Sylvie had relived yesterday. The time she and her cousin Timmy came with Jonah and Luke on a hike with those bratty kids from Scribner.

In his mind, Luke traveled the path they took that day. After Timmy and Sylvie had left them in the woods. His brother stopped to pick up the largest rock he could wrap his hands around, leaving a hole in the ground where the moss had been covering it. He chucked it as far as he could, which wasn't that far on account of its weight. The stream cut around the rock, paying no attention to the need for a sudden detour, as if Jonah's anger about his father had nothing whatsoever to do with its ability to flow.

Back then, Luke had bent down at the edge of the Penobscot to collect stones of different sizes. One on top of the other, he built a hiker's cairn in the space left vacant by the rock Jonah moved.

"Coop tell you the history of these?" Jonah had asked, adding stones to the tower.

"They let hikers know they're heading in the right direction," Luke said. "They point the way."

"Ancients used them to mark graves too," Jonah said. "This place is pretty secluded. Lots of rock formations, off the beaten path, good for hiding things."

His brother took a small stone from the dirt and closed his fist over it, tapping it with his other hand, then opening it to show Luke that the pebble was gone. "So if you don't see hide nor hair of that little shit Bobby later today," Jonah said, shaking the stone from his sleeve, revealing his magic, "you'll know where I buried him."

Luke turned quickly to check his brother's expression, to make sure Jonah was kidding, and he knocked the top rock off the cairn, sending the whole thing tumbling into the river.

All these years later, could Jonah be taking his mother and father to the place he said he never wanted to be? Maliseet Deadwater. There was an old sporting cabin near that inlet too. Back in the office, when Coop was forcing out words, Luke hadn't let him finish.

Putting it together, he knew where they were now.

Daylight had faded and the color of the sky changed, pink to gray, blue to gray. As the natural light continued to die off, it was as if his kayak began to move under its own power. Banking right where the river splits, Luke let the current take him.

*   *   *

LENA

For once Davis did as Lena asked. He kept the gun pointed at her for the trek across Church's Overlook and for the entirety of the river run.

More than once, Jonah had the chance to push Davis down an embankment. But he didn't do it. In the canoe, he could've whacked him with an oar, toppling him into the unforgiving current. But he didn't do that either.

Whether it was because Jonah didn't have full command of his body yet, or he read the fear on her face, he took his cues from her. He didn't speak or provoke Davis. Still, Lena could tell he was seething.

When they finally stepped out of the boat, Lena directed their party onward to her safe house, as if the answer to the question of what to do about Davis awaited them there.

She kept her focus on putting one foot in front of the other, the way hikers hike; she let go of doubt and trusted her faith in forward movement.

Trail maintenance in this part of the woods was neglected, so conversation centered on staying on the footpath and watching out for concealed ridges or trenches.

Davis didn't stop to catch his breath until a distinctive-looking black bird circled above them, letting loose its haunting cry as it flew upward and disappeared.

"People swear that the presence of an eastern koel means rain," Jonah said. "Around here we call them storm birds. When I was a kid, I loved the story '*The Storm Bird's Wrath.*'"

Lena would never forget those bedtime stories her boys adored. The legends about nature, and the inhospitable acts that brought sudden mists and icy blasts. Spells of strong weather, like anger, that cut and shaped the landscape.

"It's about this irascible bird that guards the mountain," Jonah said. "When things don't go his way, he creates violent storms. We read it in this book Coop gave us. Well, actually, he gave it to her."

"Who's Coop?" Davis asked.

All at once Jonah took on his edgiest voice. "He's the guy you took out back at Church's."

Bitterness opened up on Davis's face. Jonah did not yet know the nuances of his father's expressions, or that mentioning the violence he had already exacted upon a person could breathe new life into his rage.

In slow motion, Lena watched Davis coordinate the arcs and lines his body made when he was intent on hurting someone. The drawing back of one leg—the leaning in of both shoulders—the tension across his jaw. There was nothing she could do to stop him. All his movements came together fast, to gather momentum, to execute a swift kick.

At the moment of contact, Lena heard the break. She felt the fracture and fell to the ground at the exact time Jonah did. Except this time Davis had shattered their son's bones, not hers.

24

Boston—1994

THE NURSERY WAS an extension of the master bedroom, separated only by French doors that Carolina insisted stay open whenever she wasn't in the babies' room. A rare occurrence since she spent most of her waking hours and even some of her sleeping ones in there.

Whether Carolina paced the rug to settle one child, or rocked and fed the other, or sprawled her weary body on the daybed across from their cribs when the boys were remarkably asleep at the same time, hers was a life lived in confinement. Something she'd come to find she didn't mind that much. Her supporting cast included Marli and Nic. While she appreciated all of their help, truth be told, Carolina loved having the boys all to herself.

When she was solely in charge, everything revolved around the twin stars of the nursery, Simon and James, and what each unique boy wanted or needed. There was so much for her to keep track of—who'd eaten when and how much and for how long, who'd pooped and who hadn't, how long each one had slept.

Tonight she was especially tired, not because her mind was a constant jumble of baby-related info, though it was, but because Nic had once again become preoccupied with what to do about Davis.

Lately whenever he was home, Nic was justifiably exhausted from the endless cycle of long shifts at the restaurant and then helping her out with late-night and early-morning feedings. Instead of sleeping as she would encourage him to do, he'd join in parenting, parking himself in the middle of the nursery, catering to one child or the other.

Then he'd bring it up. "When do you think you might want to check in on the divorce proceedings?"

"Do we have to go over this again?" she asked. "He's totally let me go. I haven't seen him for months. If I go back to my lawyer now to push things along, Davis will land right back in our lives. Please, can we leave well enough alone?"

"Part of me knows you're right, that we shouldn't risk setting him off. But I want us to be a real family. I'd formally adopt the boys if it didn't mean Davis would have to know he's their father."

"We are a real family. I'm committed to you. You are their father. I don't need you to adopt them."

"Forgive me, *Cara*. I'm upsetting you and that's not my intent. Consider me reassured. For tonight, anyway." Nic wrapped his arms around her, swept her hair from her neck, and kissed it. "Now if only you could tell me when we can expect a full night's sleep."

"By the time they're ten for sure," she said, smiling. It was easy to excuse his preoccupation, chalking it up to how indescribably tired they both were.

Nic wasn't otherwise irritable, and he'd always been so accepting of her, such a loving man to her sons. And he had been from the moment he'd learned she was pregnant.

Paternity wasn't a concern for either of them at first. Back then, Nic said all he cared about was the fact that Carolina had genuinely committed herself to him and their imminent baby. He was thrilled, in fact, his enthusiasm contagious. He proposed they buy a larger place—a secret address that Davis would never find. It was time to live together in a real home, and not in a loft above a restaurant. They could get married, if that's what she wanted.

In the beginning, Carolina told herself it didn't matter whether the baby was biologically Davis's or Nic's. Then she got news of a twin pregnancy, and thoughts of Davis began to haunt her. What if he did have a claim on her children? But then, what if he didn't?

When her obstetrician reported the paternity test results, he'd been pleased for her. When he said, "Your husband is the father of your children," it was as though that's what he thought she'd hoped he would say.

Instead, in that cold exam room, Carolina wept. Not out of relief, as the doctor may have suspected, but because in the midst of feelings so complex and bewildering, it seemed as though Davis had finally found a way to break her. This emotional punch was the most heartless of all the other tactics he'd used before combined.

Carolina worried it was only a matter of time before he would figure it out. Despite having been separated for months, she feared Davis would somehow learn the truth.

She'd pleaded with her doctor to remove any notes of the news from her medical record. And while Dr. Michelson reassured her that only high-ranking physicians had access, she could see he was finally putting it together. He promised her that Davis would only know if she decided to tell him.

Dr. Michelson had gone so far as to refer her to another doctor at another hospital on the opposite side of the city.

In a moment of tenderness between patient and doctor, Carolina couldn't imagine going through a complicated pregnancy with a physician unknown to her. She decided to trust him and his promise.

Remarkably, Nic was selfless too. He fully appreciated how overwhelmed Carolina was, and volunteered to come with her to every appointment from then on. The only exception was the five-month visit, a day when the wine shipment had arrived late at the restaurant, and he couldn't make it across town in time.

The check-up began like all the others. Carolina was declared healthy and the boys thriving. She was to continue doing exactly as she had been, staying fit, eating well, and resting when she could.

The sense that Davis was near assailed her before she even saw him in the waiting room.

"I heard your news," he said. "When are you due?"

Carolina stood there, staring at him, trying to figure out how much he knew. He was calmer than usual, but then he looked from her face to her baby bump.

"Not for many more months." What was she doing? She knew better than to engage. Don't talk. Just go back inside the exam room.

"Let me drive you home," he said. "We shared a life, Carolina. I'd like us to end this as friends."

"Marli's picking me up. I have to go."

Davis moved closer to her then, forcing her to back up. One step, then another, until her shoulders made contact with the wall. "Is it mine?" His voice was low, and the stance he'd chosen could easily have been mistaken for a public display of affection, and not the implicit threat that it was.

Carolina pushed him aside. "No, of course not, no."

In that moment, she despised Davis more than ever. Because of him, she'd caught herself thinking of the boys as his sons. At least he hadn't read her medical record. Davis didn't know she was pregnant with twins.

"If you ever loved me," she said, "please leave me and Nic alone."

As soon as the words were out, Carolina regretted them. How could she, of all people, have forgotten his volatile nature? Waiting for a blow, she instinctively placed her hands on her stomach, a visual reminder that only a deranged person would hurt a pregnant woman.

Then Davis walked away; just like that, he gave in. Remarkably, that was the last time she'd seen him.

Six months, five days, and a number of hours that because of the twins were a blur to her.

Time was helping her to forget Davis. He may have been her history. But Nic and the boys were her present—her future.

Back when Carolina agreed to be with Nic, and to give him the gift of fatherhood, she'd done so with conditions. She would not marry him. Maybe someday, but not now. They would let the divorce happen on her lawyer's time-table; she would not push for resolution. Best not stir the beast.

Her children deserved to be loved unconditionally, and nothing anyone could say or do would change her conviction that they were wanted. Nic was never to mention to a single soul the fact that they were children born out of violence. And if he ever raised a hand to one of the boys or harmed them in any way, without looking back, like she had done with Davis, she would walk out with the clothes on her back.

Nic told her then, as he whispered his sweet name for her, that he would never need reminding. He was nothing like Davis and promised never to hurt her or the boys. It was his privilege, he'd said, to love them as his own.

She believed him. Together, they were doing a great job with the boys. Babies had a way of bringing out the best in people, even if Carolina and Nic were also dog-tired. Things would get better in time. Of course they would.

Still, that didn't mean Carolina didn't relish the nights Marli had a board meeting and Nic worked the dinner shift at the restaurant. Less than an hour ago, she'd watched with suppressed delight as he'd donned a jacket, packed a backpack, and got into his car. For the next ten hours she'd be blessedly alone with her children.

Because Simon was the bigger of the boys, who fed well and slept for longer stretches, she put him down first to buy time. Placed on his back in his antique crib with painted bluebirds, she brushed wisps of hair from his forehead and lightly kissed him goodnight. Then she turned to his twin, lying in an identical crib, wide-eyed and patient.

Carolina swayed the boy in her arms as she walked toward her chair. Once settled in the glider, she rocked her sweet baby James, staring into his dark eyes, memorizing the shape of his nose, the curve of his lips. She cherished this time with him, though it was tinged with a touch of melancholia. Because she hated to admit it even to herself: James was her favorite.

Certainly both boys were beautiful, and it had been easier to love them than she'd thought possible. But when she looked at James, Carolina recognized something she couldn't tell anyone. Deep in her heart she was more drawn to this boy, with his soulful eyes and dark complexion. Carolina could pretend that James was Nic's child. Because without question, Simon was all Winslow.

Feeling guilty for letting these thoughts linger, she rose from her chair. Standing by Simon's crib, seeing him peaceful in his bed, she whispered, "I love you too." No doubt Simon would win her over, fully and completely. In time, Carolina would work to let go of her association of him with Davis. Her children were the furthest thing from a mistake she had ever made.

"Sleep while your babies are sleeping. Isn't that one of your mantras?"

Carolina screamed, inadvertently sending a shudder through her babies' small bodies.

"Oh my God, don't drop him," Marli said. "I thought you heard me come in. I didn't mean to scare you."

Carolina placed James against her chest, his head nestled between her shoulder and neck. She rubbed his back, then patted it, rubbing it again when his little body continued to tremble.

"It doesn't take much. I'm wiped," she whispered.

Thankfully, Simon remained asleep.

"I thought you had a board meeting."

"I did. I went for a bit. But then I started worrying about you." Marli tossed her coat on the daybed, her purse on top. She met Carolina over Simon's crib. Leaning on the rail, Marli rested her hand on her nephew's tiny chest. How many times had Carolina told her not to touch him when there was even the remotest chance he would wake up?

"It's Davis," Marli said.

"What about him?"

"He's been arrested. Some overreaction to an intern challenging his orders on lab work for a patient. It got physical. He broke the man's jaw."

"Is he in jail?" It wouldn't surprise Carolina to learn that one punch to a man's head was considered assault, while repeated blows to her body were apparently nobody else's business.

"They let him out on bail. Gave him the benefit of the doubt because he's a doctor. An otherwise upstanding citizen and all that. Win did his best to deescalate the situation at the hospital. He's spent all day with the higher-ups, pleading Davis's case, asking that they not suspend him. He said Davis couldn't handle the on-call schedule. He's upset about his personal life. Win lobbied that they give him a few days' vacation. Give him some time to pull things together."

"Vacation days aren't enough to set that man right." Carolina placed James in his crib. His eyes fluttered and closed like those of a doll she'd once treasured. She motioned for Marli to move out of the path between the cribs, away from her sons and toward the daybed.

"That's why I came to check on you," Marli said. "Something's more off than usual with him. He's erratic. Missing shifts. Testy all the time. Administration is insisting on a psych workup. He's still leaving you alone, right?" Marli asked.

"He's totally let me go. Davis wants nothing more to do with me. I haven't seen him for months."

"I'm probably being paranoid," Marli said. "But I'll feel better if I curl up here with you until Nic gets home."

"You've been here the last two nights. Nic will be home in a few hours. And look, they're asleep. I insist you go home."

After promising to lock up, Marli reluctantly left, and Carolina fell asleep in the glider, near her sons. Half in and out of a dream state, her brain flitted through a catalogue of images: flickering candlelight, a lonely maple leaf clinging to the bathroom window, a clawfoot tub, Davis in the doorframe of the brownstone they'd shared on Beacon Street.

Carolina forced herself awake, chiding her mind for going back to that night. But even with her eyes barely open and the room dimly lit by her children's nightlight, she had no trouble recognizing his shadow.

Davis stood in the doorway between the master bed-room and the nursery.

"So many locked doors, and you don't close the windows? You left me an open invitation, Carolina."

The clock on the wall read 1:12 AM. Nic wouldn't be home for at least another hour. The closest phone was in the other room beside their bed.

"Something's happened at work. I needed to talk to you." Davis played calm at first. "I think I might lose my job."

Carolina got up from the glider. With carefully orchestrated movements, she worked her way toward him, moving as far away from the cribs as Davis would let her.

"That's awful. I'm sorry. What happened?"

"There's nothing wrong with me," he said. "It's your fault. I wouldn't be so stressed if it weren't for you."

Marli had been right. This was the worst she'd seen him, and the closer Carolina got to him, the more concerned she became. The look in his eyes was hollow, vacant. Davis was both in that room with her and somewhere else entirely.

"The board denied my request for time off. Even with Win vouching for me, I'm suspended. Indefinitely. And get this. They want me to submit to a psych eval."

"You've been through a lot," she said, keeping her voice soft and low, as much to keep from disturbing the boys as to not set off Davis.

"Thanks to you."

"Win will help you." Carolina tried to set aside her fear and dig deep for courage. Davis was suffering a kind of breakdown, and she needed to get him out of the nursery and away from her boys.

"Maybe you should rest. In here." She slow-walked Davis toward the master, where she might be able to grab the phone.

Carolina would call Win, or convince Davis to. Her brother-in-law was on her side and would help her get him out of here.

"Good idea." Davis grabbed her wrist and yanked her toward the daybed. "Lie down with me."

Every part of her wanted to refuse him, to run. Her mind raced, desperately searching for ideas for how to get him away from the children. Then Simon stirred, and at that moment, Carolina would have done anything to keep Davis's attention away from those cribs.

He stretched out on the daybed and patted the space beside him. Carolina positioned her body as close to the edge as she could without falling off.

He pulled her body back against his, and placed his hands on her full breasts. "When they wake up, I want to watch you feed them." His tone was taunting.

That's when she knew, he knew.

Carolina lay there without moving. She put all her energy into slowing her breathing, willing her heart to stop pounding. Eerily, her limbs felt as heavy and numb as they had a year ago in their brownstone. Except now she had two incredible reasons not to surrender to Davis.

For every eternal moment on that daybed, Carolina willed the boys to remain sleeping. But then Simon let out a throaty noise, and James began to whimper. The fussier one got, the more agitated the other became, until both boys were crying in syncopation.

At first she didn't move. Though it was foolish to think that if she didn't, Davis would stay put. With a kind of manic energy, he popped off the daybed and went straight to the cribs.

"I want you to come back to me," he said. "We can be a family."

With his hands outstretched, holding one rail of each crib, Davis blocked her from getting near the boys. His face was contorted and he began shouting. "You can't keep them from me. They're mine."

Carolina hated to give in to his irrationality, but what choice did she have? She couldn't risk him getting any more out of control standing so close to her babies.

"Okay. We can talk about it. Let's go into the other room so the boys can go back to sleep." She used a soft voice and her most agreeable posture, every inch of her trying to calm Davis.

His voice changed too, becoming monotone, almost robotic. "You're lying," he said, "You're always lying."

Simon and James stopped crying suddenly, but with Davis blocking her, Carolina was at a loss for how to check on her babies to make sure they were okay. Then Davis turned toward Simon and put a hand on his chest. "You're okay," he said. "Shh, little guy. Daddy's here now."

At the sight of Davis touching her child, her chest burned.

"The boys aren't yours. They're Nic's. You need to leave."

Carolina should not have confronted him.

In one swift motion, Davis pulled a scalpel from his pocket and began waving it above the cribs. "I know they're mine. And you can't take them away from me. If I can't have them, neither can you."

Before Carolina could make sense of what he was doing, he'd taken a knife to her tiniest baby. Carolina and James shrieked in unison, sending shock waves throughout the nursery. At the sight of blood dripping from the knife, down Davis's wrist, onto the white sheets and carpet, he seemed to reemerge from some fugue state.

"Get out. *Now!*" Carolina bellowed, her face inches from his. She pushed his shoulders and pounded his chest. With brute force she should have used the minute he first came here, she shoved Davis away from the cribs. She punched his arm, slapped at his face, again and again, without regard for the scalpel he still held above her. Carolina shoved Davis toward the French doors of her bedroom.

When all she wanted to do was go back to her howling infants and pick them up, first she needed Davis as far away from them as possible. Carolina contemplated wrenching the blade from his hand and turning it on him, but for once Davis made no effort to match her rough treatment. When they hit the threshold to her bedroom, he dropped the knife and ran.

In the midst of the horror, her mind simply stopped functioning. One minute Carolina was soothing James so she could peel back his clothing and apply pressure to the wound on his foot, and the next thing she knew, Win was there with his doctor bag. She couldn't remember having called him.

Without discussion, he took charge. Win swaddled the boy in a receiving blanket, leaving only his bloody foot exposed. He hummed softly as he sutured his nephew's heel.

Carolina stood there, one hand caressing her bundle, the other holding the phone.

"Did I call you?" she asked.

"You called Marli. She's in the other room. On the extension with Nic."

Carolina's brother-in-law never looked up. Instead, he attended to James with tender care. "You're going to be alright, little fella," he said. "Could've been much worse."

"He's sick," Carolina said.

Win nodded. "He's having a psychotic break. He needs to be committed."

Carolina didn't ask what Win suspected had set off his brother. She'd always been Davis's most dangerous trigger. Now her children were. Right then, watching her brother-in-law pierce her son's tiny foot repeatedly with needle and thread, she didn't say anything.

Instead, she left James's side to check on Simon. When he wasn't in his crib, she was flooded with panic.

"He's right there." Win pointed to the bouncy seat. Had Carolina parked him in front of the window, or had he?

"I imagine you'll want to stay here with Nic, but I'd like to hire security for you. Or maybe you'd feel safer at a hotel until I've handled things with Davis?"

As Win talked and tended to James, Carolina dragged suitcases from the master bedroom closet into the nursery. Though she didn't tell Win this, Carolina had no intention of going anywhere either he or Marli suggested.

Win could go off to hunt for his brother, and no doubt he would find him. But Davis was ill, he wasn't stupid. Once he was released from whatever stopgap psych intervention, if any could be secured, he would be back. Davis would find her.

Stuffing rather than folding, Carolina didn't pay much attention to what she packed in those suitcases until she looked up to the small bookshelf she'd hammered in place when she was pregnant. The colorful field guides to birds and flowers and trees were cherished enough that she made room for them amidst her babies' tiny clothes and warm blankets. She'd owned them since college, and maybe one day she would give them to her boys and tell them about her life before this night. She placed each one tenderly into the suitcase and then continued to fill the rest of the space with practical things.

Marli rushed into the room, though she was careful not to startle her. "Nic's on his way."

Win finished attending to James by re-swaddling him tightly and placing him back in his crib. He handed Carolina a tube of antibacterial ointment, a bottle of baby Tylenol, along with an abundance of gauze, sterile pads, and surgical tape.

"I numbed it a lot. Little guy should be comfortable for at least a couple of hours."

Then Marli urged Win to go find Davis.

When he left, she started helping Carolina pack, counting out booties and onesies, loading the suitcases with everything in twos.

"I never should have left you alone," Marli said. "You're a sister to me. Let me take care of you now."

"Does that mean you'll do anything to help us?"

Marli nodded, tears streaming. "You know I will."

"I'll need your car," Carolina said. "Take mine and park it somewhere out of town. Sell it later if you want to because I can't promise that you'll ever get yours back. And I'll need all the cash you're willing to give me."

"You're leaving? No, no. You'll be safe with us. With Nic. At a hotel. Until we get you a new restraining order."

"You know that won't make any difference. It didn't before."

"Win will get him help."

"Marli, you don't understand. Davis is never going to leave me—us—alone."

"What about Nic?"

"Whether I stay or go, this isn't fair to him." Carolina ripped the two tiny sweaters Marli was holding from her hands. She threw them in the suitcase, grabbed Marli by the arm, and yanked her toward the cribs.

"What kind of life would Nic have with me if Davis can show up at any time and do something like this?"

Carolina's voice cracked as she took in the stained sheet so out of place in her sweet babies' nursery. "Look at what he's capable of."

She took Marli's hands and turned to face her. "The day I left Davis—when you helped me get that order of protection? I had just lost a baby because he beat me. Less than a year later, he raped me. And tonight he took a knife to my son."

Carolina looked from one infant to the other, and Marli followed her gaze.

"These boys are here because Davis is a violent man. And still they are the only good thing to come out of that mess of a marriage. Nothing you can say will convince me that we will ever be safe here. That I can have this life."

"This is going to break Nic's heart." Marli reached down to adjust the powder-blue blanket covering James. His tiny foot twitched, though he continued to sleep.

"I don't want to hurt Nic," Carolina said, "but he's not safe either. Not if he stays with me."

"I love these babies. And you." Marli started to cry. "What am I going to do without you?"

"All that matters now are the boys. They don't deserve to grow up knowing the shameful thing Davis did to me. Or what he's just done to James. If I stay, they'll learn they are the sons of a monster. No matter what I do to keep it from them, if I don't do this, they will find out. No child should have to live with that."

Resolute now, Carolina wiped her dearest friend's tears and then hugged her fiercely for what she knew was the last time.

"Please," she said. "Help me."

In the quiet of the nursery, both boys blessedly asleep, Carolina heard a quiet whisper. Marli said, "All right, I will."

channel—*verb*. To be grooved, cut deeply.

Millinocket, Maine—2012

LUKE

THEIR CANOE MATERIALIZED exactly where he'd hoped it would, lodged into a break in the rugged shore-line of Maliseet Deadwater. The canoe left sticking out the way it was, with the Church's Overlook logo stenciled starboard side, meant they wanted it to be found.

The visible rise and fall of the stern in the waves gave Luke time to reverse direction, to use his paddle to draw his kayak backward toward an overhanging cluster of birch.

There was enough light left in the day that it was easy enough to secure the kayak, rope to tree, but emerging from the scrub with the backpack slung over his shoulder so he could approach from the woods wasn't trouble-free. With each step up the incline, his boots loosened dirt, sending sprays of gravel raining down onto the surface of the river. He paused to steady his breath and listen. His only hope was to come out of the water far enough away from where they were that they couldn't hear or see him.

To get a lock on their location, Luke went north, careful to stay parallel with the river, moving toward the rock formations he remembered from childhood. Brambles and thickets made passage rough in spots, and without a clear trail, Luke was trampling brush and crashing over tree roots. A few minutes in, he reminded himself stealth was his objective. So he slowed his pace and vowed to take his time, no matter what his booming heart was telling him to do.

Like a scrambled transmission, deep-throated croaking sounds dropped in and out; night birds and tree frogs were competing for attention. The rustling leaves spoke too, only softly in whispers. A few hundred feet in, below the hum of the woods, he heard familiar voices.

"Hurry up," Jonah said.

"I'm almost done," his mother said.

Through the veil of branches, Luke could see her kneeling by his brother. His left leg was extended, and he wore the same pained expression he had years ago when he'd landed at the bottom of that embankment and suffered a fracture. Now his mother had broken branches placed on both sides of his leg and up the back of his knee. She was holding the contraption together, trying to wrap it with what looked like a flannel shirt.

When Luke was sure they were alone, he stepped out from behind the cedars and walked toward them. "Are you okay?"

"I knew you'd find us." Jonah slapped both thighs with his hands, wincing on contact.

"You need to take Jonah and get out of here," his mother said to him. "Hoist him on your back. Please. Run."

"We're not leaving you alone," Jonah said.

"Will someone tell me what's going on?" Luke asked.

He heard his mother shout, "No!" at the same time he felt something hard press into the ridges of his spine.

What kind of naturalist misses someone sneaking up behind him; who doesn't sense a predator in his woods?

The man behind him moved the gun up Luke's neck to the back of his head. "Who the hell is this?"

The smell of foul breath overtook him as the man spoke; Luke gagged at the stink of it.

"Look who stumbled across our little family reunion." His voice was shaky, and being that close to him, Luke could hear him swallow.

In what could only be categorized as the worst timing ever, a few feet from them, a sheet of cedar bark loosened and broke free from its trunk, the horrible crack echoed in the grove.

He waved the gun away from Luke. "What's that? Who's there?"

For a second, Luke considered reaching for a rock and whipping it in the opposite direction to keep the distractions going. Or he could use it to take him out. Except Luke was reminded of what this person had done to Coop, and his mother; he couldn't go through with it.

"It's no one," Luke said. "I hiked out here alone. The woods can be noisy, that's all."

He stepped in front of him then, without ever taking the gun off his target. Luke was finally really looking at Davis. Where his brother's features were angular and his eyes bright, Davis's face was fleshy, his skin mottled; there was a dullness to his stare. Because they were a good distance from each other and Jonah was on the ground, there was no way to compare their heights, like he imagined fathers and sons were keen to do. It was impossible to decide who shared similar coloring with him, because Davis's stubble was coming in gray, and his hair was yellow tinged and mangy.

As if he wanted to get a good look at him too, Davis backed away from Luke, but still with the gun aimed at his chest.

His sneakers made less noise than Luke's boots did crunching over brush and stone. Quiet as his movements were, Luke could see he wasn't entirely steady on his feet. Davis took a seat on a rock and crossed his legs at the ankles. With one hand, he positioned the gun groin-level, with the other he zipped up the fly of his dirt-stained pants. The jacket he wore unzipped exposed a strip of hairless chest.

Seeing Davis wearing only the flimsy windbreaker called back into question the legitimacy of Jonah's injury. Could his mother have made up some phony ploy to convince Davis to give up his shirt so she could pretend to stabilize Jonah's leg with it? Cool air in fall was a known and formidable weapon.

"How much longer?" Davis's eyes darted over to Luke's mother and brother. While she continued to adjust the makeshift splint.

"The sporting cabin is up the hill. Half a mile tops," she said. "It's easy to get to, but he won't make it if I don't secure this tight."

His mother was full of it. The sporting camp in that direction was a rough hike away, past exposed rock and unstable cliff face.

When she spoke again, her plan was clear. Her voice so light and high, it was impossible to reconcile that it belonged to her. "I can take you. Leave these two here and come with me."

"Stop telling me what to do," Davis said. "I'm not leaving Simon here with whoever this is."

Davis jumped up off his rock seat and started pacing; the upper half of his body twitched as he rambled. "We're going to find James together. I want to see your face when he hears what you've done to me."

No one moved. No one spoke. Whether it was the whip of the wind or the rolling thunder, something shook

Davis into putting it together. Or maybe one of their faces gave it away.

He staggered backward to sit back down on the rock. "Christ," he said. "It's you, isn't it? You're James."

*   *   *

LENA

She knelt in the brush several feet from Davis, a belt of trees and both of her sons between them.

A low rumble interrupted the conversation he was having with himself. A flash of lightning followed.

Sheltered in the woods by a country of pine trees, Lena had never imagined they would be here like this. In the face of a twenty-year time gap, her instincts were to navigate terrain around Davis the only way she knew how. By being conciliatory. Keeping her voice calm and low. Orchestrating every movement with fluidity. Perhaps all she needed to do was channel a little of Jonah's successful approach, and act as if what was happening wasn't completely insane.

"It's getting dark," she said. "We should hurry. Get to the cabin before the weather breaks."

Davis stood, shaking his head, looking utterly disconnected from where they were and what she'd said.

"My boys," Davis said. "You're my sons."

Lena motioned for Luke to help Jonah. Her directives were short and to the point. "Careful. Take it slow."

"We're staying here," Davis said, waving the gun at her now.

"You have a right to say your piece," she said. "Tell them every horrible thing I ever did. But there's a storm coming. In this wilderness—coupled with the approaching dark—you won't last the night."

As if nature was on her side, and Lena a fortune teller, the next peal of thunder confirmed that for once, she was speaking the truth.

Davis took on the look of a frightened child. "You go first. And don't trick me. Simon and James, walk by me."

Simon and James. Without either of them knowing it, the Blackwell boys had been carrying their old Winslow life around the whole time in the form of their middle names. Not once had Lena ever imagined her boys would learn about their true identities this way. Because in her version of the story, they never learned it at all.

Approaching the path, Luke and Jonah leaned on each other, their steps set to the wild sound of distant loons. Their eerie song was getting to Davis, because with jerky movements he kept turning around to see where the noise was coming from.

Lena maneuvered around the boys, happily taking the lead. Better to comply and keep the gun on her back. Plus she knew exactly where they were going.

It was tough going for Jonah as the hint of a trail gave way to untraveled underbrush. They had to stop every once in a while for Luke to adjust his brother's splint. The leg was clearly broken, likely a compound fracture, so there was good reason to be grateful for whatever drugs still circulated in his bloodstream.

"How bad is it?" Luke whispered to Jonah.

"Shut up," Davis shouted. "Keep moving."

"I'd have to say it hurts way less now than it did the first time I broke it." Jonah kept talking as if Davis hadn't ordered them to be quiet.

"I'd just turned ten . . ."

It was obvious from the way Jonah told this story that he was directing the whole thing at Davis, trying once more to align himself with his father. The goal, either to keep him distracted or calm, whichever thing it was that had worked back at Emerson.

Lena remembered that day the boys went cross-country skiing with Coop like it was yesterday. The only mistake Coop had ever made was wanting to care for them. She wondered if he was okay back at the inn. If she slow-walked, could she get close enough to Luke to ask if Coop was all right? He would know. How else would he have figured out where to find them? Lena hadn't counted on Coop to break his promise, telling Luke about her safe house. As happy as she was to see that her son was okay, she wasn't sure how to feel about him being out here with them. Now both her boys were in danger.

Time crawled as they moved Davis deep into the woods, up elevated terrain, around natural obstacles. Lena didn't exactly know what she'd do once they got to the cabin if he still had the energy left to keep the gun on them. It was hard to think that far ahead. But getting Davis inside gave her more options. He had to fall asleep at some point. Three against one, they could overpower him more easily in close quarters. Plus, she had a cadre of knives.

Lena turned around once to see how Jonah was faring and caught Davis shuddering in response to nature's sound effects. The seconds that passed between flashes of lightning and rumbles of thunder told her the storm was still miles away. Nevertheless, she moved them forward.

Hiking the incline was a breeze for her and Luke. Even Jonah, wearing the makeshift splint, had an easier time compared with Davis.

During the day in sunlight, bushwhacking these woods, the advantage went to Davis. He had the gun. But as night fell, the Blackwells had the edge with everything else.

To maintain her cool demeanor, Lena practiced confident movements, in order to reassure the group she knew
exactly what she was doing and where she was going. Even
though a specific plan eluded her; the only thing she knew
to do was take another step.

To maintain her composure, she pictured the cabin,
she inventoried the supplies. She ran the list in her head.
Coleman lanterns, blankets, rope, fire starters, plenty of
water and wood.

When the slight ascent became a steep climb, their
collective breath labored. No one talked, which only
amplified the sounds of the woods. A bobcat calling to her
kittens. Thunderclaps echoing off rock face.

"A little further now," Lena said.

Under ordinary circumstances, Jonah would've been
complaining about the pain and how long it was taking
to get to wherever the hell they were going. Especially
since Lena was the one leading them in circles, guiding the
group up and around narrow ledges, venturing past steep
drops. Jonah's patience for her maneuverings was oddly
refreshing. Though she had no idea why, Lena could see he
finally and completely trusted her. It was the only bright
spot in the otherwise dark woods.

It took forever to come to a level path. Lena was
astounded by Davis's resolve to keep up in the face of such
tough going. It would've been commendable if it didn't
speak to how much he hated her.

When Jonah stopped again to tighten his splint, Davis
leaned against a tree. "I need a minute," he said, both
hands holding tight to the gun.

"Answer me this," Davis said in another breath, white
spittle collecting in the sides of his mouth. "What was so
bad about Boston that you threw the life we had away for
this god-forsaken place?"

The word *you* hung in the air without her having to say it.

"I treated you like a princess. I worked day and night to give you everything you ever wanted. And what did you do? You and that bitch Marli plotted against me. You convinced my own brother to commit me. You're the reason I lost my job at the hospital. Do you know how humiliating that was? After how hard I worked. After all I did for you?"

Lena dropped her head but otherwise remained still. She knew better than to lock eyes with him. She couldn't look at her boys either. They would want her to say these things weren't true. Jonah at least would need to hear her side.

But she would not put up evidence to the contrary. Not now. Or until she knew how much Jonah and Luke had uncovered, how much one had shared with the other. She had no plans to talk about any of it.

As inadequate as her story turned out to be, she'd kept the truth from them this long. Since Lena couldn't risk Davis telling any more of his version, she said, "We should get on now."

"I was a doctor. You know that, kids?"

"You told me," Jonah said. "A surgeon."

"Damn good one too. I still would be if it weren't for her."

Davis was the most calm when he was talking with Jonah. As clear as it was that he viewed Lena as foe, he seemed to see this child as an ally.

Luke had been as quiet as possible, choosing not to add to the family drama. Not moving unless the rest of them moved.

"Keep going," Lena said again, hoping the hike would change the subject. "It's just ahead."

Adopting his mother's stillness of speech and action, Luke let the backpack slide slowly off his shoulder to the ground. "Mind if I dig out a flashlight?" he asked Davis.

"Give it here. Let me look." Davis was shivering now, the tremors in both his arms making the gun shake, leaving a wavy pattern in the air around it.

Jonah leaned against an opposite tree so he and his brother could deftly change places on the path. Luke kneeled in front of Davis so he could watch him unzip the pack, showing him the things he must have taken from Emerson.

"See, just a flashlight, a couple bottles of water. There's a sweatshirt, if you want it," Luke said.

Lena wanted to believe it was the pickup of the wind that pulled tears from Davis's eyes.

"Okay," he said, tugging on the arm of the sweatshirt. "Give her the flashlight. And help me."

As Davis dropped one hand off the gun, he wiped both cheeks with his sleeve.

Everyone was quiet while Luke took over extricating the sweatshirt from the bag and then helping Davis out of the flimsy windbreaker. It seemed to take forever when in actuality it had to be seconds.

Lena kept hoping he would reach the limits of his endurance. The longer a hiker stands still on a trail, the easier it is for joints to seize, for icy air to seep through clothes and chill the bones. Immobility plus water brought on a kind of cold that could ignite like fire. It had happened to her.

His upper body rocking, Davis turned to Luke. "Did she tell you I came for you?" His teeth chattered as he spoke. "She was the one. She kept us apart. All I wanted was to be your father."

26

Millinocket—2012

*Y*OU THINK YOU *will forget. That time is a healer. It's not that you can't see clearly that he is thoroughly changed. His mental illness has marshaled armed thoughts and weaponized voices to destroy his once marvelous mind. For another such vulnerable person, you might be overwhelmed with compassion. Overtaken with love and a desire to speak softly, to touch tenderly.*

But every tiny bone and long limb of your body, every sense and length of your skin remembers his cruelty. As you feel again the throbbing of deep bruises and weeping cuts like phantoms—as you ache for the child he took from you—you realize that a man can be both very sick and evil. You no longer need to waste a second of your precious time trying to label which thing he is.

As he touches your adult child, you are thrust back in time to a nursery with painted cribs depicting bluebirds in flight, watching a savage person cut your baby.

"Get out," you cry.

"Shut up. Shut up," he screams as you reach for the weapon. Is it a knife? Is it a gun? The night light plays tricks

on you. All you know is that whatever it is he is holding near your face can hurt your children.

He pitches forward. With a trip and stumble, his hand is on your arm. Gripping it with a force great enough to break it. But you shake him off, easily, effortlessly. You are stronger than you thought. He doesn't know you are not the same person you once were. You may not always fight for yourself. But you always will for your children.

That doesn't mean he will give in to you. His hate is made manifest in the things his hands can do. And they are always ready to come for you.

He backhands the side of your face with a blunt object. Your cheek, your jaw—they sing with memories of other blows. The familiar smell and metal taste in your mouth calls up drops of blood on a white carpet. Stained sheets and the jagged wound on a tiny infant's foot.

You try to remind yourself that the boy is a man now. He is showing the depth of his kindness—the antithesis of his father—by helping a cold man put on a sweatshirt.

Like in a story you once read to your little boys, the river drowns the sun. Thunder announces lightning about to dress the sky, illuminating Katahdin and the Knife's Edge trail. And the rain comes.

Right before your eyes, you watch the monster transform into a harmless creature. He accepts his son's outstretched hand, and in exchange, gives him the gun.

Father and son sit on the already boggy ground. The other son leans against the angle of the slope, clutching his leg. An entire family a few feet from the drop-off.

You have a hard time believing he simply let go. He. Acquiesced.

While he struggles to put on the damp sweatshirt, when bold letters that spell "Bowdoin College" appear across his chest, you put out your hand, palm up. You tell your son you will feel better if you are the one holding the gun.

You are the mother and can pull rank when you must. Still it isn't hard for this peaceful boy to relinquish it. To hand it to his brother, who will give it to you.

But the son who needed to know where he came from is hot with emotion. His vivaciousness has been sharpened into outrage by his father's nature and his mother's lies. He looks at the gun, and you can tell he is considering whether to use it on the person who has most betrayed him.

You tell him, "Don't." Don't shoot the father. Don't be your father.

This boy is good and kind. And he gives it to you. Now the cold metal sits in your hand, and you are strong again. Your sons are on your side.

While the pathetic one who sits a few feet away, his shape diminished, his clothes covered in mud, is on a team of his own.

Whether he's off balance or dizzy from height, he leans awkwardly toward you and your children. He wants into this family, or he is abruptly hoisting his body onto one knee, looking for a hand to reach out. "Help me," he says.

You respond to the urgency of his movements by pointing the gun, first, at his thigh. To frighten him into submission. Then you adjust your aim to the apex of his heart. He would do the same to you.

One of the boy's says, "What are you doing?"

The explosion is deafening. A shrill sound rings in the night. Seconds after the gun goes off, the woods are eerily quiet. Wet leaves and mossy ground have absorbed the horrible noise. The animals that live warren to treetop have been shushed. The man, too, has been silenced. Thanks to you, he lies in a clumsy heap on a narrow path, wearing his son's college sweatshirt.

body of water—*noun*. A mass of matter distinct from other masses; embodies or gives concrete reality to a thing.

CHAPTER

27

Millinocket, Maine—2012

LENA

"WHAT THE HELL did you do that for?" At the sound of Luke shouting at her, Lena snapped out of her fugue state and dropped the gun at her feet. A bed of leaves cushioned its fall.

"We had it," Luke said. "He was harmless without it."

Lena turned her hands over and over, as if they weren't her hands. She said, "No. He rushed you. He would've thrown you off the ledge."

"He wasn't going to do that." Luke's hands were on the side of his head now, as if he couldn't get the sound of the shot from reverberating inside his brain.

Jonah stood unmoving, his back still pressed against the rock, his eyes trained on her. "Jesus, Luke. He hit her in the face with a gun. He broke my leg. The guy was dangerous."

Luke moved to check on Davis who'd collapsed on the trail. He did his best to keep his boots out of the stream of blood on the path. After wrangling the sweatshirt free from his neck, Luke felt for a pulse.

"Jonah's right. You don't know him," she said. "He would've hurt you too."

Without saying anything, Luke pronounced the state of Davis by shaking his head. Like a mirror image, Jonah shook his too.

Seeing Jonah lean down to grab hold of his shin as if the source of all his pain could be found in that one place on his body, it began to sink in what Lena had done. With the realization that Davis could no longer hurt her and her sons, years of unwept tears threatened to consume her.

She began to kick leaves over the bloody trail, not to cover her crime but because she couldn't bear to see Luke and Jonah staring at the drops of rain spattering the pool of their father's blood.

"Did you come in a single kayak?" Jonah asked Luke.

Luke used his hands to scramble backward, fumbling to get up and away from Davis.

With every bit of strength Lena could muster, she resisted the urge to shout what was in her mind and heart. *I told you not to do this. I begged you not to find him.* But she would not hurt her sons any more than she already had.

Instead, she put what little energy she had left into taking charge. She picked up the gun. Wiped it off. Shoved it into the back of her jeans.

Jonah kept talking.

"We'll ghost boat him. Send him down the slot at Rip Gorge in your kayak. No one will ever know."

"Wow," Luke said. "Didn't take you long to have a change of heart about *Dad*."

"You saw him. He was unhinged."

Lena wrenched the pack up off the trail. In a show of force, she turned Jonah around to face the boulder he'd been leaning against. Like she was getting him ready to head off to kindergarten, she fitted the pack to his back and readjusted the straps. She swiped at her tears without thinking, smearing what had to be blood across her cheeks.

"The cabin is up ahead," she said. "Take a right in about a hundred yards, where the cluster of birch starts to thin."

There she was, back to business. As Lena Blackwell, she was never at a loss for what to do.

After Jonah took direction, she turned her sights on Luke. "Help your brother. Start a fire. I can do this myself."

While she didn't point at Davis, Lena could tell Luke knew what she was planning to do. He ignored her, to bend down and lift his dead father in his arms.

"Please, no," she said. "I'm the one who should do it."

Harnessing her strength, Lena lifted Davis's emaciated body off the ground. She walked over tangled roots on an undefined path littered with rocks. Through the thick of trees to a clearing, she willed herself not to stumble. It was right that she be the one to feel the weight of what she'd done.

It was harder still to watch Luke half supporting Davis, helping her despite her request to let her do this herself.

Past the cluster of birch, the shelter came into view. More like a rundown shack than one of the Church's Overlook cabins, its shingles were weathered to the condition of tree bark, all the glass panes grimy. Or at least the ones she could see, the ones not covered by overgrown brush. Last week, she'd nearly missed it because her memory of where it stood was faded and faulty.

Lena gave into wishful thinking, desperately hoping Coop would be inside. She'd never needed him more than she did now. Why had it taken so long for her to realize how deeply she cared for him?

Despite Jonah's injury and the locked door, he'd been able to open up the cabin. Already, wisps of smoke rose from the chimney.

When they were within feet of the side windows, she pointed to the firewood stacks and let Luke help her lay the body down. For her son's benefit, she took the time to reposition Davis's limbs and close his eyes. For her own sake she was careful not to make contact with him once she'd pulled the camouflaged tarp off the wood pile to cover him.

Lena and Luke simultaneously turned away at the sound of the rain pinging the tarp.

Inside her safe house, the oversized duffle bag brimming with camping supplies sat unzipped on the floor. The Coleman lanterns were lit, and the cooler had been pulled closer to the pine table.

Jonah's efforts had a manic quality to them. Though the fire roared, he kept shoving newspaper under the logs, lighting unnecessary matches, and poking at all of it with an andiron.

Luke buried one hand in his pocket and pulled out Coop's double-steel blade. Lena wondered briefly why he hadn't thought to use the knife on the trail to wrestle the gun from Davis. Then her son placed it on the table and slid it across to her. Luke was a naturalist. He tended to the wounded wildlife he invariably came upon when hiking these woods without the use of weapons or aggressive hands.

"Did you leave it out on the path?" Luke asked.

He meant the gun. "It's here," she said, patting her back.

"What's with all the stuff in here," Jonah asked as he opened the drawer of the sideboard. Lena saw his face fall when he registered her stockpile of knives.

Pushing Jonah's backpack off to one side of the table, she motioned for the boys to take seats.

"I owe you an explanation. And I need to tell you what I'm going to do," Lena said.

"Christ, Old Man, we're *really* brothers." Jonah winced as he tried to maneuver around the bench. Luke held his elbow to make it easier, then grabbed another chair and helped Jonah lift his leg onto it.

Neither of them looked at Lena.

"How did you find out?" Luke asked him.

"After you told me the Winslows landed at Church's, I looked up that license plate and paid Marli a visit. I could tell by the way she reacted to me that she already knew who I was. But I couldn't get her to talk. I tracked down the husband, and without him realizing it, he led me to the halfway house."

"I put a spin on my story involving my film project, and the house manager mentioned that Davis Winslow was at his worksite. As soon as he said his full name, I remembered the letter you'd read to me from your collection. I figured I could get him to talk. That he could tell me how things fit together."

"At first he was calm, acting all friendly. Nothing like he was today. But then he started getting agitated. He said he'd feel more comfortable talking things over out of earshot of his supervisor. I took him for coffee. It wasn't until after I drank half of it that I realized he'd slipped me some of his medication. I barely made it back to my truck. When I came to, we were at Church's. We found Mom in the office, and then the whole thing with Coop went down."

Less disconnected from her body than she'd been in years, Lena kept her eyes on her hands. "I know now I should've told you how dangerous he was," she said. "Especially when you wanted to find him. I cut him off from us for a reason."

"Why couldn't we at least have known we were twins?" Luke's voice was pleading, momentarily sounding like a child's.

Lena took on the hushed tone she had used when her sons were little. The way she spoke when she was trying to comfort them.

"Jonah was always so much bigger; he looked a lot older than you. I thought if I changed your names *and* your ages it would make it harder for him to find us."

"What I don't understand," Jonah asked, "is why he hated you so much?"

"You said it yourself," she said. "He was deranged. That's why I left."

Lena folded her hands on top of the table, doing her best to limit how much they trembled. The only thing she dared do was shift her gaze from one son to the other. Maybe they didn't know the full story. About what Davis had done to her in their Beacon Street home. Or about Nic and how she'd stolen the boys away from him too.

Lena Blackwell, the master of intricate well-conceived lies, remained prepared only to verify facts already in evidence. She would not own up to the rape. Or to the life they might have had with Nic. Not unless one of the boys already knew about those things.

"I figured it out another way," Luke said. "Sylvie helped me get inside Win's hospital office. I found emails from the group home. I read your medical record."

Luke looked at her for the first time since they entered the cabin. His hard stare told her he'd read her entire history. Her tender-hearted son knew what Davis had done to her. He knew that he and Jonah were born of a terrible crime.

Like a glacier, the truth she'd been holding back had moved under the force of its weight, shifting on to Luke. In this new, divided landscape, she felt infinite space open up between them.

"Davis was a very ill man," she said. "I wanted a divorce. I thought I could make a new life for us. I convinced myself I could raise you boys without him and despite him. But then he hurt you, Luke. Your foot. He did that to you. He said if he couldn't have you, neither could I. That's when I knew I couldn't stay in Boston. I ran away from my whole life there because I believed it would be better—safer—for everyone if we started over."

Seeing the mask of sadness come down on both her sons' faces, Lena wanted to unburden herself of the whole of it. But what good would it do to tell them that she had tried to love someone deeply? Nic, a good man who had been kind to her and who'd loved them too. Hadn't they heard enough already? Having never known him, Nic couldn't matter to them, not like he did to her. Luke and Jonah didn't need to know that Davis had severed any chance at happiness they might have had with him. How could they ever truly know what she had sacrificed to bring them to safety?

Lena reached out to them, one hand covering each of her son's, and surprisingly, neither Luke nor Jonah evaded her touch. With her arms open to them, she welcomed feeling defenseless against their questions. "I never meant to let fear live so vibrantly inside me, or allow it to guide my every step. But I needed to do what I could to protect you."

"Did Davis ever hurt you?" Jonah pointed to the bruise blooming on her cheek. "I mean, you know, before now."

Her son who had always kept her at a comfortable distance struggled to get up from his bench. Jonah reached into the duffel bag for the first aid kit and began tending to her swollen face, gently, skillfully. The wound didn't hurt as much as she'd expected it to, but having Luke and Jonah know their father was a violent man, that was a pain that devastated.

As the wind whistled through the old cabin, Luke locked eyes with her. She refused to speak the ugly truth, but she wouldn't ask him to keep any more of it from his brother. If he wanted to tell Jonah about her rape, she wouldn't stop him.

"That's enough," Luke said to Jonah. "It's all too much."

Jonah placed gauze against Lena's cheek and taped it there. When he'd finished, he bent down to hug her. It was clear that it hurt him in every conceivable way to do so.

"What are we going to do?" Luke asked.

"In the morning, when the rain lets up, we'll head back to Church's and get Jonah's leg looked at by a doctor. I'll confess to what I did."

"It was an accident," Jonah said. "There was a struggle for the gun. He hurt you. And me. Which is all true."

Staring at the rough-hewed table, Lena couldn't take in what Jonah was saying. Back before he'd begun his search for the truth, he'd had trouble tolerating her run-of-the-mill flaws. But now he was able to rise to the occasion—to love her in spite of the irrefutable fact that for unspeakable reasons she'd been driven to violence. Just like his father. Yet Jonah had forgiven her for the worst thing she'd ever done.

And there was Luke. The son who had always defended her. The person who shared her love of this river and these woods, who worked side by side with her. With every detail she couldn't bring herself to utter, she could feel Luke moving further away from her.

As if to prove her right, he got up too. Not to join her and Jonah in some kind of ill-timed family hug. He stood and walked to the sideboard, wrenching it from the wall to unearth something that looked like a torn and yellowed piece of paper.

Luke lifted it up so Lena could see the faded ink and familiar handwriting: *Stay as long as you like.*

In that dilapidated shack, with Jonah's arms still comforting her, Luke held onto the edge of a long forgotten map, and that's when Lena knew they were free and they would never be free.

Her sons would lie for her. More to the point, they would do it for each other.

"Mind if I keep this?" Luke asked.

Jonah smiled at his brother. "Jesus, Old Man, anyone ever tell you you're weird?"

flow—*verb*. To move in a stream; to proceed smoothly and readily, keeping pace.

CHAPTER

28

Millinocket, Maine—2013

LUKE

THE SKY HELD what was left of the day, reflecting last light off the water. The pine and birch had already turned to shadow. As Luke made his way to the main inn from Emerson—the cabin he'd been living in for the last eight months—he stopped to watch a pair of cormorants glide along the surface of the Penobscot. Whatever happened tonight, he told himself, he could handle it because all of this would be waiting, right here, for him in the morning.

From outside, Luke could see the breakfast room glowing amber, a rarity for this late in the day. Which meant that's where Jonah had finally committed to showing his film. It had been finished for over a month now. He'd gotten an A from the reportedly tough professor of documentary film studies, who'd urged Jonah to enter his project into a festival competition, where it was expected to place.

Yet no one in their family had seen *Unsound*.

Not even Luke.

Jonah had told him again and again that he didn't choose the subject matter to hurt anyone. Couldn't Luke see how the topic had chosen him? Over Thanksgiving break, Jonah's chime woke him after two, and they'd resumed their pattern of early morning texting.

Driven once more by his sense of incompleteness—and guilt over his part in what happened to their father—Jonah began digging into group homes for the mentally ill, specifically life at the one where Davis last lived. The next thing Jonah knew he was visiting Waverley House with a camera. It seemed he would forever need to understand where he came from. Jonah never pressed Luke to talk about Davis or how he felt about all they'd learned about him. For all they talked about his research, and the things he'd found out about the intersection of mental health and violence, so much more between them remained unsaid.

Walking through the parking lot, Luke spotted the now-familiar Lexus, the license plate spelling out who'd already arrived.

Marli Winslow stood behind the reception desk in the lobby. "I'm so sorry," she said into the phone. "Emerson is unavailable until further notice. But Roosevelt is equally lovely. Can I book that one for you?"

She waved at Luke, then held up one finger, letting him know she was bringing the call to a close. "You're all set for the thirty-first. Expect a confirmation email by the end of today."

Whether visiting for the day or staying for several, his aunt did a great job pitching in and helping out. Luke had come to enjoy watching her take pride in what she did at Church's Overlook. Whenever Marli was there, she inadvertently gave Luke an excuse for avoiding his mother.

"Hi, honey. It's been too long. Get over here and give me a hug."

"It's only been a few days," he said smiling. "When did you guys get in?"

He went behind the desk and put his arms around her. Of the people who'd suddenly landed in his life, Marli was the one he liked the best. Despite her fancy clothes and perfect hair, everything else about her was easy.

"About an hour ago. I wanted to come up sooner to help your mother with cabin turnover, but I had a big wedding to oversee at Nic's."

Marli put a hand up to Luke's cheek. "You going to be okay tonight?"

Luke was grateful to be asked how he would handle Jonah's film, but he wasn't sure. "I guess."

"Your brother's a wreck. Why don't you go in and see if you can settle him down? I'll switch the phones over to the call service. I'll be right in."

Luke could tell Jonah was scattered by the way he hunched over his laptop, fiddling with a projector and a jumble of cables. His foot tapped the floor so loudly it almost drowned out the string of F-bombs he kept dropping.

"Take it easy," Luke said, patting him on the back.

"Help me out, will you? What the hell am I missing?" he asked. "I've done this a thousand times, and when it counts, I can't get it to show on the screen."

"You sure that's the right one?"

As Jonah bent lower to inspect the array of tangled cords, their mother backed into the breakfast room through those swinging doors, holding a tray of brownies. She scanned the room, and when she saw Luke, she smiled and mouthed, "*Hi.*" After she placed the tray down, she tugged off her apron. Lena Blackwell was once again wearing a dress.

It wasn't the same one she'd worn on that far-back Sunday supper when they'd first talked openly, though dishonestly, about adoption and her life before Church's Overlook. But at times like this, it struck Luke that there was still a lot he didn't know about her. Maybe never would.

Jonah yanked on a cord. "You're right. I must've left the one I need upstairs."

"Relax," Luke said. "I'll get it."

Before he ducked out of the breakfast room, Win came out of the kitchen carrying a silver bucket filled with beer and wine. He put it on the table by the window overlooking the river, to the right of the flower centerpiece that had a distinctly Marli touch.

"Hello Luke," Win said, waving.

"I'll be right back. Gotta get something for Jonah."

Luke took the stairs to his brother's room, a place Jonah still stayed when he came home. No surprise the place was a mess. Digging through Jonah's duffle bag, checking the bureau—no cord. Then he saw it on Jonah's bed peeking out from beneath the sheets. Luke grabbed it and took off, closing the door to the chaos.

Across the hall, the door to his old room was left ajar. Luke couldn't remember the last time he'd been inside. Before he knew it, he'd pushed open the door and entered.

Nothing about it had changed really. The shades were up the way he liked them, to let the light from the moon illuminate his space. The dictionary sat opened on the stand Coop had helped him build all those years ago, but Luke made no move to read from it. It had been months since he'd felt unmoored enough to need to flip its pages.

Even in dim light, Luke could make out the details of his collection. For years he'd hoarded things that had no particular meaning to anyone but him. Odds and ends and scraps. Feathers and leaves and flowers. Luke loved each treasure, and he could remember how and when each piece had come to him. If anyone asked, he could also tell them why something had been included. In the absence of an origin story, Luke understood now that this collage of words and pictures had been an unconscious attempt to confirm outwardly that this was exactly where he was meant to be.

His hand went straight to the center of his lost and found things, coming to rest on the final item he'd affixed there.

As if the lights in his room were blazing, he could see the picture of her arms around him; Sylvie's beautiful face turned toward his. He felt the edges of a photograph she'd given him of them, taken at the place she called *Luke's Cove*. The inlet they had visited many times since Jonah said he could live with them being together.

Then Luke's fingers felt the unfamiliar edges of a piece of paper he had not tacked there. Something coarse—a note card fresh and new—was pinned in the place where the letter from Davis used to be.

Luke flicked on the light to read it.

Dear Cara,

How relieved I am to know that you and the boys are well. I've thought of you every day since that awful night. I always hoped that someday you would return to me. It's too late for us now, I know that. But please tell the boys that I will be here for them if they ever want to know me. I adopted them into my heart all those years ago. In my mind I will forever be their father. I'll wait for a lifetime if they need me to.

Always,
Nic

Luke had heard a lot about Nic. He was Marli's friend and her boss at the restaurant in Boston's North End. But he hadn't known Nic was also the man who'd loved his mother. A man who loved her still. In a weird way, his mother had only told a partial lie when she'd said they were adopted.

Over the years, on the rare occasion Luke let Jonah lure him into imagining their father, he had hoped the man would be kind and gentle. Except the person he wanted his father to be was Coop.

"Are you thinking that if you throw the cord out the window, you won't have to watch the movie?"

Luke turned to see Sylvie in the doorway of his childhood room. Like the vision he had conjured in that space countless times, before he'd realized he loved her, she'd come to him. This time to bring him back to the here and now.

"Sorry I'm late," she said, giving him a hug. "Traffic was crazy."

"You can stay the whole weekend, right?"

Between kisses, they pressed their foreheads together, not wanting to let each other go.

"Yes, but I have to study for my last final."

"It's going to be in the mid-seventies tomorrow. We can hike up to the North Wilderness. You can study outside."

"Like I'll be able to concentrate with you there," Sylvie said.

"Jesus, do you two mind? The damn cord?" Jonah came into the room and grabbed the cable from Luke. His voice lighthearted enough.

It had to be hard for him to see Sylvie and Luke together—even though they tried not to flaunt how they felt about each other in front of him.

Back down in the breakfast room, everyone milled around, waiting for Jonah to be ready. Marli and his mother stood by the window, looking toward the river. When they turned back and stared at Luke, he could tell they wondered if he'd seen it. The note from Nic. One of them must've left it there for him to find amid his collection.

Coop kept rearranging the handful of chairs they would need, like it mattered where anyone sat in that oversized space.

Win didn't waste any time heading back over to Luke. Less than subtle, he clearly had something to say.

"Sylvie, how are you dear?" Win asked.

"I'll be better when I get through my last final. My pediatric rotation was tougher than I thought it would be."

"I'm sure you'll do great," he said.

"Hope so," she said, squeezing Luke's arm. "I haven't said hi to your mom yet. I'll be right back."

In that moment, Luke wished Sylvie hadn't left his side. His uncle seemed so serious. There was so much sadness in his eyes.

"I know this night can't be easy for you, son," Win said, putting his hand on Luke's shoulder.

"I don't mean to be rude, but can you call me Luke?"

As Win nodded, he pulled a brochure from inside his suit coat pocket. "This might not be the right time. And I certainly don't mean to push, but I'd like to make you an offer. There's an environmental sciences degree program at University of Maine. You could attend full-time in the fall, or even part-time, if you like. On me. I imagine whatever you learn there could prove useful in running this place, maintaining the wonderful thing you've got here."

"That's generous. I'll be sure and think about it." Luke reached out to take the brochure and shake his uncle's hand.

"I was glad to work with your brother. On the film. I'd like to help you too." Win paused as though the rest of what he had to say was the real reason he'd cornered him.

"I suspect this might be odd coming from me, owing to the fact that your father was my brother. It's not ever going to be easy for your mother to discuss certain things with you. I just want you to know Nic's a good person. Maybe you could give him a chance."

"I'm all set for now. I'll let you know about this though." Luke waved the brochure, before sliding it into his back pocket. He wondered now if maybe Win was the one who'd placed Nic's note in his room.

The doctor clapped him on the back. "I understand." Then he and Marli moved from opposite sides of the room, to converge on a pair of chairs near Jonah.

"Okay, everyone," his brother said. "Grab yourself a bev and pick a seat. The long wait is over."

Luke felt Jonah's apprehension in the space between them. "Hey, you want a beer?"

"Better not, but thanks," he said. "Grab me a Coke."

At the drink table, Coop came up beside Luke. "Let me get it," he said. "You know I'm not much for sitting. Why don't you take a load off? Go sit next to Sylvie and your mother. Can I get you something, son?"

There it was again, that word, trailing Luke wherever he went. Some version of the truth of it was about to fill the screen in front of him. An allusion to it was pinned to his collection. Coming from Win it smacked of so many questions; the answers of which Luke might never be ready to know.

But when Coop called him *son*, it sounded so simple. When he spoke it, the word had no double meaning, no expectations. Even though Luke and Jonah had no say in the matter, the reality was, Coop had been a father to them. The man who'd taught them how to be.

"Sure," Luke said. "I'll take a Coke too."

So he took Coop's advice and went to sit between Sylvie and his mother. The two of them had been leaning in, conspiratorially talking about what might be nice to include in a picnic basket.

Luke's girlfriend linked her arm in his. His mother went back to staring straight ahead.

Even in profile, it was impossible to miss the tension in her jaw, the rigidness of her posture. She was bracing for a movie she did not want to watch. He imagined then, how anxious she must've been from the time Jonah announced the direction his project was going in, until now, when the film was in the can. She had to have spent the last eight months terrified, not knowing how much of her life would forever be contained within those frames.

Despite her willingness to give up the details to Sylvie's cousin Timmy, and the other law enforcement officers who had questioned her after Davis's death, she'd never been indicted for his murder.

There was so much evidence of Davis's propensity for violence. Coop's concussion. Jonah's leg. The apple-sized black and blue on his mother's cheek from when he hit her with the handle of the gun. Her husband's past history. All of it confirming her claim of self-defense. All of it setting Lena Blackwell up to get away with it.

That next morning, on the walk back to their boats, before they stepped off to ride back to Church's Overlook, Luke had convinced Jonah there was no need to lie. *"Just don't embellish,"* he'd said. Owing to Luke's insistence, Jonah spoke the least of the three of them. In what could only be considered miraculous, for once his brother was able to curb his urge to ramble. Like their mother, he didn't offer any more to police than what he'd been asked to answer. As hard as it was, Luke did the same.

In the days and weeks and months since, Luke and his mother had rarely spent time alone together. In short, they preferred to go about their business steering clear of one another. Or at least he did. When circumstances forced them together, they kept the conversation centered on guests and chores; they filled the silence between them with clipped sentences about the timing of currents or the chill of the wind.

Yet sitting there, about to watch a film Luke could only imagine would humanize Davis Winslow, he finally felt something for her again. Luke could only call up a fleeting image of a very troubled man out on that trail. Jonah's account of their father would likely unearth much more about him, no doubt some of it good. Still, it was liable to be filled with the thorny details from the time before he and Jonah were born, and then right after, highlighting a part of Carolina Winslow's life she'd tried desperately to lose for good in the Maine woods.

Sitting there, all Luke could think to do was copy Marli's good example. He repeated the single phrase she'd offered him out in the lobby. The words she'd said had provided a comfort to him, and they didn't beg to be looked up in anyone's dictionary.

"Are you going to be okay?" he asked his mother.

"Probably not," she said. "But it's the least I can do to watch it. I owe him that much."

Before Luke could ask if she meant Jonah or Davis, the lights went out, and the story his brother knew but needed to know again began.

ACKNOWLEDGMENTS

I OWE ENORMOUS GRATITUDE to so many generous and talented women, including my team at Crooked Lane Books, especially Toni Kirkpatrick, Melissa Rechter, Madeline Rathle, Rebecca Nelson, and Jennifer Hooks.

Thank you to Megan Beatie and Stephanie Elliot of Megan Beatie Communications for supporting me and advocating for my work in countless thoughtful ways.

Much love and appreciation go out to my dear friends, Julie Basque, Nina Dickerman, Jeanne Crehan, Patti Donovan, Colleen Gibbons, Cheryl Reidy, Karleen Habin, and Katrin Schumann.

To all my Reeves and Griffin family members, especially Dianne Veale and Laura Griffin; thank you for your endless encouragement and goodwill.

And for all the ways they bring light into my life, I'm grateful for Caitlin Batstone, Matt Batstone, Oliver Batstone, Stephen Griffin, and Tom Griffin . . . I'm the luckiest woman in the world to be loved by all of you.

Dark Rivers to Cross examines inherited trauma, adoption, and whether parents have the right to keep painful origin stories from their children. Novelist and family counselor, Lynne Reeves writes domestic suspense about social issues to create opportunities for thoughtful conversation around the relationship challenges we find most difficult to talk about. For many readers, the trauma inheritance shapes their lives in far reaching ways. And while it is a legacy one cannot escape but must endure, inhabiting fictional narratives like hers offers readers a safe, vicarious path toward emotional resilience. When we examine the issues of our time from a distance, reading is healing.

For a book club guide with discussion questions, a Q & A with the author, and more about Lynne's work, visit her website: LynneGriffin.com.